T0359488

EPICURUS IN LOVE

The Epicuriana

A Novel of Mythos and Desire in Ancient Greece

PAUL B. DONOVAN

The
Euphorion Press

First published in 2022
By The Euphorion Press Limited
The.Euphorion@gmail.com
New York, NY, 10001

(BKR442-81) – EPICURUS IN LOVE....Digi-Rights Direct
ISBN: 978-0-578-31871-4

COVER ART: Jones, Sir Edward (artist, 1870)
'Phyllis and Demophoon' (Detail), Birmingham Museums Trust

Forget about Facebook! — Go Direct
to
THE EPICURIANA WEBSITE
at
https://www.epicurusinlove.com

Preface

Driven by a defiant Hades, erupting volcanoes at will, the gently smoking cone blows its top, belching flames and molten debris high into the sky. Suffocating rains of ash, pumice, and blistering hot gases shower down on the unfortunate luxury resort, amid rivers of lava.

Breaking news, with the byline of climate change, Live from CNN, 21st century — No, this is 79 AD, around midday. Residents are taking their noonday nap. Vesuvius, the sacred mountain of Hercules, engulfs the Roman city of Pompeii, burying everything and everyone: bejewelled aristocrats, ragged beggars, voluptuous prostitutes, bourgeois merchants, entwined lovers, horses and dogs as well — all damned, now morbid statues, encased in volcanic detritus, frozen in time. Miraculously, a hoard of papyrus scrolls, carbonized but still intact, lies buried under the ruins of a collapsed seaside villa....and one scroll in particular.

Cited by ancient authors, the object of countless searches in medieval libraries, given up as lost forever, the fabled 'Epicuriana' was recovered and returned to its rightful place in the history of ideas. The Epicuriana is remarkably, also a riveting tale of adventures, loves and losses — told firsthand by the esteemed Master himself, the 'peoples' philosopher', Epicurus of Samos. This is his human story, at once endearing and provocative, warts and all.

The wider Epicurean legacy, for which there is a weighty literature, I gladly leave to scholarly classicists and the Society of Friends of Epicurus. For some readers, Epicurus remains a dearly cherished figure, an embodiment of the art of living gracefully — any effort to portray him in mere human terms might, understandably, be offensive.

On the other hand, if we rightly regard Epicurus as a founding father of humanist beliefs, hardly seen again until the Renaissance, it is not unreasonable that he should be represented in keeping with such beliefs. Reclaiming his humanity I believe, renders his simple, profound ideas with added gloss.

The late Mary Renault, a larger-than-life doyen of historical fiction, considered that 'what these long-dead characters of ancient Greece might have actually been like as real people' to be the pivotal question of this genre. She sought to portray them as flesh-and-blood individuals, before the intervening centuries did a cosmetic 'make-over' on them, whitewashing their personal foibles and everyday oddities. Frozen in marble, they have become the stern busts — aloof on their high perches at the Louvre Museum — gazing down serenely on all comers entering the galleries.

Turning real people into idealized objects is a troubling thing, at least for me — it cries out, begging for Life in place of cold marble. I immediately think of Susan Sontag's historical novel, 'The Volcano Lover' (1992) — a reference to iconic Mount Vesuvius — for its vivid, full-page description of a marble figure imaginatively restored to the smelly, florid realism of life. A little fall from the pedestal never hurt anyone, if it means rejuvenating these otherwise remote and desiccated pillars of Mediterranean civilization. This is a special irony in the case of Epicurus, since oddly enough, it is these very same vital qualities that stood him apart from the rest: young and wild, passionate alike in his beliefs and feelings,….a smasher of idols!

Such a dynamic character lends himself I believe, to the medium of a novel, and so 'The Epicuriana' was born — an offbeat portrayal of Epicurus unbuttoned, the humanist action-adventurer and lover who more than any other, trod in the footsteps of Socrates. Separated by the vast swath of many centuries, the present storytelling calls for an informed — sometimes imagined — reconstruction of historic events and characters. In doing so, it is inevitable that Epicurus and I become melded into the one narrative — any unwitting personal intrusions, biases, or anachronisms may be tolerated perhaps, when set against the greater good of conveying his humanistic message.

A NOTE ABOUT THE ILLUSTRATIONS

Truth to tell, I admit to a 'fetish' of sorts: the first thing I do in a new city is hunt for antiquarian bookshops — the less mainstream, the better. I have spent countless lost hours rummaging through mouldy volumes, brittle and yellow with age — the feint pencilled marginalia of past owners is a bonus, as if privy to the innermost thoughts of others, voices from the past coming alive. Other times, I fossick in the stacks of library archives, whether print or online, looking for literary 'buried treasure'. There are times, precious few, when I actually strike 'gold'.

The cache of wood-cut engravings, reproduced in the following pages, are one such stroke of luck — flashbacks in time, courtesy of the Library of Congress. But there was more! The engravings, at once incisive yet naively charming, come replete with an alluring story — the fateful collaboration between a zealous, eccentric pioneer and his gifted master engraver, at the dawn of ancient Greek ethnography. Following the post-Renaissance fading of interest, the ancient Mediterranean world was once again the drawcard for well-heeled Westerners.

Anthony Rich, B.A., Esquire, was a proper English 'gentleman-scholar' in the stiff-upper-lip Victorian tradition, during the heyday of the British Empire. A graduate of Cambridge University, he was a confidant of Charles Darwin, at a time when "latterly, there has been a general disposition amongst us to recur back and investigate the customs of by-gone ages." A man of his word, Mr. Rich, Esquire, spent seven years roaming and documenting Greco-Roman curiosities, wherever he found them. From minuscule ladies' toiletries through to Attic red-and-black burial urns and monumental Doric columns, all were recorded with the blind dedication of a proverbial bower-bird. Many of the engravings, I believe, are 'objets d'art' in their own right, apart from the storyline.

At final count, this tireless artefact-hunter had depicted "nearly two thousand objects and drawings from the ancients,.... attention being bestowed upon social manners and everyday life", eventually publishing his weighty tome in 1849. Mr. Rich, Esquire, has my abiding admiration as well as my lasting gratitude, albeit posthumously. Fifty of Mr. Rich's antiquarian woodcuts are embedded where appropriate, in the text of 'Epicurus in Love – The Epicuriana'.

Paul Donovan
Santa Fe, New Mexico
2019

PART I:
"Prologue"

Chapter 1

Isle of Samos, The Aegean Sea
325 BC

I remember the searing, salty rain, whipping in from the Aegean. Wind-blown sideways, sheeting into her eyes.

Blinking in a thick pall of darkness, she struggles to find her way up the rugged, goatherd trail. Mottled with tiny windswept craters, the path veers seaward to avoid a steep ravine that slices through the headland. Raindrops are driven like darts, pelting her face, ruddy and glowing.

The escarpment is covered in mounds of tuft-matted schist, now loose and slippery on her leather sandals. As each violent squall sweeps in from the sea, she pauses to hold her ground against the blows — waiting for the lull. Crouching down on all fours, she then scrambles onward, unfeeling of the bruises, groping and clawing at the flinty layers of schist, cutting into her ankles.

She loses what little remains of the rocky trail, as the ground rises sharply. There is only one direction, windward, upwards to the crest. Grass-stalks pierce their way through her tunic, becoming needles. Thickets of scrubby garrigue scratch her with their thorn-studded branches as she pushes through them. Prickly burrs grab at her outer linen cloak, gathering in knobby clusters, made heavy by the drenching rain.

A lone holm oak, lichen-encrusted, bent double in supplication to the storm's fearful onslaught, looms up like a ghostly apparition through the gloom. The unyielding winds buffet the basalt cliffs nearby, peppering the oak — updrafts wafting salt spray and sand from the breaking surf and jagged boulders far below. She shelters behind its thick, calloused trunk, leeward, panting and gasping — exhausted, bedraggled, shivering with windchill. She peers furtively into the darkness, listening, secure that she is not followed.

Her tears, long withheld, flow now in gut-wrenching sobs. She startles, shaking. Phosphorescent streaks — like a magic show — gleam and fade above her. Thunderclaps burst furiously in peals of deafening reverberation — before growling and rumbling along the cliffs, into the faraway distance.

She reaches into a leather pouch, secured to her waist, tipping the dried black berries into the cup of her tremulous hand, gulping mouthfuls at a time in the brief pauses between gusts. The berries will soon work their spell; waiting, catching her breath as the climax of the storm passes overhead. Her heart rate begins racing — head spinning. Numbness rapidly spreads down her legs and arms, until she no longer feels the stormy buffets.

A skilled herbalist always knows her options, in this case, the bitter-sweet taste of Belladonna, the 'beautiful lady' come to take her away. Lightning criss-crosses the leaden sky, framing her hunched figure momentarily in a macabre silhouette. She stands up regardless, in a state of painless delirium and shuffles forward — now with firm resolve.

This is what I imagine — elaborating or otherwise altering images — to be my mother's last furtive minutes of life on earth. I try to feel her primal terror, as she steps off the cliff edge into the void, before eternal nothingness consumes her forever.

She may be someplace else now, transcendent, possibly the fabled Elysian Fields, among the Immortals — though I have little faith in an afterlife. Any which way, she is lost to me, which is the only thing that matters.

My father tells me, over and over again, how he discovered her sandals near the precipice. The storm has now abated. Villagers emerge, even nameless strangers, eagerly searching the ragged foreshore. No traces — clothing, limbs, torso — nothing, other than the frothing, pounding seas. Days pass in a blurry fatigue....people disperse, one by one, head-shaking and offering condolences. I can't let go.

The many lonely hours spent in my searches haunt me with their empty promises. My questing takes on a pattern — I scramble around the next craggy headland, and scan the small shingle beach, deathly afraid of what I hope to find. Deflated or encouraged — I'm not sure which — I trudge onwards, looking desperately for any telltale signs amid the foaming debris: amphora shards lie scattered in the loose sand; a broken oar loaded with gooseneck barnacles; tattered sailcloth, and lines of grey pumice in neat tidal bands. Balls of matted brown seaweeds everywhere, rolled up by the storm.... and the next headland beckons with its promise.

I want something: even a familiar shred of her tunic, examined and identified, would change everything. My mother's fate, however ghastly, would then be settled. An abrupt, alarming finality descends upon me, bracketing the remainder of my life — the time 'before' and 'after'. Between the two, lies the unknown. No parting kiss or last fond embrace. The question needles me still in odd moments — is she alive somewhere, somehow? As with all islands, Samos is given to local gossip and idle chatter. Any sighting of such a well-liked healer, 'apparently' lost to the sea, would instantly fire up the sandal-mongers, already simmering with roundabout rumors. Mutterings however, is all they are, lacking material substance — there's nary a hint of a body to fuel the embers!

Alone and motherless, I feel like a castaway — stuck on this rustic, island peninsula, with its headland of high, white cliffs, jutting out into the Aegean Sea — isolated on the windward side of greater Samos, itself remote from the cultural reawakening of Athens, my ancestral homeland, the stuff of my dreams. Somehow, Athens and my mother are melded together in my mind — she spoke of it so often, where she was born, raised, and was married — a time of happiness, before my parents' exile to this accursed speck, my wretched birthplace no less.

My last memory of her was that savage argument — really, an endless repetition of the same one — mounting variations on an well-worn theme of betrayal. I recall its effect on me: the monstrous spider of despair, an image that crawls into my mind from early years.

My reaction is always visceral.

Knees hard against my chest, I am swaying myself in a rocking motion. A residual from my infancy, I suppose, the regularity of the movement generates some primitive sense of personal control, albeit one that is illusionary.

The uncontrollable crisis descends down upon me like a hideous black spider. I hate spiders, many-eyed, hairy abominations, that entangle their innocent prey, and suck the life out of them – my life! Always, the same monstrous image springs to my mind, fed by their many past ruptures — my mother and father. This time it is worse by far, outside my door. Transfixed, I want so much to get away, as I strain to hear every word.

"Khrysokemis is my very close friend. Or so I thought she was,….until now! You know that, and you've been having her, then pretending….

"I was helping her move furniture. She's going to move…."

"…. Liar! You told me you were going to be late, 'tutoring after school' you said. Tutoring in what, I'd like to know?"

Totally powerless, I am caught frantically struggling in this sordid web of accusations. Must I bear witness to the undoing of my family life, helplessly trapped in my room?

"Since poor Zenos died, she's short on drachmas, and decided to have a sale. I was trying to help her out, since she asked me…."

"….And what kind of help has fornication as a house-chore?"

"Well, you're never here, are you? Not for me; not for Epicurus, and you're his mother! Always out on your rounds,….or too tired. Maybe if you stayed home…."

My mother lowers her voice, taking on the deliberated tone of weary familiarity common to married couples grown apart with the heaviness of too many years — a hostile dependency. Strangers to each other now, she hears herself once again, repeating the same tired insinuations.

"Just stop the lying, just for once. I saw you two together myself. You couldn't get enough of her. All over her. What a lecher…."

Never a player, always a victim, I cover my ears to allay the rising crescendo. Melanchaetes, my best friend, is also agitated, flattening his ears back against his head: his signal for danger. In one leap, he's up on the bed, pushing me back on my haunches with his muscular body, licking my neck furiously — consoling me, I'm sure of it! I hug his musty, warm body, nestling my face deep into his coat of long black fur, hiding out from the commotion.

I remain huddled on my bed. Outside my door, accusations of

infidelity and betrayal fly back and forth, scathing fusillades in a battle without mercy. Neither one is listening to the other, each with a well-rehearsed recital of hurt feelings — no quarter given or expected. The ferocity grows by the minute. Then abruptly,....

Everyone pauses, dismayed, overwhelmed by a mighty crash of thunderbolts.

A summer storm, known locally as an Etesian, often lasting continuously for days and nights, has burst in from the sea without warning, rattling the shutters. With its pummelling winds and sheeting rain, the Etesian funnels down the corridor between the high cliffs of the northern Aegean islands, past Chios, Lemnos, and Lesbos, even reaching the Peloponnesus. Speech is impossible — dampened by the relentless drumming of heavy rain on the terracotta roof shingles. I can't help thinking that Nature has imposed an eerie truce, or rather, a rage of a different kind, this time by unseen forces.

I seize my opportunity.

Throwing back my bedroom door, I burst out. Pushing my way between my parents, I plead with them, teary-eyed and distraught, to "stop the fighting". My father, Neocles, easily shoves me aside. I trip on the rug, and fall heavily, breathless but not injured. Melanchaetes barks aggressively, crouching and baring his fangs. My father is a robust man, with well-developed musculature. At sixteen years of age, I am no match.

My efforts only make matters worse.

Always protective of me, my mother Chaerestrata screams at him, and steps in between us. Unwittingly, I suddenly become the push-pull focus of the family battleground. I know my mother to be free-spirited, assertive, and even at times, abrasive. Unflinching, she speaks her mind. They are both yelling now, only louder, to outdo the thunderous competition of the squalls.

My father frogmarches me back into my room. Small as a monk's cell, it resonates the infernal screaming — mixing wind, rain, and argument into one deafening, unbearable cacophony. I return to my rocking, spider in my mind, fingers in my ears — and so it goes on.

"You betrayed me, and so did she. My so-called best friend! Zenos is dead less than a year. It didn't take you long, did it! In you go! Taking advantage...."

"....You only have yourself to blame. You're never home. Doing whatever, with whom ever! I'm not the fool you think I am. I know your dirty little secret...."

I hear a scratching at the door, and partially open it. Melanchaetes enters with his usual aura of entitlement, collapsing on his proprietary rug beside my bed with all due aplomb. Despite the commotion, he's had enough and promptly drops off to sleep, unperturbed. Intrigued and distracted, I can't help but watch him. I wait for what surely will follow. The furore outside recedes innocuously into the background.

Melanchaetes is a kinetic dreamer — it doesn't take long before his black, shaggy body is jerking, paws twitching, performing a pantomime of running movements, comical reproductions of his waking life. The calming reassurance of normalcy hangs on such everyday, simple events. Whatever happens, I will always have Melanchaetes. I lay my head down, smiling.

Just once, I would love to know what my canine companion is dreaming.

Chapter 2

My eyes open drearily, with the stout oak shutters providing only a bleak light. There comes a shiver of recognition that it must be morning.

I sit up with a start, the drama of the previous night still fresh in my mind. Melanchaetes is already awake on the mat, looking up intently, with that head-tilting quizzical gesture so typical of dogs, as if to question my stay-in-bed tardiness. I massage his thick neck muscles, our morning ritual of bonding. Exhausted with anxiety, it surprises me nevertheless, that I could have fallen asleep with so much chaos. Perhaps sleep was my last remaining haven, or arguably, it was the soothing regularity of Melanchaetes' active dreaming.

"Epicurus, at 16 years, on Samos"

I quickly awake, disturbed by the many discordant noises. The Etesian is howling as hard as ever, leaves and small branches lashing the outer stone wall of the cottage, with rain squalls pounding on the roof and shutters. Even my bedroom door is rattling.

I stagger into the kitchen, followed by Melanchaetes. No one. The house is inexplicably empty. I call out to my parents — an ominous silence. Surely they would not venture out, without telling me, in such fearsome weather? I grow alarmed, unsure of what action to take. The closest neighbours are several leagues distant. I begin to pace. Deciding that any action is better than useless hand-wringing, I throw on my heavy woollen all-weather cape and wide-brimmed petasos, tying it tightly under my chin.

Pushing against the Etesian, I open the front door with difficulty, a sudden gust slamming it back into place again. I pull down the brim of my petasos, shielding my eyes against the downpour. Melanchaetes and I scour the grounds, keeping the wind and rain at our backs as much as possible. With only blurry visibility, our search is haphazard at best. I keep the house within sight at all times, making ever widening circles until I reach the tree-line and brambles at the periphery of our property. Nothing but cold, bone-chilling rain — not even tracks in the gelatinous mud.

Melanchaetes leading the way, nose to the ground, we trundle along the narrow, stony road towards Chios. With no clear plan in mind, the tunnel of trees on either side of the road gives us a windbreak, becoming by default, the next best thing to do. Exhausted and pilloried by the windchill, we make slow, painstaking headway — until faltering doubt overtakes us — we eventually turn about, beaten and downhearted. In the opposite direction, the road contiues for a few leagues past our house, then narrows into a rutted goatherd trail.

An uphill trudge ends in a final steep climb to a rocky

promontory and high cliffs, falling away to the sea, far below. I couldn't imagine that my parents would have any reason to take that nightmarish route. I think perhaps, we may find them back home, anxiously waiting for us.

Our solitary farmhouse comes into view, as moonlight struggles to break through the relentless drizzle — casting a sinister glow over the woods, misty and impenetrable, on either side of us. Scattered outcrops of monstrous limestone slabs — all moss-covered and primordial — jut up eerily from the gloom of the treetops. Drenched and shivering, the two of us slosh and slide our way indoors.

All our best efforts have been futile — at least the freezing cold has displaced my anxiety. I call out hopefully as we enter....nothing but the constant drumming of the rain on the roof and the feint echo of my own voice. We head for the kitchen and the fireplace — empty-handed, bedraggled, and above all else — hungry.

With mighty shakes, Melanchaetes disperses the rain clinging to his fur coat — his signature halo of water-droplets. I change into a dry tunic and re-kindle the spluttering embers in the fireplace, adding pine and cypress logs. Melanchaetes is ravenous, gulping down his cuts of cured goat-meat with blissful gusto, chomping, tearing,....and slobbering. He's earned it. Strangely enough, I have little appetite. The barley and lentil broth 'leftover' from dinner, my mother's cooking, is all I need. I am too weary even to bother warming it.

We settle ourselves on a sheepskin rug around the cosy warmth of the hearth. Our storeroom is well-stocked. The mystery can wait until dawn: the weather will likely clear, so they can return safely. Warm, with a full stomach, it's not long before I helplessly succumb to sleep.

With much slamming and crashing, I am begrudgingly brought back to my senses.

There is my father, like an apparition, not so much sitting around the culina table as he is crumpled up upon it — ungainly, totally filling its area with his large frame — so that he seems to be suspended in space. Rain drips off his saturated clothing in drips and drabs, collecting in puddles on the flagstone floor.

Fagged beyond sleep, he mumbles incoherently. With obvious pain and effort, he lifts his arm and slowly fumbles with his knotted shoulder-bag draped on the floor.

Sliding his arm along the floor, without looking, he uncovers a pair of leather sandals from the bag. They are narrow, floridly embossed, as would be worn by a woman of status. I shiver, incredulous, recoiling backwards, away from them. The sandals belong to my mother, cut, sown, and adorned in her own distinctive style. She enjoys leatherwork, and takes pleasure in providing footwear for her family and friends.

My father lifts his head off the table and tries to cry but falters, making an unearthly feline mewing, then collapses back limply, into a merciful sleep. I'm left standing helpless, beside his dishevelled body.

I struggle to piece together all that my eyes have beholden, though it is perhaps, only several minutes. My mother was parted from her sandals. Something has caused her to discard the sandals. She is justly proud of her leatherwork skills, and normally would never have forgotten them, much less, lost them.

My father stirs again, this time managing a hoarse whisper between anguished gasps — rambling, seemingly directed at no one in particular.

"She's left me....She did it!....Threw herself over the cliff....

Over the cliff....Too late....Gone....Nothing I can do....She really did it....Over the cliff...." And so on.

With the long outburst now spent, regressed to mournful sobbing, he folds his arms on the table in front of him as a cradle for his head. I sit there in stony silence, doubting that he is even conscious of my presence.

My feelings towards my father normally run the gamut from wistful love, through passive allegiance, to bitter resentment. I feel only profound pity for him now. It is truly disturbing to see such a hardy man, normally resilient in the face of life's many challenges, so totally beaten down, broken in spirit.

As for my beloved mother, I have closed off my mind to the matter of the sandals, and any significance attached to them — a kind of protective numbing. I'm certain that she has run off again, as she has done several times before, and is tucked away somewhere, safe and warm with friends. I can't accept the idea — my father's story — that anyone with such high morals and zest for life as my mother, would leap off a cliff. No amount of squabbling with my father would make her do such a thing! She undoubtedly lost her way in the squall and probably kicked off her sandals to gain better traction in the sloppy mud.

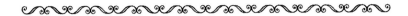

I would soon have reason enough to bitterly recall my smug complaisance.

My mother always said she would take Belladonna if she ever became incurably ill. In small doses it relieves pain and suffering, she had told me, but caution was needed. Strong dosages are inevitably fatal. Without thinking, I wander into her makeshift apothecary, semi-detached at the back of our house.

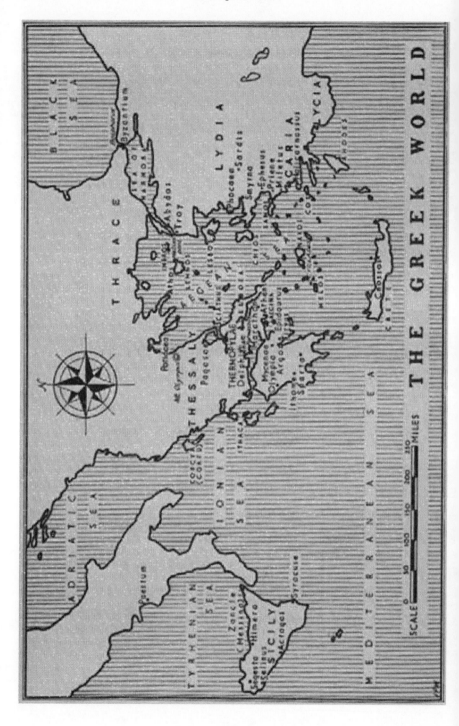

A familiar florid aroma suffuses throughout the room, a fragrance which I have always associated with fond memories of my mother. As a small boy, I watched in fascination as she compounded formulations of medicinal herbs to suit one particular client or another. Best of all were the those special times during school breaks, when I accompanied her on client visits. I witnessed incredulously, how readily people responded to her therapeutic ministrations.

While effective, the herbal 'remedy' provided the external rationale for her personal healing powers — without which her many jealous competitors would have her pilloried as a 'witch'. While they had their suspicions, spreading tacky gossip, there was little else they could do — the client happily paid for a 'herbal formulation', duly dispensed. For my part, the healing power of persuasion, body and mind, made a lasting impression on me. Unknowingly, it set the seal on my future life, as do so many seemingly innocent events in our formative years.

A very long time has passed since I have had an occasion to enter my mother's apothecary room, which was otherwise forbidden. The diminutive space, much smaller than I remember it, is unexpectedly lined with shelves, top to bottom, packed with inscribed vases, all medicinal herbs which she formulates and dispenses. With a beating heart, I take down the herbal jar labeled as Belladonna, and remove its tight cork stopper. Nothing.

I stare into the empty recess, transfixed, before I rouse myself. Yes, she has probably just forgotten to restock it! If she really did intend to kill herself, surely it would be easier to do it here, locked in her own dispensing room. She didn't need to leap off a cliff, and leave her sandals, neatly arranged, or so my father says. She wasn't a 'dramatic type', and the whole thing just didn't make sense! On the other hand, people don't always behave rationally when distressed, even my poor mother.

At some dark, subterranean level, a part of me must have recognized the improbable truth. Why else would I collect her sandals later while my father was snoring? Why did I then hide them in the woods, secreted in a convenient nook under a large rock, to be retrieved at a later time? In the following days, my father queries me several times, convinced that he had returned home with the sandals. I reassure him that it was a false recollection, born of extreme fatigue. Imagination mistaken for memory. Returning home in despair, he had promptly collapsed on the table, empty-handed and comatose. There were no sandals, I explain sorrowfully. He shakes his head, downcast, throwing up his hands in frustration.

My mother is justly proud of her leatherwork artistry, especially her finely embellished sandals. Despite many offers, she refuses to sell any of her sandals. Instead, she chooses to give them away as gifts, bestowed as a blessing for the recipient's friendship. With each gift, she says, "I am there under your feet, as a cushion between you and the hard world!". She meant what she said. Such heartfelt gestures ensured that unlike her surly husband, she had many friends who loved her dearly.

Over the years that have passed since the mysterious loss of my mother, leaving so many questions in the wake of her sudden disappearance, I have carried her sandals with me wherever I wandered. I wanted what little remained of her for myself — not to be shared with my father! If not for his betrayal, would she still be alive? I try to stop my thoughts from straying in that direction, of endless, pointless possibilities.

If I am to believe in my mother's cliff-side death, then her final act, somewhat puzzling, was to remove her sandals. It would seem to be a deliberated action, and if so, then it must have meaning attached to it. I like to think that she left them purposefully for me, as her personal blessing — also a reminder of her legacy of kindness and tolerance. A call to walk in her shoes. Since that time, my mother's sandals have become a kind of talisman, as if she is always with me, a visible reminder of a loving heart.

More than once, those sandals have saved me from plummeting into the dark abyss of bitterness and cynicism: that humanity is a corrupt, immoral creature, a lost cause. Through the symbolism of these sandals, I retain my mother as a living presence in my life — her healing influence has become the foundation of my own personal teaching, and all the providential events that have followed down the years. This is when I started to philosophise.

Chapter 3

Boston, Massachusetts
2015 AD

Despite enhanced resolution, and countless hours, the illuminated specimen — blackened, warped, and brittle with time — gives scant return for all Fiona's tedious spadework. Squinting her eyes in frustration, Fiona Roberts once again adjusts her Scanning Electron Microscope, SEM to the initiated. "SEM is fine. The scroll microscans are the problem. Kaputnik!", she thinks to herself.

'Shaped like a long dark crap', she mutters aloud, glancing at the carbonized specimen in pent-up annoyance.

Bemused at her own lapse into bawdy slang, she looks around sheepishly — an eccentric habit of talking to herself whenever she feels fatigued. Her conspicuous mop of flaming-red hair, highlighted by her white lab-coat, doesn't help her offbeat reputation.

David, her laboratory technician, standing nearby, absorbed in his laptop calculations, shows no visible evidence of eavesdropping. His only gesture of life whatsoever, is a slight adjustment to his horn-rimmed glasses. Fiona giggles aloud, tittering at the thought that the American Center for Antiquities Research in Boston, her most venerable employer, would most certainly not approve of her less-than-empirical observation.

"Well, as the bag-lady would say — it does look like crap," quips David calmly, in his best deadpan voice, eyes fixated on his laptop screen, as an impish smile spreads across his face. Only his long auburn hair is shaking. They both convulse into hearty laughter.

It was probably the break they both desperately needed, thought Fiona, after their many long, exacting hours. Their exhausting, yet meticulous work, not for the faint-hearted, left little space for a normal life. Other staff referred to their cramped, detached laboratory, only half-jokingly, as 'The Hermitage' — the techno-religious retreat of isolated hermits, whose everyday speech was sprinkled with baffling acronyms.

Professor Roberts, double-Ph.D, Rhodes Scholar, papyrologist and classical philologist, turned back to her 'crappy' specimen. It had been carbonized beyond recognition by pyroclastic flows, waves of superheated gas, that had consumed what was once a tightly-rolled papyrus scroll — one of many, two thousand years ago. So brittle was the precious scroll, that it had its own hermetically sealed plexiglass case, moved if necessary, like delicate china.

It had been recently moved many times, very carefully, in the Antiquities laboratory.

"Let's recalibrate," Fiona says earnestly

"Let's recalibrate," Fiona says earnestly, assuming her professorial demeanour once more, "and run another XPCT. This specimen shows promise. It's not as bad as the others, taken from the bottom of the original bundle, I would guess, so it got more protection. A big one too, probably sixty feet long, if only we could unwind it. We can't, of course, which thankfully keeps us both in jobs as we unwrap it digitally....or at least, that's the idea."

Fiona holds up crossed-fingers in both hands.

"Yea, boss, whatever" says David, disrespectful as ever, "but we do have a few individual letters already showing a detectable phase contrast. More distinctive than most."

He was referring to the thousands of preserved texts recovered from the archaeological site, the only ancient library with its contents still intact, where they were left on that fateful day in 79 AD. These few charred remnants are all that remains of the many grand libraries of antiquity, now gone forever.

The rolled scrolls had been crudely excavated in the 18th century, as trophies for high-end Italian politicians or doddery rich Englishmen. Enclosed in the space behind a collapsed wall, the scrolls came from a vast personal library in what was once a lavish, multi-storied seaside villa. The magnificent dwelling was one of several in Herculaneum, port of Pompeii and playground resort of rich Romans, before both towns were buried alive by the cataclysmic eruption of nearby Mount Vesuvius.

The villa was reputed to have been owned by a branch of the Julian family, most famous of Latin dynasties, otherwise known as the Caesars. Fiona knew how hard it was to separate hearsay myth from reality however, especially where money was concerned. This was one reason why she loved her vocation as an evidence-based scientist, debunking myths, or else rarely, affirming them when least expected. She thought back to Homer's Troy, a myth come true, and the vast hoard of golden treasures unearthed by Schliemann in the 19th century — still glittering, waiting for almost three thousand years.

David chimes in, reminding Fiona of the formidable task ahead, albeit with the wistful possibility of another 'Golden treasure' of a different, technological kind.

"Well, professor," he says, with mock emphasis on Fiona's title, "to get inside this scroll and delineate more letters with your SEM, we need to refine the energy setting of our microscan — much better than what we have been doing. We have to do this for each 'page' or layer with hundreds of runs, then adjust the setting again for the next layer and so on, all trial and error. It'll be a snail's pace, at best. There's no other way."

Fiona keeps silent, scowling, allowing David to have one of his unstoppable, pedantic episodes, in which he sees his role as the realist — 'putting the brakes on' as he so coarsely puts it to her. She is the dreamer, a role she cherishes. 'This is why we work so well together', Fiona thinks to herself, 'Despite appearances, David is a dedicated, research technologist, who while never admitting it, remains inspired by what we are doing'.

"Of course, each papyrus 'page' is wrinkled," David continues, "thanks to the pyroclastic gas, so that I have to be constantly re-cali-brating the settings even within that page. Next, we have to sort out what letters fit on what page in the scroll, which is never clear. Then you have this huge jig-saw puzzle, using your super-software for textual analysis — sorting out what order of letters go where, before you can begin to construct words even, much less sentences."

David catches his breath, then continues his monologue, unabated. Fiona has heard the recital before, several times over. It has almost assumed the status of a sacred recital, or perhaps, a good-luck ritual.

"On top of that, the 'helpful' ancient Greeks ran their words together, leaving no spaces. And that's before deciphering the meaning of the text, filling in the gaps as best you can. Finally, there's the little matter of translating Archaic Greek, very different to Modern Greek, into readable 21st century idiom."

Fiona's patience is rewarded, as David expends all his energies, exhausted and breathless by the mere thought of it all.

"Great," Fiona chipped in, cheerfully, "now let's get on with it! Lots to do! Hubba, Hubba!"

"God, you can be a pain," whispers David, in a hoarse voice, not quite finished with recounting his doomsday litany of the impossible. One last crack.

"All this effort, and it's going to be another dull dissertation by Philodemus, loaded with epigrams, just like all the rest." David adds, despondently, referring to the 1st century B.C scholar of Epicurus' philosophy.

In true monastic fashion, Fiona lives in her cramped glass cubicle, providing her with the silence she values for her SEM analyses. David progressively supplies Fiona with the latest phase-contrast microscans, the best that his perfectionism would permit — several dozen every week from runs of a hundred or more. He also takes up the de facto role of bringing her lunch and dinner.

Late in the evening, she drives to her nearby minimalist apartment — the only decoration, towering above her single bed, is an outsize Kandinsky print: 'a unique combination of mathematics and mysticism' — a reminder of her secret admiration for Pythagoras and the numerology he inspired. To do otherwise, to 'come out' as a rebel Pythagorean, would invite a backlash indicative of 'a sloppy mind lost-in-the-clouds', not equal to the exactitude of her profession. She would show them — her prized specimen, written in Ancient Greek, is crammed with phonetic puns, exotic perseverations, and summersault aphorisms that would surely confuse a more conventional classicist. Despite her scholarly appearance, this 'openness to oddities' is Fiona's mental key to unraveling the scroll, with all its twists and turns. Come sunbeams or snow flurries, she is back in her cubicle again by daybreak!

David has previously witnessed Fiona's absorption in her work, 'monomaniacal' he called it,....but never before, at this level of isolation. Dedication, she corrects David, pertly — and closes her door on him.

Even their daily chats, which David always enjoyed, that somehow teased out their mutual humanity, sprinkled with good humor and off-color jokes, are now brief and superficial. Losing patience, he blurts out that she 'is looking haggard and rundown', an all-too-truthful comment and one that halts their chats for several days.

David is increasingly concerned, watching Fiona slyly when he can, unsure of what to do. He thinks about calling her widowed mother, but never does so, fearful of the dire consequences. He has seen Fiona in one of her few but memorable rages, not typical of her caring temperament — enough that he doesn't want to cross that irreversible threshold.

Seasons came and went, until it seemed to David, plodding from one day's output to the next — false starts offset by an occasional breakthrough — that there wasn't much to distinguish between them.

"Days of Ennui", David moaned to his Sports-Bar friends, borrowing the flashy title of a recent Covid bestseller.

"Okay....so why do you stay?", they croon in unison, all long-suffering listeners to the oft-repeated tale of Fiona's 'relentless' work demands.

"Well....I'm all she's got!", came his stock reply to the chorus of grinning faces, keenly aware of what lay behind David's singular devotion, of which he himself was only dimly conscious.

"Yeah, what a guy! It's a great sacrifice for you alright!", sniped one of his buddies, at which the rest of the circle collapsed in side-splitting laughter, thumping the bar, rattling their beers — while David stood, nursing a confused smile, blushing red.

Springtime thawing becomes the humidity of summer — finally, the not-to-be-forgotten day arrives.

Fiona bursts out of her office, hell-bent, flinging the door open with such a wallop that topples the adjacent tower of storage boxes. David startles, as the impact resounds across their equipment-packed, wired-up space. No, not an earthquake, he reassures himself. Fiona staggers up to him, wide-eyed, totally elated, her pressured speech becoming incoherent, words tumbling ever faster.

"Eureka, David....it's Eureka! I've got it", she cries in joy, babbling.

"She's finally snapped — gone totally psycho", is David's first thought.

Dumbfounded, but not totally surprised, he holds up his flat-tened hand — waving her down to sit, quiet and still.

"Stop!," he whispers, over and over, "Stop!....Stop!"

The babbling peters out. Fiona meekly obeys, surprisingly, flopping on the chair — the giddy exhaustion of elation.

"Now, start at the start, this time very slowly," says David, speaking softly and mechanically, mimicking what he wants her to do, "and tell me what's happening."

Calmer now, Fiona proceeds haltingly, "You were right, David: the scroll was written by Philodemus, just as you had predicted.... this was disappointing at first. As more of your data accumulated however, letters emerged....at last, I could make a calculated guess on a few sentences."

Fiona pauses to catch her breathe, then rises off the chair for dramatic effect.

"David, I think that we've hit the jackpot!", she announces.

"I've kept this to myself, for the last week, reworking all the possibilities. Yes, it's written by Philodemus which was confusing me at first....It's now my considered professional opinion however, based on preliminary data, that Philodemus made a direct copy of a rare original work by Epicurus himself."

David sits bolt upright in his chair, spellbound, mouth agape.

"For real! — can you be sure?" he finally asks, meekly, protectively, "You know how competitive and bitchy you classicists can become, daggers ready, with reputations and grant monies at stake.... not to mention both of our jobs."

"Yes, yes, it's conditional on preliminary data,....but at this stage, astonishingly, it's more probable that it really is Epicurus. We need a lot more data, and funding, before we approach the journals."

Fiona adds, smirking, "I'm including your name in the journal article, so as to share the fame,....or should I say 'blame'."

They both laugh and snigger at absent rivals, at once errant children, the first time in a month. Together, again!

Gathering her composure, Fiona continues as the matter-of-fact professional classicist.

"I think the miraculous has occurred David, but there's more! It only gets better....I think? On closer inspection of the scroll, there are tantalizing hints that it may be, possibly,....a personal record by Epicurus in which he documents his struggles and trials against the odds, to found his famous 'School of the Garden'. Unlike Aristotle, he was poor and provincial, and worse still, an outsider — not from Athens. Wary of head-in-the-clouds abstractions, philosophy for Epicurus meant practical advice on living a fulfilling life. More like Socrates, really."

"So, living life in a glass cubicle is not the Epicurean thing to do!", David smirked.

A hushed pause, only briefly,....and Fiona broke into a hearty laugh.

Together, unrehearsed, they slid upwards and sideways, off their chairs, into a spontaneous hug, as brief as it was awkward. There remains unspoken, the clear understanding that in their confined quarters, such 'happy behavior' is nothing other than the natural celebration of achievement. Team-building of course, by any other name — no need for Human Resources to be alarmed!

With her still sketchy, but promising findings, Fiona is ushered into the hallowed, oak-panelled chambers of that supreme body,.... the Board of the American Center for Antiquities Research.

The Boardroom is hushed as Fiona enters, some members offering a flicker of a feeble smile. Relegated to an unpadded, straight-back chair set against the wall, she patiently waits for her turn at the podium. 'A room full of clones', Fiona muses: men-in-suits, crisp white shirts, gold cuff links, and regulation red ties. The corporate uniform! Most noticeably however, there are two exceptional women who had broken through the ethereal ceiling of corporate privilege — whose razor-sharp insights ensured that they were regarded as anything but passive tokens. Reassuring for Fiona. She takes stock as the baritone-voiced Chairman promptly calls the meeting to order and opens with the previous 'Minutes'.

The presiding Chair is a middle-aged man, with pomaded salt-and-pepper hair, ruddy complexion, cold jet-black eyes, and a pressed blue-suit bulging precariously at the seams. Fiona half-expected, half-feared that — with a resounding crack — the straining seams would burst asunder. 'Bumptious' immediately comes to mind for Fiona — she almost says it aloud as it pops into her head. It's the perfect word, she thinks to herself, as it sounds just like its burly subject, inflated and mildly comical — except,....there's a lot at stake. Strangely enough, the Chair's 'bumptiousness' gives her added relief from her jitters. Mouthing it over and over again, Fiona finds she can deflate him, bringing him down-to-earth, down to her level.

The Chair begins speaking, every syllable carefully pronounced, as if everything he says is writ large in capitals. A boorish little man, Fiona concludes, full of his own puffery. Unusual for Fiona, she dislikes him instantly. Now it's her turn - Fiona's perfectionism has all her facts primed and ready at hand.

"We have Doctor Roberts next on the agenda today, presenting her....ah....recent findings and — he pauses here, lamely — her 'provisional' interpretations".

The introduction continues at length, with several unsettling references to 'budget overruns' and 'red ink'. An arrogant 'corporate type if ever there was one' Fiona muses, buttoning down her contempt at his pompous game-playing. She had heard of his gender conservatism and reputation for LGBTQ misspeaks ('A sad case of repression' — Fiona is delighted with the mischievous thought that popped into her mind — a private chuckle whose only giveaway is an inscrutable smirk).

The Chair concludes with another signature pause, turning the floor over to "Doctor….umm….Roberts, one of our….ahem…. hard-working academics".

Her dander up, Fiona launches into her PowerPoint presentation, describing as briefly as she can, her many months of exacting research. An hour passes and heads start to nod, while others are busily clock-watching. Taking her cue, Fiona skips the 'statistical tables of probabilities' — it's time to hammer home her breathtaking conclusion.

"If…and this is a big IF, this is indeed Epicurus' own story told by himself autobiographically,…."

Fiona hesitates in mid-sentence, then drops the punch-line, a universal, never-fail appeal to self-interest.

"….it will add immediate lustre and renown to the Antiquities Center."

Heads perk up, elbows retrieved from the Boardroom table. Chins are cupped and rubbed, faces stroked. Fiona knew the Center was currently lagging in institutional status (she didn't mention this), which diminished the personal prestige of Board members — not to mention their career aspirations to move ever upwards. It had been a long drought since the last groundbreaking Press Release.

With a toss of her fiery red hair and raised voice, Fiona makes a theatric appeal for additional funding — swinging her arms in a wide arc, while looking steely-eyed at the Chair.

"We need a larger team, many times over, papyrologists,

classicists, sub-specialist textual scholars, maybe even a forensic archivist."

The Chairman sniffles loudly, rubbing his chin. More coded communication.

Most importantly, Fiona requests 'access funding' for trials with the Grenoble synchrotron (at David's insistence), which would "vastly improve the accuracy of the energy settings for the microscans."

Coughs, splutters, and mutterings.

"Yes, yes it will be expensive, no doubt....," she adds.

"....but the the synchrotron will speed up the project immensely."

The Board members have sat restlessly through 'the ordeal' of the scientific data, chins propped on the table, shifting in their plush leather chairs to stay awake. The last statement however, is the clincher that abruptly galvanizes their full attention. Weary of endless talk and anxious for tangible results, it's the 'bottom line' they have been patiently waiting to hear.

Sensing the momentum, Fiona shrewdly launches her punchline with perfect timing, plucky as ever.

"I think we are all standing on the threshold of a wonderful discovery," she announces, heart in her mouth, "I'll stake my reputation on it!"

Where once a strained silence reigned, now everyone is talking at once, elated to finally have a newsworthy project....with their prominent endorsement. Scanning the room, sensing the shift in mood, the Chair congratulates Fiona on "a fine presentation,.... Doctor Roberts,....may I say, Fiona?" — calling for a 'vigorous' round of applause.

Funding is duly budgeted, conditional upon progress of course, and a 'best of the best' team is recruited, hand-picked by Fiona as Team Leader, complete with "Team Epicurus" tee shirts (David's idea). The bumptious Chair — after first losing his way to Fiona's office, "it's a rabbit warren!" — now becomes a frequent visitor: "just to keep up morale".

After one year, the team reaches consensus that the text is indeed, a copy of an Epicurus original, moreover, of a likely auto-biographical nature. At four years, despite the bleating of the Board for quick turnaround results, Team Epicurus has assembled a 'digital simulacrum' of the original manuscript — letter by letter, sentence by sentence, page by page, from countless thousands of carefully calibrated microscans.

It is indeed, the 'Epicuriana', one of the great lost works of antiquity!

At long last, the Antiquities Board launches a major Press Release that takes off like wildfire, grabbed by all the news agencies across the United States, and internationally. In eye-catching hyperbole, headlines trumpet the digital recovery of an 'invisible diary', an ageless Epicurean masterpiece. Board members beam while Alumni fight to provide endowments, that nonetheless, carry their illustrious names.

At the obligatory black-tie cocktail party, the major fund-raising event of the season, Fiona runs the gauntlet of gratuitous smiles and finger-pointing. The once pretentious, now affable Antiquities Chair shepherds his prized researcher between groups of potential donors, Fiona finding herself responding tirelessly to the same predictable questions. An obese Saudi in traditional garb pats Fiona briefly on the shoulder, and strokes her arm affectionately several times during their conversation. David shows restraint, telling himself that it's nothing more than cross-cultural differences, though this doesn't stop him from intervening, calling Fiona aside for an 'urgent call'.

Amid the glad-handing, Fiona encounters for the first time that bugbear of all researchers: those partisan agencies who wish to conflate classical studies with geo-politics. While the Chair is waylaid by eager journalists — with David holding forth at the bar — a stylish, handsome 'official' from the Greek Embassy button-holes Fiona into a corner. At first, Fiona is relieved by what seems to be an innocent conversation, as a welcome break from the monotony of rote questioning. It's actually refreshing, she thinks to herself, that he is less concerned with her academic research — Fiona gathers that his interests lie with some tenuous Greek claims to claw back several small Aegean islands lying off the coast of the Turkish Republic.

She listens attentively but disinterested, concluding that he's just another ardent patriot, which makes for a pleasant, but harmless interlude. Her passive listening receives an unexpected jolt however, when the ancient kingdom of Ionia, a proto-Greek state, slips into the discussion.

"Would the Epicuriana", the handsome 'official' inquires, "contain any dated references to these Ionian islands, especially relating to ancient commerce and trading routes, which might bolster our righteous case for annexation? Turkey grabbed the islands illegally when Ataturk overthrew the Ottomans in the aftermath of World War One. The West was so anxious to embrace the new Republic, even at the cost of its old allies."

Suddenly uncomfortable, Fiona finds herself plunged into the murky waters of international intrigue. With beating heart, she quickly excuses herself for the ladies' 'powder-room'! Making her way, she notices that her prior exchange had not escaped the notice of the Turkish Ambassador who makes a point of smiling benignly — nodding graciously at her as she passes.

Months slip by, as Fiona settles back into her laboratory research, preparing her overdue monographs between an onslaught of media interviews. It's not long before other blandishments follow, considerably more substantive: a hefty salary increase, tenured professorship, plush office, and even a private secretary, as incentives to retain her services (She places several recruitment offers in her top drawer). Moreover, she is granted a six month sabbatical which also allows ample time for a tour of ancient Troy, especially arranged by the Turkish government.

"A professional courtesy" says the Turkish archeologist, her personal guide on the Trojan site, now that she is a momentary celebrity. "....Or a bribe by any other name", Fiona thinks to herself.

A bright young man, he coyly asks her many detailed questions about her work on the Epicuriana, not in itself, an unusual thing in exchanges between scientific colleagues. As time passes however, the conversation subtly converges on her Ionian findings. Fiona is prepared this time.

"Just to clarify any possible misunderstandings," she states nonchalantly, while intensely examining a tiny ceramic potsherd, "You should know that Epicurus makes no mention whatsoever of the disputed Aegean islands."

Fiona looks up with an impish smile. The young man nods innocently, as if the matter carries no importance — merely friendly chitchat to pass the time.

High above them, the red flag of the Turkish Republic, with its prominent crescent moon of Islam, flutters over the hallowed battleground of Greeks and Trojans. Ancient history and modern politics, while seemingly strange bedfellows, are uniquely difficult to separate.

"Treasure comes in many forms" mused Fiona, as she wanders amid the dusty ruins of Homer's Troy, stratum upon stratum of long ago lives, which not surprisingly, remind her of the delicate layers of a carbonized papyrus scroll! She thought too, about her many years of tedious research — excavating Epicurus' life from the dustbin of history — her very own Trojan odyssey.

Epicurus' voice was lost in time — suppressed, disparaged, and distorted beyond recognition — finally brought to vibrant life from the Athenian 'Golden Age' of philosophers.

"For I am he, born Epicurus of Samos, son of the Athenians, Neocles and Chaerestrata, of the Athenian deme (village) of Gargettus, and clan Philaidae, and this is my true voice."

"Herewith, I lay aside my reed pen, having recorded my thoughts as well as my lived life, such as it is, which is merely the pallid interlude between such thoughts. Neither poetics nor rhetoric, I turn my testament over to the Fates, in the hope that while I am now nothing but dust, these erstwhile thoughts may yet continue to live, and find a gentle heart amidst an uncertain posterity."

PART II:
"Beginnings"

Chapter 4

Notium, port for Colophon, Ionia
310 BC

With a lightness of spirit, and young heart beating with the prospect of adventure, I bid farewell to the licentious city-state of Colophon.

Plans have been laid, and promises made. I have no regrets — save the teary wrenching apart from Servilia. Despite her tenderness and support for my future plans, I feel guilty for leaving her. Parting is always more difficult for the one left behind.

Valerius of course, forever the merchant businessman, has a quite different response.

"I've got a proprietorial investment in you, Epicurus," he remarks, in mock severity, accompanied by his signature winking, "and I look forward to a handsome return!"

I am startled, even amused, to find that both Valerius and my father are together, chatting away in animated discussion, on the dock. My father has come to accept the inevitable, still ambivalent at my departure, but without the opposition I had once dreaded. Valerius' beneficent funding and patronage had clinched the arrangement, undercutting his objections.

My father gives me a furtive, parting hug, a vicarious admission that he will miss me, unstated, though appreciated all the same.

The cargo is now secured, hawsers are cast off, sails set and trimmed, billowing and flapping as we pick up speed, amidst the parting shouts and farewell waves. Only when the last faint outline of Servilia dies away in my eyes, a lone disappearing speck on the horizon, does the enormity of my decision strike home to me — a nagging, fleeting thought pushed away for the moment — overtaken by the immensity of a glittering sea beyond sight of land. My first dawn at sea, crisp and inviting, an omen I hope, of the new, adventurous life that awaits me. For the first time in a long while, I feel free and light as if anything is possible.

Merchant Galley, "Hector"

I watch enthralled, as the arched prow of the Hector knifes through the crystalline waters of the North Aegean. In the distance, the grey-green smudge of the Ionian coast becomes visible in the growing daylight, as our stout vessel gently heaves and yaws in the following sea.

The Hector is one of Valerius' commodious merchant galleys, complete with a second bowsprit mast. It's captain, Master Panyotis is nuggety and sun-wrinkled, with a memorable paunch and that jolly disposition that comes with unimpeachable authority. The cargo manifest shows three hundred amphora below deck, mostly wine and olive-oil, while the rest are grindstones — serving the dual role of trading goods and ship's ballast.

A small cabin, seemingly appended as an afterthought, rests disproportionately at the stern as shelter for the ship's master and the few experienced freedmen, "old hands". Linen awnings, flapping loudly as the ship rolls, provide the deck-crew's only respite from the sun and fluky weather.

The billowing mainsail is the typical Attic square of coarse linen, with twin rudder-oars for steerage. When Aeolus, god of all winds, leaves us becalmed, then the crew turn to oars with leather skirting, set below the high gunnels. Mostly enslaved, but well-treated and cheerful, the crew are swarthy types: unshackled, barrel-chested Scythians, jowly Thracians, and a few long-necked North Africans, burnt to darkest ebony by the Mediterranean sun. We all take turns baling the bilge, a daily chore, including the master himself.

Such a glorious day, fresh, clear, with a blue, blue sea fading invisibly into a cerulean sky. It's Spring, the prime season for voyaging: few storms, fair winds, and warming weather, making for a pleasant passage. The melodic slip-slap of the sea on the hull sets me to musing about Homer's poetics. Servilia and I would read 'The Iliad' and 'The Odyssey' aloud to ourselves, taking turns, sometimes even play-acting characters such as the aggrieved Menelaus or doomed Iphigenia. It was 'our thing', that became a coded inspiration for the personal conduct of our future lives — with added lashings of melodrama. These were our stories! We gloried in our shared Attic - Ionian heritage — we were treading in the footsteps of our Homeric ancestors, charged with the same unflinching audacity.

Now here I am, sailing the 'wine-dark sea' of Homer's epics, the Aegean at its finest — dolphins gambolling, tuna shoaling. Flights of cormorants and kingfishers dive and feast on the gathering pods of sardines. There's even a semi-resident Pelican perched on the stern, awarded the moniker of "Ulysses" by the crew — all affirming that I too am an integral member of Nature's great Chain of Being. I fear that I'm already slipping into mysticism, or worse still, becoming a Platonist! I've heard that the immensity of the ocean — boundless blue in all directions — does this to people.

Even the ship has eyes, vividly painted on each side like all our vessels, so that the Hector can see its way around dangers for safe guidance, or at least for good-luck, if nothing else.

We will need this assurance when we enter the narrows of the Hellespont, encrusted with heroic legends and cyclopian myths, past the ancient remains of Troy, en route to our final destination: Lampsacus. Shipwrecks are not uncommon in the Hellespont, due to the fast-flowing waters — riptides and swirling eddies, which unpredictably, degenerate into roaring maelstroms.

Such tidal occurrences are far from being the only danger. Pirates also, with a reputation for cruelty, are an ever present scourge in the confines of the Hellespont narrows. Sluggish, heavily-laden trading vessels like the Hector, caught in tidal races, with little ability to manoeuvre, make for ideal prey.

Master Panyotis and the freemen crew are armed of course, but inexperienced. As a hoplite warrior, I am the only one trained in heavy infantry shock combat in full armor, or hoplomachia. By Valerius' insistence, I am carrying on board, my javelin, sling, short-sword, and aspis, a large dish-shaped wooden shield. Carefully oiled and stored below, is that most precious of military belongings, my bronze breastplate, shin armor, and vivid crested helmet. I, a fresh-faced philosopher of the tranquil life, have been designated to lead the phalanx in our defence — I'm tickled by the exquisite irony. Then I remember that Socrates was a hoplite warrior also, a veteran of many savage battles, even acclaimed as a hero on at least one occasion.

With a fair wind and a following sea, the redoubtable Hector gently rolls and pitches, sails bellowing: full-speed ahead for a gallant old tub! Pirates, be damned! Poseidon is with us, god of the seas and storms, protector of poor seafarers — for we will surely soon need his protection!

By mid-afternoon of the second day, an ominous line of black storm clouds, with dense, towering thunderheads comes scudding over the horizon, accompanied by sheet lightning and booming thunder. The once luminous blue sky has now turned slate-grey, ugly and foreboding — heavy rain squalls hiss across the white-crested seas of the oft-treacherous North Aegean. Ahead of the storm front, close at hand, I catch sight my first waterspout, a spiral column of air and water funnelling upwards, dazzling and giddy to watch. The Master is less impressed.

"We're in for it now," Master Panyotis growls instructions, above the howling of the wind.

"Lash and stow everything loose on deck. Secure the hatches. We'll be on our beam-ends, if we're not careful."

The crew have followed the same storm protocol countless times, and know it well, anticipating the master's orders. They spring into lively action, each knowing his place, hard-reefing the mainsail, and tightly furling the small mizzen-sail. I try to help where I can, though I feel like useless cargo.

The heavily-laden vessel is now wallowing comfortably between blue-green combers, her sails reefed, with an occasional white-capping sea wave breaking over the deck. Master Panyotis tells me calmly that the Hector has weathered a hundred such tempests — purposely built to withstand these conditions, and much worse. I hope not, mercifully, since my stomach is already roiling.

"Play out the hawser," he orders, "a sea-anchor will reduce our yawing and risk of broaching."

The hawser is run out to its full length, so that the bow remains pointed in the direction of the swells — we are to hunker down and ride out the storm. Then matters take a turn for the worse, much worse.

"Sail Ho," comes the strident cry from a crewman, "Pirate off the stern, close in on our port quarter."

Master Panyotis curses loudly, very florid and inventive — the mark of a true sea-dog — though it does little to abate the waves or ward off the pirate.

"It's the Sea Wolf," he says, now assuming the deadpan voice of quiet authority, "a well known predator in these waters. The worst of the worst — daring, speed, and savagery. These vermin use the cover of a storm-front, thunderbolts and heaving seas, to close in on their prey, undetected in the blinding downpour — coming out of nowhere. The fury of the storm then further adds to the shock and menace of their attack — when their prey is buttoned down below decks and most vulnerable. With our hawser out, loaded down with cargo, we're like a big fat cow stuck in a bog. These wolves will be on us shortly. No time for all your fancy armor, m'boy, just grab what weapons you can."

I go below, and return with my spear, sword, aspis, and sling, as well as a pouch of lead shot. I am eager at finally been assigned a role — a deadweight passenger no more! The crew are all grim-faced however, armed with makhairae, the short stabbing-swords favored by sailors. I get my first glimpse of the pitch-black hull of the rakish pirate vessel, lightly-constructed for speed and manoeu-vring. Treble-reefed, with little cargo, it's riding high and fast over the cresting waves like a racehorse, bearing down upon us.

The pirate crew, a misshapen, ghoulish lot, have grappling-hooks at the ready, as they prepare themselves to come alongside for a forced boarding. I ready my sling, and hope that I give a good account of myself. I had been trained by a Balearic slinger, the very best, renowned for his deadly accuracy.

Master Panyotis now takes the helm. Much to my surprise, for a man of such restrained authority, he immediately screams into the wind, defiantly, deafeningly.

"Now! Now!"

With that, one of the ebony crewmen wields a heavyweight ship's axe, severing the hawser. The Hector instantly leaps forward and comes about, manoeuvrable once again. At the very same time, the Master swings the helm hard over. The Hector veers sharply to starboard, broadside to the waves, directly into the path of the Sea Wolf, making boarding impossible. A collision amidships is inevitable. I look at the master with growing concern: I'm no sailor, but whatever is he doing?

I brace myself for the collision....and keep my sling handy with lead shot.

The Hector is a deep-draft, wide beam, high freeboard vessel with a frame and outer hull of sturdy oak, designed to transport heavy cargos in all weathers. Slow, but robust, and very seaworthy. Conversely, the Sea Wolf is sleek, purposely built for speed and pursuit.

In practical terms, this means a shallow-draft, narrower beam, lighter frame, and lower freeboard, to reduce displacement weight. Like many things in life, enhanced speed is a trade-off, at the cost of sturdiness. Master Panyotis of course, knows all this instinctively, and now uses this knowledge to his advantage.

Matters then play out, in rapid succession. The pirate vessel plunges into a deep trough, flaring mists of spray as it falls. The following wave then catapults it forward, lifting it up to the foaming wave crest, as it comes crashing down upon our ship. The sturdy hull of the Hector heels over as expected, absorbing the massive impact, before rightening — with its high freeboard, the leeward port gunnels remain safely above the waterline. Driven onwards by the wild sea, the pirate's bow mounts the Hector's hull before slamming into the upperworks. Never before have I heard the spine-chilling, sickening cacophony of splintering, exploding beams.

Our weather side gunnels hold firm however, as the the pirate vessel rides up and over them, lifting its bow and keel. Listing to port, waves now break over the aft quarters and gunnels of the Sea-Wolf, risking capsize. I can plainly see the pirate crew, most of whom have been thrown off their feet by the impact — at least one is washed overboard, a momentary scream before he disappears in the raging surf. The pirates' confusion gives me a brief opportunity to pummel them at short range. I bring my slinger into lethal action. Several slinger shots find their mark, much to the jeering satisfaction of the Hector's crew.

My status on board, formerly one of quiet tolerance and condescension appropriate to a landlubber, has now become that of comradeship, even deference.

Chapter 5

Master Panyotis performed an astonishing act of seamanship, based on the ridiculously simple premise of doing that which was least expected — turning towards the incoming pirate vessel, rather than away from it!

Setting the two vessels on a deliberate collision course, he wagered the sturdiness of his solid galley against the light-framed pirate vessel. With the capping waves of the storm driving them forwards, the pirates had the weather against them, with no time to manoeuvre. Master Panyotis' timing was impeccable.

The pirate vessel was first bludgeoned at the bow by the high-speed collision, losing several of its crew to the sea, then a few more to my slinger. Soon after, comes the second act of the Master's entrapment tactics!

Having smashed the bow of the pirate vessel, the stern is next. Immediately following the collision, the Master swings the helm hard to port. No sooner does the pirate vessel slid back into the sea — once more on an even keel, if only briefly — than the heavy stern of the Hector rams the aft quarters of the other ship. Incredible.

The Hector is now to windward of the Sea Wolf. With each capping wave, its huge displacement weight pounds down on the stern and upper-works of the lightly-constructed pirate ship, shattering gunnels, spars, and deck beams. Finally, the mast itself falls. Seizing the opportunity, I bring my versatile slinger into action again, cracking heads.

The pirate chief stands sword in hand, defiant, glaring in disbelief at his toppled mast. He turns, and we lock eyes, wide and glaring: a moment frozen in time — little did I realize then — that will come back to haunt me. He makes for a striking profile, with a moonlike, tattooed face, piercing black eyes, and block-shaped, deformed earlobes protruding from his head. Completing the exotic image, tufts of wild red hair are scattered across his otherwise bald scalp. Most unforgettable however, is the scarlet red tunic he wears, bright and conspicuous, as if to say, invincibly, omnipotently: 'Here I am, a rosy-red target for all to see, and you can't touch me'.

I take up the challenge with my slinger, aiming at 'Red'. He watches my swing as it builds momentum, waiting for the telltale finger movement that signals an imminent release of the ball. Standing firm and unflappable beside the toppled mask, he dodges the projectile, with calculated disinterest.

Not a total miss however, since it grazes his right cheek, blood running down the nape of his neck. 'Red' continues his gaze unflinchingly, fierce and nonchalant. Enemy he may be, I couldn't help but admire his courage.

In that moment, we register the other as deadly adversaries, imprinting the the image for a future reckoning. I try again — a close miss, as he twitches his head quickly to one side! He's playing a deadly game with me, in which all my best efforts only serve to demonstrate his skill and bravado.

Much to their astonishment, the pirates find that their easy prey, apparently defenceless, turns out to be a tactically-managed armed merchantman.

The Sea Wolf limps away, driven by the wind and waves, dragging flotsam behind it, still attached to the mast rigging. Our crew jeer and whoop excitedly as the pirate passes out of sight. Not mortally wounded, it's certainly badly damaged, decks awash, with several crew injured, dead, or missing. I see 'Red' scrambling about, frantically issuing orders.

The Hector has sustained only superficial damage, with no injuries to the crew. The sea battle is over: the breaking seas ensuring that it finishes as quickly as it started. This stirring feat of seamanship will surely pass into legend, entered into the annals, told from one generation to the next.

The proud Hector's crew raise a loud cheer for their audacious master, who used his otherwise vulnerable, lumbering vessel as an unlikely weapon, to cudgel the Sea Wolf into submission. It would seem that 'the big fat cow, stuck in the bog', has a lethal wallop.

⁂

Mytilene is our next destination, the principal port-city on the island of Lesbos — a two day berthing to offload cargo, our only detour, then onwards to Lampsacus. Our proud Hector will be considerably lighter by the time we enter the treacherous Hellespont.

The sea is no longer roiling and breaking with white combers, as it was yesterday. Come morning, it has settled down now into that long, rhythmic heaving familiar to all mariners. The crew talk of little else other than the recent encounter, that they were 'witnesses' to something momentous, 'history in the making', and so on. With the conflict over, I retreat into the anticlimax of weariness. Exciting, yes, but also fatiguing.

With little to do now, I stretch out slumberous in the morning warmth, cushioned on a coil of camel-hair rope — ample time to review the rapid-moving events and choices that have placed me on this unexpected course.

The amniotic warmth of the sun, the lap-lapping of the bow-wake against the gunnels, and the steady rise-and-fall of the deck on which I'm sprawled, all induce a dreamy relaxation. Idle thoughts float into my mind, childhood memories leap-frogging back in time: playing 'hide' with Servilia, laughing together, become muddled with fearsome snapshots of 'Red. I struggle to keep myself in this half-awake state, fighting back against Hypnos, god of dreams — at some point however, my previously random thoughts take on a definite, surprising direction. Has the battle upturned my too-cosy view of life? Whatever was the trigger — whence came these unexpected thoughts? — is lost to me now, though my life will be altered forever.

Epicurus as a Young Man

Valerius is shoring me up as an egalitarian act of goodwill, he says. When the time comes, I can then enter Athens as an independent teacher, fully established with my own followers. It's a well-reasoned plan that I must reluctantly admit, makes a great deal of common sense. Can his motives really be that simple, so transparent?

I'm no longer a credulous child however — I know that self-interest drives much of human behavior. I ask myself then, what does Valerius have to gain by becoming my self-appointed patron? A debt of honor, so he says, to be settled in my mother's name, which makes little sense to me, nor does he explain any further.

My mother and I were close and she never once made mention of him! I obviously can't check this with her, so corroboration is impossible. What if he has misrepresented her, to hide his true motives? If true, then I resent his use of my mother's name to manipulate me and bolster his own covert designs. In fact, this dishonors her!

If this so-called 'debt of honor' is just something he invented — a bare-faced lie! — then I need to consider other reasons underlying his generous patronage. The question then becomes: 'Why me?'. There are plenty of ambitious young men in Colophon with more talent than I. It's not as if I came to him unbidden with a proposal. Instead, he sought me out! For what reason?

I know him to be a savvy businessman if nothing else — I wonder if his designs on me may be more self-serving than he presents. Experience has taught me that usually the most obvious, straightforward explanation is the correct one. The immediate assumption that springs to mind is Servilia.

Valerius is a possessive parent, which makes it plausible, even compelling, that his 'patronage' is a cleverly veiled attempt to separate Servilia and I! He may be hoping that my prolonged absence will put an end to the romance: as time naturally dulls my memories of Servilia, the nubile young maidens of Lampsacus can only gain in their seductive charms — or so he thinks! He may already have some 'velvet traps' lined up — waiting for me.

Yet Servilia insisted that I take this lifetime opportunity, to fulfil what I pompously called 'my destiny'. She vowed to continue loving me in my absence rather than feeling forever guilty if she held me back. As she put it in her own words,

"I already have my fill of guilt over my mother's early death. If you were to remain here, you will end up resenting me, no matter what you say. It would kill our love, and that would be the greater loss. This way, I keep you alive in my heart, always, until you come back to me."

Valerius' obsequious devotion to Servilia presents as a comic mix of operatic care, paternal protection, and overripe affection. It's all too much at times — as if she is the reincarnation of his dear, departed wife. I understand that he may want to split us up as a couple. Is he offering me the fulfilment of my deepest wish as a favor, when it is really a bribe in disguise? While my obedience to his wishes may further my life's goal, the cost of losing Servilia is a very high price to pay.

If the simplest explanations are always the best, then Valerius' goodwill is nothing other than a baited trap, in which case I owe him nothing. My dander is up!

Time for me to reclaim my own self-interest, ex-Valerius. A plan, just an idle thought at first, begins to gather momentum the more I think about it. My very own plan! If not Athens, then let the alternative be of my own choosing — instead of Lampsacus, where I will be hemmed in by Valerius' cronies, reporting on me. My balmy days on the Hector are regrettably drawing to a close!

I will 'jump ship' and begin my public teaching at Mytilene, much closer to Colophon, quickly get established, then call for Servilia to join me. The Mytileneans include several important philosophical schools, which suggests a ready-made level of acceptance. Surely, there is room for one more teacher, offering fresh and original doctrines — with the prospect of opening my own school in the near future.

Aristotle himself taught there, before becoming tutor to the great world conqueror, Alexander of Macedon. Aristotle used

Mytilene as a 'bridge' to gain greater recognition. He then used this reputation to establish his school at the Lyceum in Athens. If Aristotle used Mytilene as a steppingstone to Athens, then so can I. This alone makes Mytilene a better option than Lampsacus — if Aristotle's success is any guide, then it's the obvious place to start for me. To further bolster my decision, Mytilene is now governed by a Macedonian general, whose territory also includes Colophon, enabling an easy transition between the two cities.

Master Panyotis will object of course — Valerius had appointed him to personally ensure that I reach Lampsacus safely. However, the master is good-natured and will surely understand the ambitions and adventures of a headstrong young man, especially one who has given honorable service as a maritime slinger.

At the age of thirty, my time has arrived. I sense that Mytilene, whatever may come, is a turning point in my life, something that I must reach out and grab while I can. There are no second chances in life.

For me, life is an adventure to be lived fully. Yet every life-adventure involves some risk, albeit a calculated one, otherwise it's not an adventure. Of course, the outcome of a life-adventure, as it is so often the case, might not be what I expect. No matter. Better an adventure, even one driven by a rebellious impulse, than stuck in a helpless rut! Otherwise, I remain a mere puppet for a devious Roman master, pulling the strings.

Playing life too safe. Not for me! I want to live life contagiously, spreading the contagion. Otherwise, life remains secure enough, though vapid and stagnant, overflowing with possibilities never taken.

I don't want to die with regrets, in life or love. While my yearning for Servilia is palpable, I will return to her — but it will be a triumphant homecoming as my own man,....not a pawn of her scheming father.

The pulse of life beckons, onwards to Mytilene.

Chapter 6

Mytilene, Aegean Isle of Lesbos
309 BC

Shoved and elbowed, carried along by the crowd, I find myself entering a covered colonnade. I am dazzled by its length, exceeding two hundred cubits, with ornate barrel vault ceilings, and a promenade of fluted Doric columns on one side.

A seemingly infinite jumble of shops jostle together noisily on the other side, separated by partitions. I wander along dreamily, hustled by lame and misshapen beggars, amid what seems like a gauntlet of colors, cries, and the babble of furious trading. Anything can be purchased, bartered, or else, deftly stolen from the unwary vendor — if one is willing to risk the loss of a right arm!

This is the famous Stoa of Mytilene on the mythic island of Lesbos, a cornucopia of riches: the staples of corn, olive oil, honey, wine, wool, and papyrus but also hemp for rope, pitch for sealing decks. Then come the goats with their strident cries, cattle bellowing, game-cocks scratching and crowing. All manner of gemstones catch my eye as I wander along, especially the intense deep-blue of lapis-lazuli, the cinnamon-red of garnets, or lustrous amber from the frozen northlands. Most precious of all, beyond gold and silver, are the fine silks from China, following the ancient trade routes, over deserts, skirting bandits, by caravans of camels.

Remorseless slave traders parade their finest Scythian specimens, the wretched batch of recent raids in the Pontic steppes:

cowered maidens whose once long, beaded hair is now close-cropped and spiky, the telltale mark of slavery. Defiant paragons of masculinity still struggle in their chains, all to be auctioned off to the highest bidder, in batches, or singular if the specimen is exceptional — including one formidable hulk, still unbroken, from faraway Germania.

Stoa of Mytilene (entrance), Lesbos

Dye and cloth merchants are here aplenty, as well as fishmongers, farmers, weavers, and leather workers. There are artisanal foundries in bronze, iron, and glass with sculptures of favorite gods in abundance. Potters too, with bright red-glazed pottery, or Aeolic grey wares in all sizes.

Sleazy charlatans offer the ubiquitous electrum coins and figurines, dip-coated, not pure of course, at 'unbelievable' bargain prices. There is no shortage of gullible foreigners with deep pockets, and poor judgement. Such ersatz wares also seem to have a special attraction for the self-proclaimed 'great negotiators', who believe something for nothing is just a question of glib trading. The errant merchants love them, artfully playing the game of bickering over inflated prices. It's entertaining to watch.

This is the beating heart of the city, the bustling, cacophonous agora, complete with a public address platform, even boasting its own lending library. It was here that the celebrated Sappho shared her lyric poetry of love and sexual longing, sung to the accompaniment of a kithara. I follow in the footsteps of the young Aristotle who loitered down the same agora promenade, only a generation before me, wondering what life may have in store for him. Sappho and Aristotle: if only the stones could speak! Now it's my turn, waiting for me — I enter alone, knowing not a soul: the commercial, political, and spiritual center of the boisterous city-state of Mytilene,....soon to be my home. Pshaw on Valerius!

❦❦❦❦❦❦❦❦❦❦❦❦❦❦❦

The good ship Hector has already discharged its cargo, sooner than expected, and will slip out of harbor early tomorrow, gauging a flood tide for the Hellespont narrows. While their stay in Mytilene is brief, the master and crew are justly feted as conquering heroes. The warring exploits of the gallant Hector, embroidered with each telling, has fast become 'the talk of the town'.

Most importantly, Master Panyotis has shattered the myth of the pirates' invincibility and opened the sea-lanes around Mytilene. The local traders are fulsome in their praise! In the hands of a few, well-chosen seamen, the master had demonstrated — to everyone's astonishment — that the pirates can be soundly beaten. The lamb turns out to be a lion. Beaten no less, by a defenceless, old hulk, straight out of Homer, Hector by name, Hector by deed. It is a moment to savor, in which the whole community joins in the merriment.

I have purposely dodged the wild celebrations: trumpets sounding — noble speeches by self-important dignitaries in honor of the heroes; staged dancing in the agora, spilling over into the raucous crowds; heavy drinking, back-slapping, bonfires, and carousing in the docklands. The city is consumed by this spontaneous festival of goodwill. The Hector and her crew are awarded the perpetual 'Freedom of the City', by which all meals, wine, accommodation, or any other 'personal services', present and future, will be paid by the city-state. My own status however, is an awkward one: any acclaim will necessarily 'position' me as a seafaring hoplite in the public perception — not the reputation I am seeking in my newfound home. If I am to gain renown, I want it to be on my merits as a philosopher, not to be immediately branded as an heroic slinger and pirate-hunter.

I needn't worry, as the Fates intervene once again.

Shuffling my way laboriously through the jubilant crowd, I catch a brief, tantalizing glimpse of a bright, red tunic, topped with ringlets of red hair. The face is only a distant blur. Whoever owns the tunic is situated on the far periphery of the crowd, lost amidst the merrymaking on the opposite side of the dock, furthermost from me. So fleeting is the glimpse, I can't be sure about what I have seen.

Has my imagination conjured up a ghostly apparition from last week's dramatic events? I am still finding my 'land-legs' after a week on a rolling deck. As with my legs, my vision may also be a little wobbly? Could it really be 'Red'? Would he be that bold? Even wearing his signature tunic? Is he scouting the enemy for information, looking for a second round?

Repairs to the heavily damaged 'Sea Wolf' will take at least several months, according to Master Panyotis. Thoughts flash across my mind: should I give chase to some innocuous Mytilenian who by happenstance, has an unusual preference for bright red tunics? Moreover, the city is a busy crossroads port — there are any number of celts here with red hair!

I could spend my time wondering, or just simply find out, before the moment is lost!

It is now or never.

I instantly change direction, cutting across, as quickly as I can — even pushing people aside — heading towards my last sighting. As I draw closer, I note that the outer fringes of the crowd melt into a particular alleyway, one of many.

I can see the figure clearly now. It is 'Red', no doubt, trotting away, at the far end of the narrowing alley.

He breaks into a run, even as I watch, past the stone ramparts of the ancient city wall, into the squalid docklands, on the outskirts of the Agora. With its population of shadowy types: cutthroat robbers, prostitutes, pickpockets, and rough-edged brawlers — the ghetto is a sprawling and ramshackle place. It offers the perfect roost to hide out in plain sight. No one asks questions in these close quarters. Moreover, everyone expects a notorious pirate to be living a private life of princely excess — certainly not secreted away in a decrepit slum under the noses of the law.

Has he seen me? I need to be careful.

I am the one eyewitness who could take him to the gallows — or an impromptu lynching by a vengeful mob. With an infamous reputation for unspeakable violence, he has even garnered a local alias, 'The Red Devil'. No one has actually seen him, and lived to tell about it. Weighing up the risk, I stay back, tailing him from a discrete distance, just sufficiently to keep him in sight, and with luck, avoid detection.

The opportunity will be lost if I stop and call for assistance. Eyes watch me suspiciously, from half-closed doorways — denizens lurking on the margins of society. I have no plan, other than the vague idea of tracking him to some underworld hideout, where if possible, he would later be surrounded and captured. I struggle to keep 'Red' in sight, following him doggedly up the empty, narrowing alleyways — ever deeper into the irksome ghetto, sprinting and puffing as I go.

Staying in the shadows as much as possible, I turn a blind corner....straight into an ambush! Tripped by an unseen leg, I'm sent sprawling heavily on the cobblestones.

I yelp in pain and shock.

Cunning as ever, Red had purposefully increased his pace, forcing me to choose between losing him completely, or else, relaxing my guard as I run headlong after him — luring me into a trap. Bleeding and disoriented, I am dragged upright, finding myself in the sweaty clutches of two hardball muscular types who hold me tightly by the arms.

Dazed as I am, I see the 'The Red Devil' leering at me, waving the gleaming, curved blade of a formidable kopis dagger before my eyes.

"The Red Devil,....his guttural Phoenician accent"

I struggle to put together his words, made more difficult by his guttural Phoenician accent: he comes from a nation of sailors and traders — also, infamous pirates. This explains his seafaring expertise, apart from his recent defeat by the Hector. He won't make that impetuous mistake a second time.

"The gods have decreed that we should meet again," he gloats, sneering in my face, "A big red target, and you couldn't get me with your puny little slingshot. Just a little scar on my cheek is the best you could do. Now it's I, who have you at my mercy. But sadly, after the damage to my poor ship, there is no longer any mercy left over for you."

He runs the blade gently across my throat, scratching the skin. I feel a small trickle of fresh blood.

"No. No mercy for you, my little slinger. I will throw your life-less body into the harbor at midnight,....so that it washes up on the mud flats of the tidal basin. Fish will feast on your fingers and toes and ears,....then come low water, seagulls will pick out your eyes and entrails, leaving what remains for the crabs with their pincers ....to gnaw away the rotting flesh from your bones."

He is laughing now in my face, crazed with malice and vengeance, shaking his matted, curly red head vigorously from side to side. His stench and spittle fill my senses in nauseating waves.

Chapter 7

I stop breathing, surreal, as if none of this is really happening. 'The Red Devil' looms over me, waving his kopis before my eyes — he wants me to beg for my life, or at least, a quick death. His varieties of ritual torture, played out on the bodies of his many victims, earn him his devilish title.

"Should I just cut you now, you know, from ear to ear, and make it quick and easy for you? Otherwise, I could slice you down the middle, but you will still be alive....then, I can send you off, with your intestines trailing behind you in the dust — the dogs and rats nibbling away at what's left. That way, you can watch yourself slowly dying in agony from the inside out. How nice — a grand feast for vermin."

He is cackling with amusement, self-absorbed by his own monstrous game of death.

"Hmm....What will it be for my little slinger? Cut out your tongue first, then your ears, nose, and then we go lower, whatever you have hidden between your legs? I wonder where to start — which end first, eh?"

Thoughts flash through my mind in quick succession. This is not something new to him — he's done it before many times, I realize with a shock. A lust for cruelty, lacking all feeling, a domination that excites his passions — he has become Ares, god of brutality. I am nothing but his private plaything, no more than a toy for his sadistic amusement. I balk at the thought that this will be my inglorious end:

lying mutilated in a pool of my own blood, dead in a filthy, harbor-side ghetto. As it so happens, the shock of this dreadful image spurs me into action.

I snap back to reality. What follows is a blur. A burst of action, no more than it takes for a few snaps of the fingers, yet it seems as if time stood still.

'Red' withdraws the kopis temporarily from my throat, waving it before me absentmindedly. He is totally engrossed in the gory details of my impending death — wide-eyed, half-crazed with satiation.

He gabbles to himself about the aesthetic virtues of a knife thrust under the armpit, to partially sever an aorta, leaving no visible injury! Happily playing his deadly game with me, he intends to prolong my despair as long as possible, or until he tires of it — a cat toying with its mouse. Instead, his self-absorbed reverie gives me all the opportunity I need.

Whether driven by a desperate preservation instinct, or a dim reflex from my hoplite training, I lash out deftly with both feet, using the elbows of his henchmen as a fulcrum to pivot my weight. I score a direct hit on his gonads (no missed target, this time around!).

'Red' recoils in excruciating pain, falling to his knees, screaming piteously. Much to my surprise, his two blockheads promptly drop me hard on my hindquarters — a 'none-too-bright' reflex action — and rush to assist their downed pirate master. I fall to the ground with a dull thud, jarring every bone in my body.

No matter! I leap up, hobbling at first, then running for my life, helter-skelter, back down the alleyway. Panting and bruised....but free! Strangely, there are no sounds of pursuit. Better than I could have hoped.

I plunge headfirst into the crowd, pushing and shoving as I go, people screaming and cursing behind me. I don't stop, until panting, bloodied, and inarticulate, I reach the custody of Master Panyotis. My trusted savior.

I stay aboard that night, where I feel safe, my last respite on the Hector before we both part ways. I have grown attached to the old tub that despite the odds, mauled the racy 'Sea Wolf'. Strange are the ways in which affectionate feelings become attached to an inanimate object, magnified perhaps, by my near-death experience.

In his workmanlike manner, Master Panyotis peppers me with a barrage of questions, a frustrating ordeal for both of us. I'm jittery and embarrassed, and the trauma still feels so real for me. I wince at the thought of it all, and how very close I came to a gruesome death. Try as I may, I have great difficulty recollecting any useful detail. My bruised hindquarters are aching. The master gives up, and notifies the city authorities.

Only much later, do I recall any useful details, long after the Hector had departed. Oddly enough, as so often happens in such out-of-body situations, the mind fixates on one particular item that for some reason captures its wholehearted attention; in this case, one of the thugs possessed only one ear.

I think to myself interestingly, that my mind fixated on the missing ear as a way of retaining some sense of personal control in what was otherwise a powerless situation. Attention becomes constricted to a single object that's present, or in this case, conspicuously absent when it should be present, so that everything else is relegated to the distant background. The matter-of-fact philosopher in me takes over — relentlessly teasing out the metaphysics of my own near-death experience!

Nevertheless, I can still feel that razor sharp blade on my throat, which remains to this very day, my closest experience of imminent death.

I had made friends aboard the Hector, as we became comrades-in-arms. Our victory over the 'Sea Wolf' bound us closely together, so that when the time came, we parted with sad farewells. I sought out adventure, thinking I would have it on my terms, and when it came in abundance, I had no say in the matter.

My only safe home (and bunk) is now gone! Homeless. Exciting, and scary. So begins my public life as a philosopher-teacher at the stoa, come what may. If 'Red' wants me, then I won't be hard to find. I can't live my life in fear, hiding out as if I am some snivelling coward. The agora is mine. If I fail, or am slain in the process, then let it be on my terms — my decision, as Master Panyotis would say!

Mytilene is impressive enough, somewhat rough and coarse,.... but vibrant and exciting, like any frontier city. While prosperous now, it has suffered many invasions in the past, notably Persians and Athenians. What's left is the uprooted legacy of an unruly and volatile population, now governed by a harsh Macedonian general. If Master Panyotis' suspicions are true, the pirates are tolerated by the scheming Macedonians in return for a share of the booty. He's usually right!

What I find most disturbing however, is the throng of teachers — vying competitively for the attention of shoppers. A ragtag mixture of Platonists, Aristotelians, Sophists, Cynics, Zoroastrians, and several nondescript others, even a singular Epicurus, have established themselves between the massive columns of the stoa.

Whether it be the regular spacing of these columns, or in compliance with some unwritten etiquette, these philosophic competitors space themselves equally apart. They resemble nothing so much as booths of motley hawkers, selling their ephemeral trinkets and baubles. I am quickly relegated to the only remaining space, on the periphery of the stoa.

One side of the promenade is mostly concerned with material objects, of one kind or another, utilitarian things like hoes, jewellery, or cornbread. While across the way, the learned philosophers, each in his allocated 'booth', usually a swatch of matting and small platform, aspire to 'ethereal matters of profundity', or so they tell themselves. Not however, without a disturbing lack of civility.

The Aristotelians, for example, condone slavery as natural and inevitable, as do the followers of Plato. Meanwhile at the adjacent 'booth', the Sophists, in strident opposition, condemn slavery as barbaric and morally corrupt. Each teacher has a coterie of devotees, though most people just stop and listen momentarily, then move on. Others chose to heckle the teacher, in a ritual diatribe that seems to be an accepted part of the spectacle.

What begins as a calm debate soon regresses to a heated contest of wits, one shouting over the over. I observe again, what I have long noted: when seemingly reasonable people gather together, the loudest rabble-rouser takes over. Before long, the scattered group becomes an unruly mob.

Finally, the crowd disperses, tired of the theatre. Each party, finding no appreciative audience, cease the pantomime, without any show of bad feeling. Whatever the message — on the nature of Being, the transience of all Truth, or even the impossibility of Knowledge — it is surely lost in the greater comedy of delivering that message.

Others take a different tack, less debate and more populist demagogy, pandering to the mob in what they want to hear. These 'truth-tellers' are keening for donations, more bent on selling their omnibus message, 'one size fits all', than seeking to discriminate truth from falsity.

Then there are the hair-splitting pedants, who befuddle their rustic listeners with artfulness and quackery. Sophistry for sale as legalese rhetoric, packaged under the noble banner of 'Philosophy'!

A few listeners however, always remain detached, outsiders for various reasons. Some of these are totally self-absorbed in a world of their own construction, half-crazy and witless. Others are cerebrally impaired, due to glaring head-wounds, the gruesome work of a battle-axe, war-hammer, or slinger. Sadly, there are many of the latter, just as the wars and invasions are many, the Macedonians being only the most recent.

There are also listeners, a diminutive few, that I deem to call 'mindful individuals', who have a singular consciousness of their own, rather than the ranting of the mob. These few, precious few, are the seekers that I in turn, seek to find. One in particular stands out, a solid, young man of quiet demeanour, moving between 'booths', listening attentively, nodding occasionally, or shaking his head distastefully. Now he arrives at my station.

After carefully watching the boisterous antics of my rival 'competitors', I decide to speak in muted tones, only sufficient to be heard above the chattering crowd! I refuse to be drawn into any screeching debate — my message of tranquillity and equanimity must be consistent with my presentation.

A small group gathers around me, waiting for the show to begin, no doubt taken by the presence of a new face in town — another scrappy upstart. They are sure to notice that I have no 'old guard' of established supporters, who if the need arises, will act as 'peace-makers'. Too late for me to back out now!

I am the latest recruit, fresh blood for the metaphysical circus.

PART II: "Beginnings"

As I wait for the crowd to grow, my thoughts go back to Servilia — back in time, to Colophon where it all started....but that's a heartbreaking adventure of a very different kind!

PART III:
"Failures"

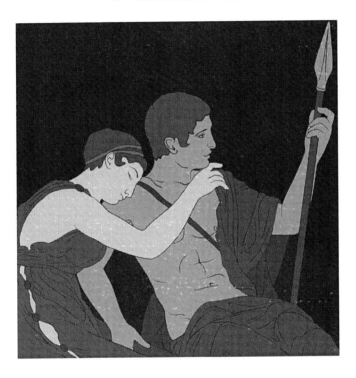

Chapter 8

Colophon, Ionia

311 BC

The enormity of the dread, coming so abruptly, so excruciatingly, plunges me into a misery beyond any past experience.

I still grieve for my mother, lost for several years now, but this is something different: as if my heart has been wrenched from my beating chest, leaving nothing but a black, gaping hole! That monstrous black spider, a forgotten relic of my childhood, flashes across my mind out of nowhere. I manage a few words, barely coherent, with each breath.

It was a foregone conclusion that Servilia would give her love to no single man — with the naivety of young love, blinded by wishful fantasy, I considered myself to be that special, singular exception. Older heads had warned me, so that I might avoid the pain of certain rejection; all too plainly, they saw through my smug facade. Now that impossible moment is upon me — brash reality intrudes on my carefully nurtured fantasy.

When she speaks, lashing out, all I hear are harshly-pitched sounds, like the cacophonous shattering of crockery, dashed into myriad shards on a cold, hard, unyielding floor: yet how fervently does she speak of Critolaus! There is little else, but tales of Critolaus — as if I am absent, left with nothing but the cold, hard shards of her rejection.

Servilia shrugs, using her lithe body in a particular feline movement that is wholly her own, blending affectation with nonchalance, accenting her curves under a diaphanous, murex-purple toga. I follow the outline of her breasts as they move: proportional, tight, and full. Several of the resident Theban cats — rat-catchers all — have emerged out of hiding, mewing and gambolling as they go: a comical, playful retinue trailing behind their stylish mistress.

"Servilia Melia: A Feisty Aphrodite"

She says nothing, walking but more like gliding, a gentle dancing movement, over the marble mosaic floor, in her delicate, bare feet. Her thick mane of hair tosses gracefully from one shoulder to the other in step with her artful promenade: a sensual exhibition that instantly and unforgettably, captures all eyes. Servilia's willowy enactment exudes no less, an aura of the vengeful Furies, a certain ill-defined danger — contained and concentrated such as one sees in a wild predator, coiled and ready to spring at its cowering prey — eliciting at once, an oddly mixed response of rapt temptation baited with wrathful punishment.

Past the fluted columns, she glides soundlessly into the vestibulum, the sunny, leafy quadrangle of her father's elegant country villa.

I watch her performance-art, holding my breath, heart beating hard, as if in a stupor. She speaks again, and the allure deepens further: a startling cadence, raspy and resonant, her gravelly voice serving as a counter-point to her otherwise nubile presentation, heightening the overall sublime effect on all around her. Despite my torment, or perhaps more so because of it, I lose myself in her: smitten! — my own personal 'Great Goddess', transfigured into Artemis, Cybele, Athena, Venus, and not least of all, a feisty Aphrodite.

❦❦❦❦❦❦❦❦❦❦❦❦❦❦

I cringe, even to think about it now — embarrassing, if not downright ridiculous — then ruefully shrug it off as my long-delayed entry into adulthood. Painful but necessary, as so often is the case. It seems that I grow more by my missteps than I do by my gains. The positive contribution of such 'embarrassments' and losses is only fully appreciated from the healing perspective of distant time — no longer an insipid, innocent lover.

The unknown circumstances of my mother's death, I think, retarded my development — followed not long after, by my obligated military service in Athens. Due to the Macedonian invasion of my homeland island of Samos, in the wake of Alexander's conquests, I was compelled to return to Colophon upon completion of my two years training as a hoplite warrior.

The city-state of Colophon, urban and sophisticated, lies on the mainland of Ionia. Only a few days journey away, by ship and wagon, Colophon is a world apart from impoverished, provincial Samos — the island of my birth and my poor mother's final years. A key trading center, handling all manner of goods from Persia, central Africa, south-east Asia, as far away as the Indus Valley, Colophon is a true cosmopolitan city dotted with palatial villas.

Never before, have I witnessed such peaceful coexistence

between races and ethnic groups. Greeks, Armenians, Jews, Celts, Persians, Syrophoenicians, even Lombards and Berbers, are interwoven under the universal banner of 'trade' — resulting in unique trading routes that span the known world, from the exotic East to the burgeoning West. Such trade brings great wealth of course, though not without its excesses and vices — fleshpots on every street corner, with their waiting throngs of eager customers.

No small surprise then, that I was unprepared for the culture and verve of Colophon — any more than I was prepared for Servilia and the merciless ways with which she dispensed her favors. Her libertarian views were shocking to my bashful innocence and sheltered upbringing on Samos. Servilia's rejection in favor of Critolaus stands out as one of those abysmally dark events of my life.

The aftermath of that rejection marked my entry into the real world. It was impressed upon me, however painfully, that people are themselves, complete with their own agendas. Other people follow their own authentic star, rather than how I wanted them to be for me — as seen through the prism of my youthful self-absorption.

There lies the crux of the adjustment for which I was wanting. In my unformed, callow state, it simply didn't occur to me that other peoples' self-interest may not be aligned with my own. Call it selfish, perhaps narcissistic, but certainly a large part of my problem was a lack of life experience. I was naïve, vulnerable and easily hurt — selfish I admit, but on the positive side of the ledger, I also suffered from an excess of trust. I took the goodwill of others for granted. For better or worse, I was missing the 'social virtues' of tactfulness and calculated reserve — testing the ground before I put my boot into it, so necessary for survival in a worldly city like Colophon.

She turns, her blue-green eyes smiling seductively into mine, puckers her lips, and blows me an air-kiss.

"Come along", she whispers, coyly.

I know that Servilia is taunting me in some veiled way — yet I am too confused to answer, even to think. All I can do is follow like a lamb; embarrassed, as if I am outside myself, watching my own meek compliance.

Five months have passed since our last torrid meeting, and once again, wide-eyed, I am back at the villa. I miss our intellectual exchanges, and convince myself that our reunion is not solely out of love.

She sits down, ever gracefully, on a granite bench. Several olive trees in large terra-cotta pots are clustered together to form a shady, private bower. She pats the space beside her — a loaded invitation, one way or another. Time itself seems to have slowed, in pace with her own fluid, sensuous movements. I hold my breath, waiting for a revelation, I know not what.

The faintest zephyr of breeze rustles the olive branches gently above her head, hardly noticeable, adding their small contribution to the soft carpet of dappled leaves at her feet. Maybe the breeze isn't chance at all, but a timely intervention of the gods — I still think about that divine possibility to this very day.

Whatever happened, divine or witchery, it feels as if I am now waking from a dream. The alluring spell is broken, so abruptly. People say that 'you snap out of it', and so it happened, just like that: I snapped back, out of my old piteous, fawning state. My breathing, barely perceptible before, now becomes rapid, though my speech remains measured and clear. We both need to come to some understanding.

"You were busy bedding Critolaus, a sponge-diver no less, that your father took in from Leptis Magna. You lied to me."

"I thought he was your friend. He likes you."

"Yes,....and so he will continue to be my friend, despite your mischief. He sails to North Africa for your father, diving and harvesting sponges for rich people, outrunning Phoenician triremes, storms, and pirates: an exciting life full of adventure. You want me to compete with that? Well, so be it....I'm the drab son of a poor school-teacher, a grammarian with no prospects, marooned here forever in Colophon....I'm not playing your game of competition, one against the other!"

"O Epicurus, my love! You are much, much more than that. Some day you will be famous," she croons, softly, imploringly.

I smile, or smirk,....yet the nearness of our bodies overpowers my objections. Words drop away.

We sit, huddled together silently on the hard bench, cheek by jowl, our arms overarching, for what seems like an infinite time.

Chapter 9

"You think I can't love....that I just use sex as a substitute for love", Servilia purrs, softly and gently, even factually, as if she is reciting an everyday matter — common sense that should be obvious to any child.

"You want to freeze my love," she whispers into my ear, " to take hold of it, putting it away securely in a box on the shelf, to take down when you feel like it. This kills my love, and turns it into the very lie, of which you accuse me. I am not made that way."

Strangely, I no longer feel angry, just empty and absent,....very flat, as if all this really isn't happening.

She pauses,....takes a deep sigh, and squeezes my hand.

"Like the great Sappho, I've even written a poem about me.... about us; I call it, 'Where Love Lies'. I do so much want you to read it, please....please."

She is kissing me lightly on the lips now, barely touching, yet the delicacy of the act carries with it, the demure promise of rapt sensuousness. She speaks in hushed tones, stroking my forehead and hair leisurely, with soft tender motions.

"So we get married, dear Epicurus — and surrender our individuality, our birthright to choose the pleasure of real spontaneous love. We trap each other, ensnared by all the empty promise of procreation,....that takes more than it gives."

It all sounds so rehearsed, building momentum as she rattles it off like a solemn lecture.

I lose patience, throwing my head back in frustration — in a huff.

She doesn't like my interruption to her well-practiced rhetoric, pulling her hand away, recoiling from me, with a visible wince. Servilia is in fine form now, raising her voice angrily, unstoppable.

"Nature tries to use our own fertile bodies against us, at the cost of who we are as free individuals. Why can't we make our own independent choices? I'm sick of family lies, and their hypocrisies and false values. Life is too short to have our young love made into a guilty, shameful thing by others."

Clearing my throat, I find my voice, tremulous at first, then rising in pitch and volume. My confidence is returning, as I warm to my response, finding myself on surer ground — speaking calmly, with measured words.

"My dear Servilia, I'll gladly read your heartfelt poem. If it's about us, as you say, then I'm asking you to look at your great fear of been with me, just me! You're afraid of losing your liberty — to be treated as chattel like a piece of furniture, until I grow tired of you. But none of that will ever happen, dear Servilia. You have known me now since we were both young children on Samos, so you must have some sense of who I truly am...."

I end my avowal of love with an inflection, calling for an answer — but she sits, hunched and inert.

She fears attachments: that she will end up dying in child-birth like her mother — 'killing my own mother', as she point-edly calls it. Servilia and I have been together since she was a little girl — childhood playmates. Over the years, a little at a time, she has confided the emotional upheaval in which she lives out her daily life. I attempt to comfort her — for a deep-searing guilt she carries through no action of her own: only the primary fact of her mere existence, for which she had no choice in the matter! How does one atone for such a guilt that remains unassuaged with every breath of life that she draws — when her very first breath of life came at the cost of her mother's death? Yet the bare fact lingers, locked within the shadowlands of her soul, beyond the reach of words.

Sad enough,....but then, there's more to her dilemma! Servilia's 'guilt-by-existence' is further reinforced by her father — kept as a raw, festering wound — never intentionally, but in so many subtle ways that will lie forever, beyond his recognition — fed by his denial. When Hypetia gave birth to Servilia, Valerius lost his beloved wife and his world crumbled, leaving him withdrawn and moody. While loving his daughter dearly as his only child, he remains conflicted: unable to reconcile the joy of her birth with the deep loss of his wife. Servilia's very appearance, her striking similarity to her mother — at every glance, rekindles his morbid grief; while at the same time, his daughter's spunky, irrepressible spirit gladdens his heart.

Servilia in turn loves her father — who vacillates between adoration and veiled, unspoken resentment — yet feels the judgement passed down upon her, an unspoken curse that defies discussion. Love, guilt, denial — all entangled, tied up in knots. I doubt if she will ever heal — even if such a thing is possible?

I understand — touching on my own struggles — why she can't trust love! She always needs someone in reserve: either Critolaus or myself, keeping us at a distance, both needy of her.

Servilia avoids any attachments, any depth, playing men against each other — setting hearts on fire, not out of caprice or malice, which isn't her true loving nature. Rather, she is riven by fear, that depth will make her vulnerable — the risk of yet another blow to her acute sensitivity. Despite her lively banter, she feels doomed; better a lonely spinster, intact, than an embittered soul, broken on the wheel of 'love'.

Servilia's Private Bath

We sit side-by-side quietly for a long time — I mull over the inner conflict of love and rejection, in which Servilia hides, beneath her surface merriment. I finally summon up my courage and make an effort — as blunt as I can — to cut through to the frightened, loving person cowering within her.

"There comes a time to let go of the past, to start afresh; the dead shouldn't dictate to the living! To live is to love, and the avoidance of love, is not to live fully. We need to break out, both of us,....and be together, trusting each other. This is our shared destiny since we were children."

I pause, to make a final heartfelt plea, couching it in her own terms.

A heavy, ominous lull descends upon us, as if we are both suspended in time.

"That's the real meaning of your poem....that's 'Where Love Lies'."

I can't say how long I sat there, motionless, ruminating. Waiting.

Arms flinging about wildly, Servilia abruptly leaps up off the bench, clawing at me, shrieking I know not what.

I step away in astonishment, reflexively, but not quickly enough — she shoves me violently with both of her arms outstretched. Her surge of strength catches me by surprise.

I lurch backwards in retreat, struggling to regain my footing.

She is pummelling me half-heartedly with her closed fists, her shrill cries accompanying each lashing. Shocked by such ferocity, I counter her blows as I pull back into the atrium of the villa. Servants watch their mistress, eyes wide open, agog....still as alabaster statues, not sure what to do.

Gaining some composure, I grab each of her arms tightly and hold her still. I ready myself for the inevitable kicks. Nothing.

Servilia's whole body goes limp and seemingly lifeless — so completely that I almost drop her. I lower her gingerly to the floor, without resistance: an untidy tangle of limbs, torn fabric, hair and spittle, with her toga bunched up around her groin. Her eyelids are twitching, mixed with spasms of rapid blinking.

I'm relieved — her eyes are not rolled up into her head. I know from my hoplite training that 'seeing only the whites' would be a grievous sign. She is sobbing and gasping deeply now, struggling to catch her breath, her bosom heaving and convulsing, as I stand helpless beside her.

What has happened? Everything spiralled downwards so rapidly. I hear the steady leaden beat and grunts of someone running hard.

It's her father, Valerius Mela, as he races towards us, heavy-footed, calling out frantically for help and support!

WHERE LOVE LIES

Life as ephemeral
shallow
when I crave depth
Where Love Lies

What IS
IS
while it IS
then
IS NOT
Where Love Lies

Not doing
not thinking
not feeling
NOW only, still and quiet
Where Love Lies

Any more, beyond NOW
Begets IS NOT
emptiness only

The Lies of Love

-Servilia Mela, 312 BC

Chapter 10

I kneel beside Servilia's sobbing, contorted body, stroking her arm.

Valerius enters the Atrium, breathing heavily, yelling out incoherent orders, servants scattering obediently in all the directions. All manner of thoughts and feelings race through my mind.

How did it get to this so quickly, I wonder?

Servilia is no longer crying, but staring up at me, dazed, with a puzzled expression. I lean down, embracing her gently, tenderly, intoxicated by her rose-petal perfume.

"We are both of us without a mother," she murmurs into my ear, "both trying to break away from our fathers."

She pauses, then continues in a hissing little voice — entreating me to listen, as if confiding a dark secret.

"These fathers are in our heads….controlling us with guilt and the promise of love, so long as we do their bidding. They want to own us, and live our lives from the inside."

I silently mouth everything she said. I'm bewildered….Valerius has stopped now, standing under the entrance pediment of his private office, the tablinum. He is watching intently….though I'm not sure that he can hear us.

I wonder silently, what he plans to do?

Valerius Mela is neither Greek nor aristocracy.

Proud to call himself an entrepreneurial merchant, he was raised in Ostia, the ancient harbor city of Rome, on the estuary of the Tiber — his family was illustrious but far from rich.

Bearded, with close-cropped hair, olive skin, and broad-shouldered, he is widely respected as a savvy trader. Unnerving to other merchants, he possesses an unforgettable craggy, somewhat surly face. His steady, canny gaze would abruptly, when least expected, burst into a lustrous, disarming smile, beaming out goodwill to all. Many have asked themselves with dismay, caught unawares in a torrid exchange, whether this toothy effusion is natural or a wily manipulation.

A crafty businessman, descended from a family of crafty shipowners, Valerius built up a lucrative trade in North African sponges, considered to be the best of their kind. While other traders laughed at his 'loony' ideas, he shrewdly invested in a fleet of

dhows. Constructed near the Red Sea, in the region of Arabia, the dhows are especially designed for sponge-diving, with an outsize duckboard mounted to the transom at sea level. Most significant of all is an innovative (and 'secret') viewing portal to magnify and pinpoint sponge clusters from the surface.

Twin-masts, with lateen-rigging, his dhows can navigate the shallow coastal waters of Mediterranean Africa, otherwise inaccessible to deep-draft vessels. Using the viewing portal, his crews then easily harvest the vast accumulations of premium sponges, as well as the occasional, much-prized red coral. The dhows are particularly vulnerable to sudden squalls however, when crossing the Mediterranean from Notium, the port for Colophon. While he may lose a few dhows, his handsome profits more than make up for this, 'the cost of doing business', with a generous endowment to the families of lost sailors.

Valerius' base in Ionia suits him well, as a major trading crossroads close to the bounteous sponge harvests. It has the further advantage, never to be underestimated, of keeping him a safe distance from the poisonous (literally) politics of Rome. While accumulating great wealth, Valerius knew that money and ability could never atone for his lowly birth while he remained in Rome. Despite his sociable nature, his opportunities would always be limited, if not openly resented. Even his devoted marriage to an aristocratic 'princess' drew sneers of contempt from the privileged orders, as a crass attempt to convert his money into status. He said it best that 'the only way of moving upwards was to move outwards', first to Samos, thence Colophon. Having established himself with a large trading fleet and opulent villa, his well-heeled credentials are now beyond dispute.

He has also taken an active interest in civic affairs, contributing to the construction of public baths and aqueducts as well as gaining favor by employing local artisans whenever possible. As an exotic Roman import, ludicrously wealthy, Valerius makes for a curious exception within the rigid social strata of Colophon. Since he is not hidebound by local prejudices or familial ties, he possesses that advantage shared by all Outsiders — which ironically, gives him ready access to all levels in the community.

Valerius' wealth, munificence, and Roman credentials soon pushed him into the closed circle of the provincial gentry — as ranked by the outrageous grandeur of the family villa, befitting an emperor. He enjoys being a big Roman fish in a small Ionian barrel, a prominence shared by his only daughter. Unfortunately, Servilia is not endowed with her father's added gift of discretion, especially when it comes to 'affairs of the heart'.

Servilia's sexual appetite, is an open secret. The wealth and indulgence of her father — despite his strenuous but futile objections — continue to enable her numerous liaisons, while her social status remains the envy of her well-heeled peers.

For someone so young, Servilia is remarkably facile with arguments, turning them around seamlessly, so that they end up supporting her brand of morality. She juggles her many suitors with ease — playthings of the moment, otherwise dismissed and put back on the shelf. This is especially true when it comes to her nominal betrothal to one such frustrated suitor: Epicurus, me. Servilia's aristocratic bearing — olive-bronze complexion and aquiline nose — was inherited from her deceased mother, Hypetia of Smyrna, descended from ancient Ionian royalty.

Whether Valerius overheard Servilia's imploring rant on "fathers in our heads", or simply because he saw that she was safe, albeit in my embrace, he retires quietly back to his tablinum.

I assist Servilia back to the bench, where we sit close by each other, lightly touching. As she speaks, her breath gently caresses my face. I feel her bodily warmth under my tunic as she places her hand in mine, and looks wistfully into my eyes.

"I don't pretend to be a soothsayer, Epicurus....but I have a strong premonition that we will both become great healers, you and I," she says, stroking my hand softly, accenting the rhythm of her speech with each gentle stroke, "helping people in our two different ways, you with your philosophical reasoning, and myself, as a kind of spiritual channel to the gods."

"You will become a legendary priestess," I announce, in mock seriousness, "like Pythia, the Delphic Oracle, high on Mount Parnassus, the place where heaven and earth meet, prophesying the fates of gullible mortals, who run around like frantic ants, down below."

My attempt at humor falls resoundingly flat. Looking into her bland stare, I instantly regret my ill-chosen words. She promptly withdraws her hand — timing is everything, and this is not it! I apologize, and plead with Servilia to continue.

"Actually Epicurus, you're right in a way," she muses, lost in thought, "I do see myself as a kind of oracle — but without all the sacerdotal trappings and trickery."

She raises her voice passionately, partly in annoyance at me, or Delphi, or both of us? I'm not sure.

"I don't need to breathe hallucinating gas venting from the ground, as happens at Delphi. Or wander around in an altered state, mumbling incantations, while a band of accomplices struggles to make sense out of nonsense,....depending upon the size of the client's donation! Poor dupes, high as a kite, every word of prophecy charged with an otherworldly aura, hanging in the air, pointing the way to a glowing future, while in the meantime, their coffers are picked dry. Putting all the mystery aside, that's the real business of the 'theater' at Delphi — not the kind of sleight-of-hand oracle I want to be. I went there once with my aunt. It's all about soothsaying....and making money!"

"You want to help people live happier, fuller lives in the present," I add, prudently, "not some fairytale future."

"The oracle at Delphi delivers cryptic predictions to mighty princes and great city-states under the name of Apollo, a male god of mastery, separate over Nature," Servilia explains, flushed with enthusiasm, shaking me by the arm, "I want to provide guidance to ordinary people through the auspices of those goddesses who follow the feminine principle of Nature. Demeter invites us to embrace the organic connection shared by all living entities on Mother Earth, such as trees, fish, worms, and of course, people."

"The connectedness of Nature," I ask, "rather than the separateness of Apollonian mastery?"

"There's a place for both, inclusive of each," Servilia answers, quietly now, "Both are needed in this world, depending upon the circumstances. It's about the balance between them. Much of the time, there's an imbalance which leads to universal misery for all."

Our conversation pauses, as if by mutual agreement. I savor this moment of tranquility and connection between us — particularly the core values that we both share. I feel as if we have made an implicit pact with each other that lends an order and direction to our future lives.

Little did I realize then, in my besotted, incurable state, that Servilia was no mere youthful infatuation.

The love that we share would take on various forms across the passage of our eventful lives, from the giddy sexuality of young adulthood to the nurturing companionship of elderhood. Through to the end of my days, I have desired no other all this time.

She remains for me still, an embodiment of the eternal feminine, tempestuous and incomparable.

~~~~~~~~~~~~~~~~~~~~~~~~~~~~~~

In the mean time, Servilia perks up, ending our intimate reverie.

"I was very young at the time, merely a toddler, but I vaguely remember a woman healer who came to our villa regularly and administered to my father's grief in the years after my mother's untimely death."

Servilia recalls, with a melodious laugh, "She always made me smile, and had humorous names for different people: I remember my father was 'old Rush n' Rouse' — I'm still not sure what that means, but it somehow fits him. I looked forward to our meetings, though I was soon ushered out of the way."

"She was very beautiful, soft and caring," Servilia continues, "My father gradually improved with her visits and herbal potions. He came alive, and was present for me again when I needed him. Those early impressions of real care-giving remained with me as an inspiration. Then she stopped coming, no goodbye, and I never found out the reason. When I asked my father, he just shrugged as if it was nothing."

She pauses, bewildered.

"Funny that I remember her now, talking with you, after all this time," she adds, "Those memories have laid dormant, half-forgotten, all these long years. The mention of healing must have brought them back to the surface."

As I listen to her recollections, an unaccountable wave of nausea passes over me. I shiver involuntarily, thinking of my mother and her herbal ministrations on Samos. We were very close — she would have surely mentioned the Villa to me if she had ever gone there?

Servilia notices my change in mood.

She asks if I am well, though in truth, I feel inexplicably sad. I nod that I am fine, embrace her warmly, and depart amidst a shower of kisses. As children, she and I had played in the villa courtyard of one of Valerius' friends — curiously, I had never been to her residence or met the master himself, until recently. Servilia was always escorted by trusted servants.

I can't tell her of my suspicions, because that's all they remain. There were several herbal practitioners on Samos at that time. If it was indeed my mother, I should be proud of her legacy in motivating Servilia at such an early age — it would also be another connection that binds she and I together. I find it deeply unsettling nonetheless. Probably grief, I conclude. It never truly goes away: that unforgettably horrible night on Samos!

That was not where matters ended, however. As I leave the villa soon after, a slave bows with a message from Valerius. He would be pleased to have a private audience with me (meaning: no Servilia) in the morrow at the ninth hour.

While presented as a gracious invitation, its true nature is that of a command. It seems as if today's events are not without consequences: perhaps only social, but more likely to be serious — if not a thinly veiled threat!

Chapter 11

Valerius Mela is that larger-than-life father I had always wanted — despite his autocratic temperament, and absolute rule over his household. He possesses that most significant trait, woefully lacking in my own father: he loves Servilia above all else, even his own life.

In our humble farmhouse, the comparison could not be greater. Where love should be, there is only a solemn, suffocating silence, in which I am neither seen nor heard by my father. Failings are treated with quiet disdain, while ambition and initiative are merely 'vanity in disguise'. I would rather be rebuked — any pitiful recognition that I have some scant significance — than merely ignored.

Am I nothing but an obligation lacking any commitment, to be discharged as expeditiously as possible — a duty imposed on him under sufferance, as a single parent? It doesn't help matters that I assist him at his school on occasion. I prefer the freedom offered by my private tutoring, which provides a meagre, though independent income for me.

Whatever lay in his past, I only know my father as a moody, introverted man, whom I have tried to love — much as a naïve, young child does naturally. I was raised with tales of the family misfortune: that he had picked the wrong side in one of those seemingly petty, yet torturous disputes, for which Athens is infamous. His self-righteous stubbornness had ended with an exile to the Athenian colony of Samos.

Isolated on the island, fuelled by a temperament of austerity and perpetual melancholy, my father's misfortunes festered into a paranoia that saw conspiracies everywhere. Any remaining friends were driven away, leaving only Marius, our long-suffering but ever-loyal slave. Good Marius would take the brunt, patiently listening to my father for countless hours until he was finally spent — exhausted by his own litany of forebodings! Matters only got worse. First and foremost, there is my mother's untimely disappearance, then my compulsory military service in Athens, and finally, the Macedonian invasion of Samos, followed by a further exile to Colophon. At the same time, Valerius also relocated to Colophon, by his own choice, using Notium as the base for his trading fleet.

Following my mother's disappearance, the rumor has gradually trickled down to me — usually in hushed tones, behind my back — that she had taken on a secret paramour as a last refuge from a loveless marriage. My mother's body was never recovered, and questions continue to linger, as is their wont in such unsolved cases. A vacuum calls out to be filled, even if only by wild speculation. While my father certainly has his problems, I truly can't believe he would harm my mother. His grief was pitiful to behold, and he has never fully recovered. For that matter, neither have I.

Whether it be raging storms sweeping inland from the distant sea at Notium, or else, in my panic-laced dreams, images of my mother lonely and afraid, atop the cliff, I wake up shaking and sweaty. I find myself looking to the door as if she will walk through at any moment, though we left Samos years ago. My mother's death has become a part of my life that I try to seal off, as if that horrid night never happened. Her sandals have become a symbolic inspiration for me — to fill her shoes!

On the other hand, if my father had not been so quarrelsome in Athens, he would never have moved to Samos in exile. I would never have been born there and Servilia would not be in my life now, such is the quirky happenstance of life.

PART III: "Failures"

"Chance and Choice collided," says Servilia, primly, mimicking one of her private tutors.

Chapter 12

I stare listlessly at my mug, with its infusion of herbs — collected by my mother in past, happier times. I am seated in the culinary, half-asleep, daydreaming.

Thinking of her, I steer my recollections on a different course — To 'swerve' away, rather than regressing once again into a hopeless, maudlin state. Then….a sharp rap on the entry door of our rustic stone cottage. We don't get many visitors now, since my mother's disappearance.

Large by local village standards, it is nevertheless, a hard-scrabble dwelling by comparison with the palatial villas reserved for the Colophon elite. Apart from our single servant, Marius, I am the only one at home — father is teaching at his classes.

I open the door, not without its customary squeaking hinges.

"Hail Epicurus," declaims Servilia in mock-formality, a legacy of her Roman heritage, "I thought that you may be in need of some feminine company."

"Why yes, of course," I reply in a snap, teasing her, "any feminine company whatsoever is always most welcome here, day or night."

While it sounds like rapid-fire banter, Servilia knew what was coming — we are play-acting comedy lines from Aristophanes, a favorite pastime. We love "The Birds" for its smart satire and gaiety — comic relief that makes for a hopeful start! We both chortle away, like a pair of mischievous schoolchildren who have just deposited a frog in the teacher's desk. I actually did this once — only the teacher was my father, who was not amused.

Servilia is known for her 'drop-in visits', with its subplot of catching you by surprise, covered over by innocent assertions of 'just passing by'. No matter — she's here, now!

I usher her into the culina, haphazardly furnished in clutter as becomes most cosy kitchens. Defying proportions, its dominant feature is the oversized hearth of umber-colored, rough-hewn granite. Occupying almost one complete wall, with iron cauldrons and ladles to one side, it's an impressive luxury when the village standard is a primitive fire pit. We sit down together on backless stools casually facing each other across the rough-hewn oak dining table.

"I've been doing a great deal of thinking," I announce, in a serious tone, "why you and I end up having so many spats. You feel rejected, then I feel rejected, and so on. It's a muddle. I know that you need to feel independent and free, but it leaves me wondering if you will ever settle down….,with anyone?"

"Uh Oh." Servilia's only spiky reply, while she shuffles ominously in her chair.

Silence. Servilia is staring into my face, keenly focused on my eyes, 'reading my aura' as she calls it. I find it unsettling, since matters often take a dramatic turn after such a 'reading'. She is listening attentively, though her face remains stony and flat. I need to change direction, another 'Swerve' — Marius, ever reliable, beats me to the rescue.

He had busied himself in the meantime, clattering plates as background noise, ensuring our privacy in such a tight space. He seizes the opportunity offered by our pause.

Stepping forward quickly, Marius offers our esteemed visitor a goblet of rustic Samian wine. Certainly not a wine varietal that would be found at the Villa. Acting as our host, he explains that it is "known locally as 'moschato', jammy on the palette at first with a lingering dry finish.

"The divine gift of Bacchus!", he announces as he pours gleefully, wearing his whimsical half-smile that never fails to amuse.

Servilia beams back at him, sipping the Moschato, and complements him warmly. He bows in grand style and with a flourish of elegance, places the large kantharos serving pitcher before us. We may refill our own goblets now, dispensing with his services. An accompaniment of delicious goat cheese — sweetened with rosemary-scented honeycomb from my father's beehives — completes his etiquette of welcome.

"Servilia….an accompaniment of delicious goat cheese"

Servilia raises her goblet in an overacted gesture of salutation, very graciously, all sweetness, in accordance with her mannered upbringing — Marius' wrinkly smile widens even further, a rare feat. Servilia then turns to me, inscrutable as ever. She's still wary.

Marius dutifully pours a last goblet for me, then discreetly retires with a sly grin, ostensibly tending to the farthest garden. Good, faithful Marius, the household diplomat and erstwhile host, taking over from my mother.

Despite the wine, my mouth is parched.

We both sip our wine in silence. Servilia tilts her head, thoughtfully, stroking her chin, but says nothing. I pick up the thread of my 'Swerve'.

"I must apologize," I say slowly, bluntly, looking her squarely in the face, "I've dumped my insecure, painful feelings on you.... when I look at them closely, they all lead back to my own family battleground....so much betrayal and hurt. I've absorbed it all like a sponge over the years, so that I don't know anything different.... then I hurt you."

Unexpectedly, Servilia reaches across the table, pulling me towards her — followed by a wordless, soft kiss on my forehead, and of course, her signature, bewitching smile. I'm disconcerted, blushing, but only momentarily — I should finish what I have to say.

"Even when you don't like it, I want my reaction to be mine, and mine alone,.....not something that's driven by my loony childhood. That's no way to live,.....and offers no future for me, or us."

I feel depleted, and pour more Samian wine for both of us. Servilia makes no mention of my 'revelations' other than gulping down her wine copiously with a broad smile. Now it's her turn.

It's obvious that she is feeling in high spirits, bubbling with good humor. I sense that she has appreciated my wine-soaked ramblings.

She begins an animated conversation, mostly minor gossip and updates on mutual acquaintances. Like a true Roman, descended from the race of Romulus, her dusky arms, hands, and fingers are in constant, graceful motion. Swirling, gesticulating, and jabbing the air repeatedly, as if every thought is assigned to its due place. I remain somewhat guarded, going along with it, waiting and watching. I try to inject a word or two, but I'm beating against the tide.

"Walking the Sacred Pathway"

When Servilia slips into one of her periodic garrulous states, I'm never sure what will follow next. Thoughts fall over each other in the pressure to convert them into words — as if she is punctuating the air — ending up as unconnected ideas. I try to smooth out her utterances, making allowances for them, as part of her mercurial character.

Over the years, I have come to realize that like myself, Servilia is riven by inner conflicts. Inherited from her family — not of her doing, blameless — yet she carries these conflicts along with her as a heavy burden. This deeper understanding gives me the patience to listen, quietly and attentively, just as she did with me.

I recount to myself what I know about Servilia, those experiences which, if I listen to her own words, have shaped how she sees herself.

I know for example, that she is an avid devotee of the Eleusinian Mysteries of the goddess Demeter, the primal earth mother, and the cycle of the four seasons, aligned with birth, life, death, and rebirth.

Accompanied by a paternal aunt, she made a grand pilgrimage to the sanctuary outside of Athens, at Eleusis — a gift from her father, on her sixteenth birthday. Valerius had begrudgingly agreed, after the intercession of the concerned aunt, acting on behalf of her motherless niece.

Arriving at the sanctuary, Servilia had become agitated: only those without sin are eligible to enter the inner circle of initiates and must be vetted by the Eleusinian goddesses.

Since her aunt was already a member of the inner circle, she acted as sponsor — Servilia was duly inducted into the mysteries despite her young age. Afterwards, Servilia walked the arduous Sacred Pathway, along with the many other supplicants, weeping frequently as she went — a purification and cleansing of her long-held regrets and sadness.

It would seem that without any conscious plan, Servilia and I have entered into an intimate exchange, an openness about ourselves and our inner lives — a new experience for both of us, aided perhaps, by Samian wine and the 'magic' of our rustic culina.

Snug and inviting, the culina is replete with assorted pots and pans hanging haphazardly from the rafters. Sea-shells, carvings, specimen rocks, and colorful jars fill the mantelpiece, above the fireplace, while straw-brooms and pans in the far corner complete the domestic scene. The golden rays of the late afternoon sun come streaming through the open back doorway, filling the small kitchen with a luminous glow. Swirls of dust motes sparkle and dance amid the sunbeams. A peaceful silence imbues the space between us, and we both savor its wordless serenity — Servilia etched in profile by the waning twilight! We sit spellbound, as time passes, becoming meaningless, hardly breathing, not one of us willing to disturb the otherworldly enchantment.

It's a rare, unforgettable occasion, a moment so unexpected, so precious, frozen forever in our collective memories. I feel as if this is our time and place, that we will always belong here, always together, detached from the rest of the outside world. Finally, I know not when, I clear my throat and gently mention to Servilia that I was thinking of Eleusis and the Mysteries, breaking the genial communion that had overtaken us.

"As you know, dear Epicurus, I am an only child and lost my mother at birth," she speaks calmly now, "one life exchanged for another, which carries its own perverse burden of guilt. At least you got to know your mother before she died. I never had the chance to hear my mother's voice, feel her touch — even to know what she looked like!"

She hesitates, her top lip quivering, but carries on.

"Sorry, but you should be thankful for whatever time you had with your mother. Yes, I am attracted to the Mysteries. They focus on fertility, and the special relationship between mothers and daughters, womb begetting womb."

She sips her wine, then abruptly screws up her face into a sour grimace.

She waves off my concern, to indicate that it's not the wine.

"When I think about it, my life consists of endless acts of contrition and sacrifice. Whatever I do, it's never enough to make up for 'killing' my mother, and 'robbing' my father of his beloved," she snorts, shrugging her shoulders — a gesture of hopelessness — followed by a short, hollow laugh.

"I never told this to anyone: what really happened at Eleusis, so it can be our secret. As part of my initiation into the Mysteries, I was given a potion which put me into some kind of trance. I can't tell you everything,.....and so much happened that I can't even recall. I remember that all the gods and goddesses were present, as if I had died, and my mother too was present, smiling at me. I heard her voice for the first time, so sweet and inviting, telling me that she and I will be united forever in the afterlife."

Servilia paused, wiping away a few tears with the back of her hand.

"It was a blessed experience, and so helpful. But despite everything, I still fall back on my old patterns of thinking. I still feel selfish, as if I don't deserve any enjoyment in my life, even my time with you. Like I have to make restitution for my guilt. Even right now,…. here with you."

Tears trickle down Servilia's pale face. I pass a towel to her. I think about hugging her, but feel that she needs her space.

Pitiless self-judgement I think, must always be the ultimate measure of punishment. No one can scourge another person as effectively as that flogging metered out by one's own self — for which there's nowhere to hide. Well-guarded secrets and unrequited yearnings become the branding irons of that most personal of mental torturers.

Servilia goes on to describe in detail, the pilgrimage to Eleusis. It became a milestone in her life, a rite of passage to womanhood, but moreover, a symbolic redemption of her own identity. She describes it as "Promethean", alluding to it as a fiery gift of the gods, that of divine forgiveness, burning away her sacrificial shrine of endless guilt. For the first time in her life, she felt free, lightened in spirit, unburdened. The experience didn't last — but nor can it be erased.

She knows now how it feels to be truly free.

This was as unexpected as it was welcomed by the many, many people who love her, not least of all by myself.

Chapter 13

While Servilia's experiences at the Eleusinian Sanctuary were life-changing, her fainting episodes nonetheless continued.

Taking a steely attitude, Valerius concluded that a different approach was needed — an alternative to the magical 'atavism' of the Eleusis sanctuary. Against her vehement objections, Servilia was compelled to attend the famous Hippocratic School of Medicine on the Aegean island of Kos.

"I was told, much to my disgust and disbelief, that I was suffering from a problem with my uterus. They described it, with the condescension given to a child, as a case of 'wandering womb'? My 'hysteroid womb', is supposedly floating around freely, unattached within my body, causing all kinds of problems."

She shakes her head reflexively, in dismay.

"It doesn't make any sense, and only applies to women of course. Never men. So if a woman gets 'emotional', it's not really an appropriate reaction to events, but rather her floating womb that's the culprit. Everything is lumped unto the evil womb."

By this time, Servilia's voice is racing, reaching such a pitch that she is screaming. Her much-maligned body shudders involuntarily, limbs agitated, as if casting off a putrid garment.

"They told me on another occasion that my womb was wandering because I had lost who I was as a woman, wanting to be a spiritual healer instead of settling down and having a normal husband

and family....(she pauses, sobbing)....just so that I could die in child-birth, like my poor mother."

"When I objected, that it wasn't helping, they even quoted Plato in an attempt to convince me. Apparently, he refers to the uterus as a separate creature living in a woman's body, especially if she is older and childless! That's the end of Plato for me!"

"They applied a brew of foul smells to my nose, and then....these men wanted to rub a fetid ointment into my genitals. I put a stop to that. Can you believe it?" Servilia asks rhetorically, with flashes of anger accenting her words.

"I try not to hate all men, after what happened — but it's hard, and that experience affects me still to this day,....and they said I was the sick one! Homer said that Circe, goddess of sorcery, enchanted men with her beauty, then delighted in turning her lovers into swine to reveal their true natures. There was a time when I found that story disgusting, but now I totally understand her reasons."

Again, she shakes her head vigorously, frowning.

Her brunette mop of hair is plaited with gold and silver beads. With each shake of her head, a shimmering aura lights up, as the flickering beads catch the slanted beams of the late afternoon sun. More than anyone I have ever met, Servilia speaks with her eyes — sparkling huge blue-green eyes, narrowing or widening most curiously, with every ebb and flow of emotion. Never was anger so breathtaking!

"It seems to me as if their repulsive conclusion, my evil, wander-ing womb, was deliberately intended to undo much of the good that came from my Eleusinian pilgrimage — so I just ignore it, as much as I can."

"It's made me even more angry at my father. He sent me to Kos only because he was losing his control over me. He resented my newfound confidence and self-determination following my pilgrimage. My time at Eleusis totally altered my life, and still does."

"Wandering womb!," Servilia snorts incredulously, throwing her arms up in disgust.

"Can you believe that? Such nonsense!"

❧❧❧❧❧❧❧❧❧❧❧❧❧❧❧❧❧

I remember the time immediately after Servilia's return from Kos, when she first told the story of her 'wandering womb', to the accompaniment of much merriment from our friends. It sticks in my mind because sadly, it wasn't one of my finer moments.

"....turning her lovers into swine"

At some point amidst the general hilarity and cackling, I thought of another part of Servilia's anatomy that like the womb, had a habit of wandering about, unaccountably. I was the garrulous one on this occasion, brimming with a heady mix of good fellowship and abundant wine — so much that I couldn't resist mouthing the obvious flippant remark.

"All in the spirit of good fun," as I protested later in my pitiful defence.

While our friends had all laughed heartily at the insinuation, Servilia's petrifying stare would have turned the mythic Medusa into stone. There could be no doubt that my little joke would cost me

dearly. Caught up in the merriment, without thinking of the consequences, my mouth became disconnected from my brain!

I soon found out about the meaning of 'hubris'. I had gone too
far, and with my tongue loosened by wine, I didn't know when
to stop. That was several years ago, and my crude slip has been
forgiven — though not entirely forgotten, as Servilia once again
reminds me. What was originally an unthinking quip in very bad
taste has now taken on a legendary life of its own — it lives on irre-
deemably, much to my everlasting shame.

I plead with Servilia to reconsider my 'grossness' as an imma-
ture throwaway remark — just petty juvenilia, arguably a necessary
part of growing up.

"Can't we both can then dismiss it with a laugh,....or even a
groan?"

To no avail! She is unwilling to relinquish a useful item that
carries such leverage.

The only thing that matters is that she is here with me now:
flashing eyes and lustrous olive complexion, happily yielding to
the pleasures of the grape in my father's cozy culina. Whatever may
be its other attractions, this time with me offers a temporary relief
from her father's suffocating scrutiny. Her 'minders', sympathetic
to young love, turn a blind-eye.

As for my own father, he is all the family left to me — though
I must admit, I still fear his formidable dark moods. I have made
up my mind to leave Colophon, whenever my tutorial earnings will
permit it. The pull of Athens, my ancestral home, yet still largely
unknown to me, has grown irresistible of late. The newly minted
Parthenon, decked out in many bright colors, has turned out to be a

lucrative attraction. My cache of silver drachmas however, remains woefully small.

Meantime, I have my own Athena beside me, a warrior goddess with a generous heart. She and I had decided together, as children do, spontaneously assigning roles which remain for life, that she was to be Athena, the virgin warrior — rather than Aphrodite, goddess of sexual desire.

I wonder about this sometimes, whether there is some ambivalence in her roles — occasions in which my stern, vestal Athena is transformed into a seductive Aphrodite. The lover of Aphrodite is Adonis, the irresistibly handsome male god of beauty, and I can't compete in that arena. I eventually console myself that her inevitable flirtations are nothing but the outrageous behavior of a worldly warrior goddess. After all, she had adopted Athena to please me, as she knew of my familial origins in Athens — surely a tacit acknowledgement of her commitment?

"Adonis, the handsome male god of beauty"

With her pedigree of Latinate and Ionian cultures, I have always cherished my stormy dialogues with Servilia, all through our shared childhood. She would feign apparent disinterest, followed by a startling flash of enquiry that always pushed me to think further.

Whatever the ways and uses she makes of her body, Athena or Aphrodite, wandering womb or not, her brain is a different organ altogether. At once cocky and inquisitive, she never hesitates to challenge what she can't intuitively understand. Smitten by her alluring beauty, I had never previously thought of her as a muse — someone who would encourage and tease out my philosophical enquiries. Until now, I had never even considered that I needed such a thing — though implicitly, she had always been my mental sparring partner....and equal.

The thought grows on me now as I begin to appreciate her as a complete and unique personality. She has changed, grown in maturity, and surprisingly, against the odds, so have I.

On my side, I must learn how to tone down my defensiveness,.... and yes, my 'always-right' intellectual arrogance.

I know only too well that Servilia is not always the bouncy, whimsical creature that she presents to the external world. She usually has an ulterior motive in most of her actions, such as her present apparently 'random' visit. I didn't have to wait very long.

"About my little poem on the art of loving; what does it mean for Epicurus the budding philosopher, I wonder?" she coos in my ear, an inviting Aphrodite — with a warlike Athena, armed and waiting in the wings.

"I called it, 'Where Loves Lies': but where indeed for my Epicurus?" She queries, in her best dulcet tone, sweet as honey.

I sigh with relief. I had expected this at some stage, and had a diplomatic, yet affectionate response, ready to go. While I enjoy Servilia's poetic talent, this particular piece is keenly personal for both of us. Not only a declaration of love, but also a baited trap of sorts. I choose my words with great caution.

"Loving someone must always be an act of free-will, which applies to both parties, if it's to be authentic. They go together."

She is nodding now, and smiling broadly. I feel relieved, yet with a lingering pressure to perform, to say the right words. I carry on.

"You are right in saying that being spouses can degrade love, turning it into a lie, when people take love for granted, just because they are spouses. This is what happened with my own parents: what was once free-will turned into a cruel prison for both of them — which ended up as a tragedy."

In mouthing Servilia's self-serving views, I struggle with my own growing impatience. I know also that these views are nothing but a thin veneer. At one level, they hide her own doubts — whether she can have a 'normal' loving relationship. At a deeper level, she has her father Valerius in her sights, especially his oppressive scrutiny over her life.

The importance she places on free-will is not coincidental. She doesn't want to replace one controlling male with another. To that end, she plays other suitors against me. It only happens infrequently but sufficient to maintain her sense of independence — and my sense of unease! I understand her ambivalence, especially in light of the gross 'treatment' she experienced at Kos.

All these concerns come together in a patchwork quilt, begging to be disentangled. When I reach out, as I have done several times, all too often I end up as the target. I try for a singular shift in the discussion:

"You speak wrongly of Eros, Aphrodite, and Adonis, as if there is no love outside of the erotic 'Now'. There are different types of loving relationships, whether the lovers are spouses or not, just as there are different types of love, and love-making."

I've had more than enough esoteric discussion on the varieties of free-will! Putting discretion aside, I close the awkward moment by cutting straight to the unspoken heart of the matter: the very personal issue which lies hidden behind all this talk of 'free-will'.

"Look, Servilia,....it comes down to this: I am not your father, seeking to control you....And you....you are certainly not my mother,....so that I should feel forever guilty, always trying to prove myself to you."

I hit the nail on the head....Or not!

Servilia raises her eyebrows now, at the same time affecting a disdainful drooping of her mouth, matching her infamous body shrug. Surprise and disinterest, all rolled into one. Her range of expressive gestures is a language unto itself, worthy of the best theatre. It is this 'Otherness' — her defining characteristic — that is so unfathomably attractive to me.

I'm perplexed! What am I missing here?

Knowing Servilia to be an accomplished poet, I understand that she is lyrical by temperament yet also wily by nature. With all this tedious talk of free-will, fathers, and mothers, it dawns on me, if ever so slowly, that there may be an altogether different meaning between the lines of her poem — hidden in plain sight.

A meaning that is simple and obvious, rather than deep-diving into the sophistry of overripe philosophy. Moreover, a meaning that calls out, albeit forlornly, for an immediate response.

Slow indeed, but I eventually get it.

In the 'Now' of her love-making lyrics and the spontaneous

'free-will' of her visit, she is expressing an invitation that requires less talk — one that's more natural and instinctual. The clod I am! That's the simple, straightforward reason she asked about my reaction to her poem!

The Now is right now!

Chapter 14

Carefully untangling myself, I gently roll over in bed to avoid disturbing Servilia — exploring our conjoint free-will has surely been a most pleasant exercise in philosophy. The 'Now' has at last, been adequately laid to rest — 'Where Love Lies', indeed.

Servilia wakes, tousled and bleary-eyed. Propping myself up by the elbow, I ask for her assistance....someone to help clarify my philosophical mullings. She replies coyly, purring with satiation.

"Hmm....what further assistance could you ever possibly want?"

As if offering a reply, she whips off the cover with one hand, exposing her nubile young torso. Placing her other hand on my scalp, she pushes me slowly down in the bed, despite my stubble, rubbing me along the length of her lithe body. I'm enthralled and speechless, totally helpless — an appetite that seems unquenchable.

She nibbles my ear. I can see little above the crescent outline of Servilia's generous cleavage. Genteel she is not, when despite her inherited wealth, or in rebellion against it, she practices the exotic arts and skills of Aphrodite and Eros. My sensuous world is reduced to her greedy little mouth.

Idle rumor has it is that Servilia happily surrendered her virginity to an eastern mystic-cum-businessman. The story goes that he mysteriously arrived from Byzantium and was offered lodging by Valerius during their lengthy trade discussions. Whether oriental scoundrel, or racy liberator to womanhood, who is to say? Whatever her prior credentials, Servilia's eroticism is all-consuming: I surrender myself hopelessly, to her florid generosity.

"Servilia wakes, tousled and blurry-eyed"

Gripping my head between her legs, she arcs her back, digging her long nails into my neck. Squeals like newborn piglets, at first — becoming throaty, shifting to a rising crescendo of open-mouthed groans. Disheveled, her blonde locks fall over her face, brushing my nose as she nimbly swings her torso upright — shoving me roughly on my back. Manhandling. Mounted now, and riding me with a steady rhythm — poised, as if taking her favorite stallion for a trot at the Villa. The trot increases in pace, growing into a frenzied gallop. Thinking stops — all of me is absorbed, lost within her. The climax comes as a elemental scream, as of a birth or death — both of us, together.

It is rumored she takes woman lovers as well, uninhibited — all are equal in the eyes of Aphrodite, the icon of democracy!

Ionian philosophers believe that all things are in constant flux, beginning at the atomic level thence working their way upwards to worldly objects, which sadly, includes lovers. Only too soon, I have firsthand experience of this inconvenient truth as it breaks upon us.

The telltale squeaking hinge of the front door announces the return of my father, home early from school.

Impeccable timing, as it couldn't come at a worst moment. Shocked, I come to my senses — only to realize that it's already approaching sunset, Servilia's curfew.

Valerius will begin searching. The thought flashes across my mind: to be compromised and caught between two formidable fathers. I have never before appreciated the sublime 'squeakiness' of our front door, as the warning bell of imminent danger. I sit up, listening for movement in the house. I hear my father padding about in the culina, followed by his typical sunset regime — outdoors to attend to his vegetable garden with Marius. We have a short reprieve. Servilia nevertheless, covers herself demurely. After all, she comes from noble stock.

Our pleasurable suspension of time has an untimely end. 'Now' is over. Decorum is restored. Bacchanalia terminus — back to bucolic boredom! Dressing quickly, I again invite Servilia to work with me in teasing out my ideas — for our mutual benefit as well as the 'fun' of spending an afternoon together.

Half-naked, at once rumpled and voluptuous, Servilia wrinkles her face sternly,....correcting my request with her best gravelly voice.

"Partner, not collaborator!"

Ever defiant, with an intellect to match, my own personal Athena. I keep one furtive eye on the door, and the other lingering on her resplendent nakedness.

"You're a good one…."

She cuts in, to finish my sentence with a question, inquisitively,

"....despite all the rumors?"

A bear-trap opening, if ever I heard one — recollections of hubris, and her 'wandering womb'.

I choose my words very carefully, "....because of the rumors!"

Her beguiling smile lights up the room.

"....my own personal Athena"

Servilia and I are sitting side-by-side atop a volcanic hillock, a vast swathe of pitch-black basalt boulders.

A bird's-eye view of my father's house is laid out below us, made conspicuous by its roof shingles of red fired clay. Neither of us speak, absorbed in the serenity of our hidden lookout.

We both startle by the shock, as if suddenly awakened from a dream.

The pristine stillness is abruptly ruptured — an otherworldly squeaking, high-pitched, noxious in its intrusion. It's the front door-hinge of the farmhouse.

"I need to oil that damn thing!"

"Shhh!! Please don't!" Servilia cries in dismay, breaking out in one of her saccharine smiles, crinkling her eyes, as she turns to wink at me. She's right, of course....the proven alarm system for our daytime dalliances.

Our amorous encounter of the past week appears to have gone undetected. Marius of course, sees everything and ever scrupulous, says nothing. We gloat and nudge each other, as small children — and lovers — are prone to do: breaking a taboo, then dodging scrutiny from the grownups.

Looking down from the hill, I can see my father clearly, a match-stick figure in his sleeveless tunica, tending his beehives while Marius busily tills the vegetable garden, ready for planting seedlings. Whether harvesting his own honey, picking ripened fruit, or gathering olives for pressing — these are my father's favorite pastimes upon returning home from the mental strain of schooling all day.

Our black hill also serves as a private retreat for my philosophical reveries — the famous 'seven hills of Colophon' as a vermilion backdrop in the hazy distance. The physical height of the hillock somehow enhances my ability to 'look down' at complex matters, or else to 'rise above them'.

Delusional I admit, but it seems to work nevertheless. At other times, the hillock offers a temporary refuge from my father's wrath during his dark moody episodes — those fearful times when he becomes unapproachable.

"Well, let's get going on your so-called Swerve," Servilia

announces, with her customary gusto, "it fosters the choices made by our free will, especially how we handle rejection. So it's about determinism....how we are born with our instinctual reactions versus free will, and how we consciously choose to react."

"You have it," I say, impressed with her rapid-fire summary, better than I could do. Knowing myself, I would cloud it over with a needless mountain of words.

"Recognizing this fact consciously, gives us greater choice in how we perceive events and what action we take: like a column of dominos, we may wobble in the face of rejection, but remain upright — we choose not to react, or else take a problem-solving approach."

She pauses for dramatic effect,....then as if it was a mere afterthought, drops her own personal fireworks.

"But what if for instance, you have done something that justly deserves rejection?", she murmurs, glancing sideways at me, with a wicked sardonic smile. Servilia is, by turns, exotic and maddening.

We both know that she is referring to Critolaus, of course. She alludes to him now in an offhanded remark, coming out of nowhere, that catches me by surprise — seemingly, to create 'distance' between us — playing him as a kind of Adonis. Servilia wants to trigger a jealous reaction from me, I think, since we have become too close? At a deeper level, I suspect it's her old guilty self-negation — that denies her any real joy in life — which like a poisonous arrow, pierces straight to her heart.

Though she won't acknowledge it openly, Servilia maintains an eerie relationship with the 'spirit' of her dead mother. Hypetia's death, giving life to Servilia, has left an unfortunate legacy of lasting guilt and self-hatred. Then there's her controlling father, whose overt 'love' belies a clawing possessiveness, fuelled by an unspoken blame.

The end result is a witch's brew of guilt, anger, and melancholic isolation — which in turn, feeds her uncertainty about any emotional attachments. The closer she becomes to someone, such as myself, the more it raises her hackles....the primal attachment to her deceased mother, as well as a primal loss — a rejection by any other name.

This much I have gathered over the years, putting the pieces together: a confession of sorts, but also a warning.

Attachment to anyone, even her father, places her at risk — along with the pangs of love comes the pain of further loss, which is unbearable for her. Pushing the other person away becomes more pressing than the desire for closeness. A most infernal paradox, forever caught between desire and fear — wavering between the poles of intimacy and estrangement.

I ignore Servilia's provocation: using poor Critolaus to evoke a jealous reaction in me.

This is something I have never done before: it's true that I am quietly annoyed,....but not overwhelmed with emotion! On the other hand, Servilia's desperation and fear, masked by a veneer of smugness, is sad for me to witness. I plainly see the pitiless, powerless trap into which she was born, haunting her everyday life.

While the Eleusinian pilgrimage provided a measure of relief, her visit was too brief,....her inner conflict, too severe. Any lasting healing requires a longer stay. The experience nevertheless, gave Sevilla a sense of hope — for the first time. For his part, Valerius was indignant, perhaps afraid of losing her. A true man of his times, and rich merchant to boot, he sided with the doctrinaire physicians of Kos, promptly forbidding any further visits to Eleusis. The fallout between father and daughter was a bitter one.

Valerius has gradually come to realize, to his great dismay, that such attempts to reign in his troubled, charismatic daughter only serve as a launching platform from which Servilia catapults herself onwards and outwards — an unstoppable, fragile force of nature that despite all his paternal misgivings, he secretly admires. Just as he did with his beloved Hypetia, to whom the daughter shows a remarkable resemblance. This is the woman I love, a plucky show-stopper — with the gentle sensitivity of a penniless beggar.

Thoughts and emotions tumble headlong through my mind — as I muster my answer to Servilia's loaded question. My heart goes out to her: now is not the time for outbursts — jealousy will have to wait its turn. I decide instead, to turn her 'projection of rejection' away from me, back to its source: her own self.

"Your question does you great merit. Sometimes, we just need to drop our defences and accept rejection behavior by other people, even if we don't want to hear it,....even when it's true."

Despite my best intentions, I can't help drawing out my last few words.

Servilia pokes out her tongue, nonplussed, mimicking her distaste, smiling puckishly, as if my words were sour wine. I have not reacted impulsively this time as she has expected I would. Ignoring all the emotional loading, I simply answer her question.... literally and concretely.

She pouts, with aristocratic disdain. Servilia thinks that I'm lecturing her with my dry observations, or 'recitations' as she calls them. Things are getting a little heated.

I shudder that our discussion may be striking too close to home. She makes incoherent grumbling noises. What began as a calm discussion of rejection has now become something much more personal and unsettling. Things are becoming sticky, no longer flowing — I can feel us sinking into heaviness. Alarm bells are ringing in my head.

I think back to the recent emotional collapse at her villa, with her father watching us so intently (I still have a meeting with Valerius tomorrow!). I feel the pressure is on me to do something. Things have gone too far, too quickly. I must close the rupture that I have unwittingly opened. I can't heal the deeper wound: only she can do that, in her own way, when she is ready.

A tense, long silence settles over us — a stalemate. I sense that both of us are taking stock, aware that a shakeup is occurring between us. Servilia played the old game, tempting me with jealousy to bring on a rupture — and it backfired, exposing her further. For my part, I pushed too hard into her personal space, where I had no right to go, taking her to the edge. We are both on new ground.

Where do we go from here, I wonder?

Chapter 15

Servilia is quiet now, even docile,....so unlike her.

She is particularly skilled at cutting through the complexity of word-play to nail down the essential ideas, however painful they may be....an ability I can use perhaps to lessen the strain between us. I sigh, and catch my breath.

"In my opinion, perception is the key to managing rejection,.... oneself in relation to the other person," I declare, wryly, hopefully putting matters back on track, "I would like to suggest an important idea for handling rejection."

"Yes....so I'm waiting....", she interrupts, agitated, swirling both of her hands for me to get on with it — patience never being one of her great virtues, while wordiness is undoubtedly one of my great vices.

"It's a simple, short statement, easy to remember when we encounter rejection behavior: Whatever other people think of us, or what we think they think of us....it's still none of our business!"

She appears languid, dreamlike, eyes half-closed — I carry on, not sure if she is listening. Strangely enough for a wordy person, brief, matter-of-fact proverbs appeal to me.

"We don't know what other people are really thinking, since we can't get inside their heads. It's arrogance for us to think otherwise. So we project our own self-rejection, and load it on the other person — setting up a vicious cycle of mutual blaming — since the other person is doing the same thing at the same time! So destructive."

I find her oddly attractive at such times, transformed into the guileless young girl I remember, pensive and withdrawn, vulnerable, crippled by emotional insecurities. I also observe, despite the noonday heat reflecting off the rocks, that she is trembling.

"Well, it's nigh impossible for anyone to know what the other person is really thinking," I repeat myself for good measure, "regardless of what the other person says or does. We are not omnipotent gods, living on Mount Olympus,....at least not yet! Moreover, we don't really live in the world, only the perception we create in our minds. If we train our perception — that what other people think of us is none of our business — then we alter the world in which we live."

I put it very bluntly, perhaps too clumsily. My stomach heaves. I gently reach out and take Servilia's limp hand, holding it steadily, passively. No response, so I carry on.

"In trying to guess what the other is thinking of us, we become caught up in our own wild projections of self-doubt. We are so busy putting ourselves in the other person's mind, we lose any real sense of ourselves,....our own solid grounding."

She squeezes my hand several times. I hold my breath.

"Aha! I get it," she says, breezily, as if we are discussing what's-for-dinner...."Yes, of course....that's what happens." More smiles.

We both laugh, contagiously....relieved that the tension has passed.

Servilia's mental labyrinth is no different to my own self-defeating paralysis: when my repetitive thoughts drift aimlessly, heaping one negative thought upon another — such as my recent rumination about the meeting with Valerius. I think about the fable of Sisyphus, a lot of mental effort, repeated endlessly, for no gain, leaving only frustration and exhaustion..

I reach out, and grab both of her hands in mine, my eyes catching hers.

"No one can reject you, Servilia, only your own self-perception; not your father, and especially not me....Nor your mother, who lives within you every day, through you, in everything you do — she is there, with you."

She throws her arms around me, irrepressible as ever, though still tremulous and obviously shaken. I'm left in a bewildered state myself, an absurd combination of care-taking and arousal. Not so bad, really.

We trek back down the hillock, hand-in-hand, light-hearted, following the crooked trail of steppingstones, dodging the pitch-black basalt boulders, slipping and sliding on the loose scree. Servilia stops to pick a bouquet of blood-red poppies as we go: "perfect for the tabletop of the culina", she says.

It's Servilia's idea, as if she is claiming the culina possessively, tellingly, in her own words, as our special place. "It needs a feminine touch", she adds.

"So you are marking your territory?" I ask, laughing kind-heartedly — a snide reference to certain feral animals.

She winces visibly, then breaks into a roguish smile — the imp that lives in Servilia's many-layered personality.

"Your gross lack of delicacy, Epicurus," she sneers, gloating in mock severity, "So typical of you men. You just can't help being coarse and vulgar. It's your base nature!"

Servilia has made precious few complaints, if at all, about my 'base nature'; rather, I would say she has purposely cultivated it.

Revelled in it, actually, if the truth be known. However, the truth would ruin our little one-act play.

I instantly revert to role, becoming the crestfallen, aggrieved lover, whimpering at the injustice of a scolding, castrating Medusa. Servilia responds to my victim role with a solid, rather painful punch to the shoulder. I love it when we play, albeit not so physically.

"We are talking about Poppies, which symbolize blood," she declares, fancifully, "and blood means passion — matters of the heart, love, and longing."

Unbeknown to her, Servilia is more correct than she could ever guess. I don't tell her that blood-red poppies were my mother's favorite wild flower.

If not my father, then surely Marius, discrete and ever observant, will appreciate the sad-sweet sentiments belying our simple gesture.

Chapter 16

The Villa is surrounded on three sides by massive stone walls of white fine-cut limestone, criss-crossed with a latticework of brick-red terra-cotta shards.

The overall impression is that of a giant dice-board made for a Homeric Cyclops, a metaphor that probably wouldn't please the Villa's master.

Beyond the stone walls, the grounds are surrounded by a semi-circular caldera, a geological feature formed by a major eruption eons ago. The walls of the dying volcano toppled in upon themselves, creating what is most aptly described as a giant bowl, or cauldron. In fact, the local name for this lavish villa is 'The Caldera'.

I have never been able to pin down with my Colophon neighbours, rural and reticent by nature, whether this local name is a geological reference to its volcanic origins. Could it be a veiled sleight directed at one of Colophon's most prominent outsiders, a vociferous personality and a Roman foreigner to boot? The Villa's Latinate name is conspicuous to any visitor, Domus Solis Domina, 'home of the sun lady', writ in bas-relief across a monolithic boulder of pink marble.

The opulent country estate was originally built to please Valerius' wife, Hypetia — she of the 'sunny' disposition — dying in childbirth before its completion.

I ask myself whether the caldera site was chosen for its association with Hephaestus, infernal god of fire and brimstone? The god of smithery also, beating raw materials into the desired shape. I wonder if this fiery association is a portent of things to come — then I catch myself, overthinking again. This long-awaited meeting with Valerius has once more stoked up my anxiety.

Quadriga of Valerius

I trudge onwards, along the familiar white gravel ramp, made wide for oxen-driven carriages or the master's quadriga, a chariot drawn by four horses, hitched side-by-side. I hear guard-dogs barking ferociously in the distance, tethered I hope, announcing my presence, or sealing my fate, as the case may be. Too late now to turn back.

Passing by the ornately-carved lions-gate, into the walled garden, I marvel yet again, at the grand panorama opening up before me: a landscape designed to awe visitors with its overripe trappings of status and beauty. The collapsed walls of the caldera form a natural bulwark, enclosing a sheltered space, filled with black, mineral-rich soil. An access promenade of flagstones follows the arc of the caldera, planted with hedges of thyme, myrtle, and rosemary, so that a waft of scents immediately engulfs the visitor.

The eroded volcano walls are lined with sharp-pointed cypresses, ancient oak spotted with lichen, stands of parasol pines and manna ash, amid the silver-grey leaves of ageless olive-groves.

On the other side of the promenade, there are scalloped terraces of scrubs, including juniper and pink oleander, mixed with thorny acacia with its fragrant white blossoms.

Here and there, oaken benches are placed, sited for contemplation, to capture a particular alignment of variegated color. Sometimes, a full-figure statue of Aeneas or other Trojan hero is the focus. One feature however, is given pride of place, situated atop a small embankment, visible throughout the estate: a ceremonial, octagonal temple, gleaming-white in the afternoon sun.

At its center rests the monumental pink marble sarcophagus of Hypetia, princess of the royal family of Smyrna, mother of Servilia, beloved wife of Valerius. I can imagine the master of the estate, in somber mourning: crumpled on one of the benches, mired in helplessness, his worshipful gaze fixed on the temple vista — visible through the carefully manicured foliage of that regimented garden — where they had agreed to spend eternity together, along with their pet African leopard, now mummified.

"Sarcophagus of Hypetia, mother of Servilia"

Slaves scuttle about, carefully avoiding my gaze, watering, pruning, potting, irrigating, and all the other myriad tasks necessary to maintain such a lavish garden. Gravel paths wind between raised beds of narcissus, anemones, asphodels, lavender, and saffron crocus, as well as numerous tropical exotics from faraway Africa.

An elaborate system of irrigation canals, siphons, waterwheels, and aqueducts source water locally from mountain springs.

To complete the spectacle, an orchard of figs, golden apples, and pomegranates sweeps around the villa itself, offering superb fruit within easy reach. A lush strip lawn provides ready access to the orchard and abuts the tiled loggia incorporated into the villa.

Finally, the mandatory vegetable garden is sited at the back, between promenade and villa, artfully concealed behind extensive vineyards, producing several varietals of house-wine. I am daunted by the sight of the garden 'potting shed', considerably larger than my father's humble house.

I promise myself that one day I would own such a garden of delight, simple and less ostentatious, to fill with friends and pleasant talk. In place of Valerius' palatial porticus entrance, I would have a plain hardwood door, with a pediment above it and a grapevine trailing over the garden wall. On the doorway of my fantasized home, facing the pavement, I would post a conspicuous sign, "All are welcome here."

I inherited my spirit of greater humanity, inclusive of all nations, races, religions, and class, from my mother: my imaginary home with its welcoming open door, reflects her positive influence in my life. My poor mother has no monumental pink marble sarcophagus to mark her passing: in fact, no monument whatsoever other than the boundless immensity of the ocean. Her legacy requires no hard marble, yet her kind-hearted goodwill and influence linger on, alive still, in my heart as well as the many who loved her.

I turn now into the propylaeum, the forecourt and reception for the villa, and find a slave patiently waiting for my arrival in the atrium. I am led along a central colonnaded arcade having a low entablature with niches inlaid with porphyry, for statuettes or ornamental red pottery. The floors are paved with mosaics of multicolored pebbles, of various fishes, whales, dolphins, and other aquatic life. Everything about the villa is oversized and overstated, designed not merely to impress, but rather, to overwhelm.

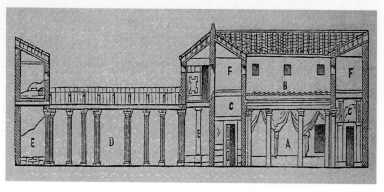

"Domus Solis Domina" (Valerius' Villa — partial cutaway view)

Passageways intersect the arcade at regular intervals, providing access to the many rooms of the main house, or domus, with a heated bath complex off to one side.

I am escorted into the tablinum, the male inner sanctum.

The master of this sumptuous estate is waiting for me.

Chapter 17

As I approach, Valerius greets me with a half-hearted version of a Roman military salute. Forever the showman, as I came to know him later.

His right arm is closed to a fist on the heart, then swung fully outstretched and upwards at an angle in my direction, with a flat palm, held rigid for a few seconds, then released to his side. The chivalrous ritual of the Roman salute is intended I believe, to convey a message of loyalty or friendship such as 'my heart belongs to you'. Time will tell, in this case.

Caught off guard, all I can manage is a weak wave of the hand, nothing outstretched,....and certainly nothing military. Besides, I'm an impoverished Athenian Greek, trapped in Colophon forever , not an affluent Roman who can choose when he comes or goes.

Mine host lies half-reclining on a couch, under the shade of a rose-colored damask canopy. My Greek image of sybarite Romans is completed by the sight of a tattooed Thracian maid standing nearby. Clad in diaphanous silk, bare-breasted with gilt edged loincloth, she is serving her master from a box of imported figs.

A trellis of grape vines, bearing purple, ripe fruit, lies within reach, as well as an ornamental fountain, capped with a statue of the god Poseidon armed with his trident. Tortoises, alive and jostling, fill the fountain reservoir. The cascading levels of fountain-water, eurythmic and relaxing, provide a counterpoint to my tense anticipation of the meeting.

As a self-proclaimed patrician of Colophon, Valerius is kitted out in full-length woollen toga and scarlet-trimmed linen cloak, draped over the shoulder, wine goblet in hand. The goblet immediately catches my eye with its brightness. I recognize the unique sheen of 'green gold': a precious gold-silver alloy, also known as 'electrum'.

"...clad in diaphanous silk"

With a gracious tilt of the head, I am invited to join his libation — soon reclining uncomfortably on an adjacent couch. I muster as much aplomb as I can manage, or endure. The ability to relax on Roman couches must surely be an inherited skill not shared by us poor Greeks. A slave is summoned, and returns promptly, placing a matching electrum goblet before me.

I recognize the offering at first tasting — a special combination of two rare red varietals, home-grown on the estate: the Phochian and the Retinian grapes. He is signaling the significance of his agenda, while I sample his 'house wine', and struggle to conceal my nervous tremor.

Greetings, libations, and small talk soon follow, on those safe topics for which mutual agreement is assured. We start with the costly repairs to the foundations of the Heraion Temple, always a problem — constructed upon low marshy ground, verging a river delta. Valerius is contributing generously to its restoration.

"What were the ancients thinking when they built it there?" he queries, rhetorically.

Attentive listening is surely a polite compliment, a hallmark of culture. In Valerius' case however, it becomes something else, the veiled instrument of a penetrating intellect — subjected to such focused attention, I feel physically uncomfortable. He must know that I sleep with his daughter,…. his sole offspring.

No sooner have my fleeting words left my lips, than his inquisitional mind bears down upon them. Culling through my unguarded remarks, I am left with the impression that he is cross-referencing and tabulating for contradictions, slips of self-disclosure, or other revealing foibles.

Such 'interrogation', even though it may be dressed up as 'goodwill', fosters its own defences. The impulse to mentally censor everything I say, for example, before actually saying it, becomes paralyzing. What should be a flowing exchange in other circumstances regresses to a string of stilted, anxious mutterings! I find myself instead, shooting out words under pressure — involuntarily, to beat my own mental 'censor'.

Lyre-players provide sweet music at a distance.

I express my admiration for his floor of tessellated tiles, classical black-and-white, a favorite of the Romans. An otherwise innocent remark — just a polite throwaway — yet it feels awkward and contrived even as it passes my lips.

My words hang limp in the air.

"There's no hurry," says the master, smiling and somewhat bemused, "Take your time before speaking. I find that a sip of wine always helps to free up the right words." I still feel as if he is the cat, playing with me as the helpless mouse.

I appreciate his good-natured advice, intended to put me at ease — while at the same time, it asserts his total control of the situation. This is a personage for whom wielding great power comes as naturally as breathing. Having established his power base, he adds several humorous anecdotes related to the estate. I am glad to follow his lead, laughing or retorting on cue. An understanding of sorts, is forming; perhaps, the beginnings of trust. I follow along.

The wine is excellent indeed, and seemingly endless. With such a generous opportunity for indulgence, my goblet is never empty. We parley back and forth. I begin to relax into the couch — interestingly, it seems to have become a good deal more comfortable .

We then get down to business.

Chapter 18

Valerius abruptly raises the prospect of my future plans, partly I suspect, to catch me by surprise. He leads off by making the assumption that I am probably intending to remain in Colophon. Tricky.

"What is an ambitious young man like yourself doing here, in a lascivious backwater like Colophon,....so far from the seats of power and influence? You should be in Athens, where you are already a citizen. Why would you come back here of all places?"

His surprise ambush works. I'm dumbfounded. He hasn't finished yet, however.

"While Colophon is a paradise of sorts, with its mild climate, charming seaport, and rich patrons, it's also a place where young people end up marooned. Seduced by all its shallow pleasures, they remain stuck here for the rest of their arbitrary, short lives — dying fat, stupid, and drunk, with a surprised, incomprehensible stare on their blotchy faces. What a waste!"

He pauses from his fiery tirade, just sufficient to catch his breath. I'm still reeling mentally, trying to catch up with a sensible reply to his sudden outburst. I feel like I've run into a crazy man, yet I know from his esteemed reputation, that he is anything but that. He's deliberately altering the tempo of our meeting.

"I've witnessed it myself many times in other young people," Valerius adds, "and I don't want that fate to be yours!"

I must admit that everything Valerius said is patently true, plainspoken by a somber businessman. The entitled sons of the political elite provide me with a small but steady income from my private tutorials. Their lives of superficial luxury, living from one debauchery to the next, are not the stuff of serious thought.

The 'ruling class', mostly Ionian and Macedonian, assume an unstated superiority, so subtle that they are hardly aware of it themselves. On the other hand, I feel it keenly, despite their feinting attempts at friendship. While I bridle my true feelings, such elitism is deeply offensive to me. My hoplite conscripted service in Athens honed a natural sense of 'demos' — as did my mother's teaching when I was a child.

It's true: I'm impatient to move onwards — though right now, I have a more immediate problem: what reply should I make to Valerius? I hesitate, faced with a dilemma. If I don't acknowledge my plans (assuming Servilia has unwittingly disclosed them), then it marks me as evasive, even secretive. If I am open with him, it is inevitable that sooner or later, Valerius will speak with my father — as the rich, outsider Roman, Valerius makes a point of meeting regularly with groups of teachers as part of his acceptance in local circles.

My departure, 'if and when', remains a volatile subject with my father. I'm sure he can read the signs, but has been reluctant to ask me directly — somewhat out of fear of being left alone. His depressed mood always simmers like a dormant volcano, just beneath the surface. He knows me well enough that the act of raising the question may end in a nasty confrontation. This in turn could hasten my resolve, and bring on the very event he most fears. So we live together in an awkward state of truce and mutual avoidance.

On the other hand, if he were to find out about my plans 'second-hand' from Valerius, my father would feel compromised, even humiliated. This would trigger an explosion of accusations we would both later regret. It is truly a marvel that all this 'double-thinking' passes through my mind, thought after thought presenting themselves, in the space of a few seconds. I know that I must face my father eventually,....so I may as well be done with it now!

"Just as you say, Colophon has no attraction for me! I'm thinking of leaving and joining one of the philosophy schools in Athens, my ancestral homeland", I declare bluntly, as wholeheartedly as I can manage, in keeping with Valerius' own matter-of-fact style.

"During my two years of hoplite training in that great city, I took full advantage of my spare time to visit the different philosophy schools. With help from friends, I attended the famous Lyceum of Aristotle — the so-called "walking philosopher" — whose seamless flow of thoughts was aided by his eccentric habit of pacing rapidly back and forth as he spoke. The symposium was then continued by his aristocratic followers, debating the selected topic as they also paraded to and fro, imitating their esteemed master — each in turn outdoing the previous speaker by adding his own quirky habits: shuffling, twirling, gesturing, and so on.

"So much for 'free thinkers'! I came away both enlightened and amused! As it so happened, I was exceedingly lucky to hear Aristotles's thoughts in his own words — the symposium turned out to be his last appearance before his final exile to Chalcis, that small city-state just north of Athens on the island of Euboea. The great man died a few years later, never seeing his beloved city again."

I continue in this vein for another goblet or two, adding my sometimes intriguing, often boring experiences with the Platonists and other sophists of various stripes! I notice that the nearby Krater of wine has be been quietly refilled.

Valerius remains patient throughout my self-absorbed rambling, listening attentively as ever. I had not expected this receptive response from such a hardheaded businessman. I have certainly benefited from his largesse in other ways: his endorsements have granted me tutorial access to the upper echelons of Colophon society.

I had always thought of this assistance as an veiled favor to my father, rather than myself: more as a recognition of my father's many years of community teaching, repaid to the son. Yet there is something indefinable in the conversation today, even the way he looks at me, that makes me wonder if his motive is more personal?

"....the nearby Krater of wine "

We have been 'wrestling with the air', to quote a popular saying in Athens, which makes its own statement about talkative Athenians and their effusions of 'hot air'.

Chapter 19

Valerius asks after my father — tellingly (was it my father who arranged this mysterious meeting?) — then adds as a seeming afterthought,

"Why was your Athenian-born family on Samos in the first place, then ends up as refugees in Colophon? Didn't the Athenians go to war with Samos and many Samians were then exiled?"

"Samos was originally a prosperous city-state with a proud history of naval warfare," I reply, promptly "which made sense because the island is a hub for many trading routes."

I inserted the lure of 'trading' to shift the focus back to himself:

"That's surely the same reason that you settled here in Colophon. The harbor at Notium gives you easy access to the busy trading routes. Unlike Samos, you also have the bonus of a luxury-goods local market."

Valerius nods his agreement, artfully ignoring my ploy to change the subject,....so I continue.

"Athens has invaded Samos several times. Eventually, Attica installed its own colony of settlers, which included my parents, and I drew my first baby breaths a few years later. All went well for a while. Then the Macedonians took over while I was away with my military service in Athens. In my absence, my father fled to Colophon. My mother had already died on Samos."

I begin to wonder about Valerius' series of questions, first about my future plans and then now, curiously, about my family history. His lengthy enquiries are socially appropriate for a genial host, and appear to be innocent,....nonetheless, I'm feeling uneasy. Is he really evaluating me as a possible son-in-law? Or else, could it be the controlling father wanting to 'know your rival' — gathering anything he could use to undermine me in Servilia's mind?

More sparring. Nerve-wracking yes,....but I sense that we are converging on the main event, step-by-step, as we take the measure of each other. He changes the subject once again, becoming more personal — and provocative!

"My Servilia tells me that you have helped her,....for which I'm grateful. She also says that you waste much of your time just thinking about thinking."

The possessive 'my Servilia' is duly noted — nor would she ever say that I 'waste my time thinking'. Valerius is inserting his own opinions, the scoundrel, using Servilia as a proxy. He is scouting me for weaknesses, I think, to see how I defend myself.

"It may be 'thinking about thinking' as you say,...but I remain grounded in present reality. What separates me from other philosophers is that I start with 'things as they are' — the world of 'What IS'. Many thinkers waste their time with giddy imaginings of 'how things SHOULD be'. Divorced from the world, they live only in their minds."

Valerius stares at me blankly, expressionless, silent, waiting for more — he needs to sink his teeth into something more concrete than 'the world of IS'. I forget his reputation as a boilerplate practical man: abstract thinking isn't his thing.

"Better a life of thinking, than that of a sex-crazed playboy," I retort, taking the moral high-ground, "....there is no shortage of them in the young Colophon elite — I encounter them every day in my tutorials. When existence is reduced to sensory pleasure — sex for the sake of sex, a new partner every night — life becomes nothing but blandness and apathy. Their life-weary faces say it all."

Introducing the idea of sex to a possessive father may not perhaps, have been a wise choice. I am indeed dating his only daughter. My host remains as inscrutable as ever, making no comment — other than pausing to sip his own wine, sucking his lips, pondering as he goes, ever so slowly. It almost seems like he's waiting.

We need to be talking more spontaneously — free-flowing, instead of butting heads. Come what may, I decide that it's my turn to take the lead — I throw a diplomatic sweetener into the mix.

"I suspect that you yourself spend a lot of time thinking....reading peoples' characters — which is what our little meeting here is all about! Otherwise, you wouldn't be the successful businessman who lives in such a grand villa, enjoying such delectably, glorious wine!"

My animated compliment on his choice of wine produces a smug but jovial smile. Was he waiting to see how far he could stretch me — before I had the nerve to seize the initiative? One can never be sure of anything with Valerius.

We begin a lively, friendly discussion on wine varietals, a subject that makes it necessary for us to share yet another round of imbibing. The ice is definitely thawing — I sense that Valerius also, is relieved.

Whatever his obscure reasons, Valerius desires a close connection between us. He would not invest so much of his valuable time if this was not the case.

Chapter 20

Valerius, ever dramatic, raises his goblet.

"I salute my young philosopher who, like a skilful slinger on the battlefield, aims his words with such accuracy, to take down his target."

"As hoplites, we were trained in all forms of combat." I reply, goblet in hand, returning the compliment.

"As Hoplites, trained in all forms of combat"

"The training includes slinging of course," I add, earnestly, reminiscing of past times, "though actually it was my weapon of choice. Strange that you chose that comparison without any foreknowledge."

"Not so strange, really," he replies, as he grows more soft-spoken with wine, "tell me about slinging, and why it's your favorite."

"Slinging appealed to me simply because a warrior-slinger can unleash a hailstorm of leaden projectiles, with a greater range than arrows. They cause terror as they whistle and whoosh in flight,.... until they strike, almost invisibly, leaving little outward sign of their deadly impact, unlike arrows, swords, or spears. This causes further panic in the enemy ranks."

Valerius' listening skills immediately ingratiate him with the speaker. Everyone likes to be heard, and I am no exception.

With that goodwill shared by fellow wine-lovers, Valerius at last gets to the point of our meeting. He speaks now in a firm measured voice, probably his 'business voice' — to be taken seriously.

He reassures me that he feels under no obligation to disclose our private discussions with any "third-party, including Servilia", or my father. I thank him for his discretion.

"The golden years of Athens as the center of erudition and arts is declining," he tells me, "and will eventually be overtaken by Alexandria with its wondrous library. I appreciate nevertheless that you are an Athenian by heart, descended from an ancient lineage."

I interrupt to remind him that my grandfather fought alongside Socrates in the ill-fated Peloponnesian War.

"Yes, yes" as he quickly nods his understanding. I detect a hint of impatience that such anecdotal remarks are redundant now — that it would be timely for me to listen.

"I know that whatever may come, you are driven to return to the city-state of your ancestors, but I would strongly suggest that you delay any impulsive action at this stage. It's too soon."

I don't tell him that my sorry dearth of silver drachmas puts a damper on any immediate return to Athens, impulsive or otherwise.

"You speak of your future, Epicurus — you want entry into the scholarly circles of Athens. You wish to be accepted as a fully-fledged thinker and debater in your own right — to have your very own school of philosophy. I believe you have that potential."

I thank him, ever so briefly, for his confidence in me. Apparently, I have passed 'the test',....but to what end ?

"Philosophers however, in my limited experience of them, are just like everyone else when it comes to outsiders" he continues, "Regardless of your ability, they will treat you as an ignorant rustic from the provinces, to be belittled, ridiculed,....and then slow-roasted."

He pauses to allow his message to incubate, before summoning up his punchline. He must know that's not what I want to hear.

"Simply put, you are not ready for Athens yet!"

An unblinking judgement I had not expected, hitting at the very heart of my dream. I struggle to filter the hopelessness welling up from within me — I understand now why Servilia calls him 'hardheaded'.

"You may be right," I concede, rather plaintively, "I am originally from Samos, now Colophon, and it's true that I have a nasally provincial accent, or so I'm told. That's my background however. It's who I am, and I can't change it now. I don't see any alternative, other than clawing my way up the Athenian ladder."

"That's not going to work either," he fires back, remorselessly, "You have to start the way you want to finish. You think you know

Athens, but previously you were there as a conscripted recruit. That places you under the protection of the Ephebic College, since you were receiving military training as a prelude to citizenship. All Athenians respect that role, a noble thing, since they have graduated from it themselves. This time, you have no role other than the one you wish to impose,.....no College status,...and no support. Athens is a voracious city."

He pauses for emphasis, as if more was needed!

"They'll tear you apart for breakfast!"

A cutting remark — is there a need to be so harsh? — that dashes all my hopes in one fell swoop.

"You invited me here to tell me that!" I exclaim, with Valerius' judgement ringing in my ears.

Chapter 21

Valerius sidesteps my objection, responding shrewdly, unexpectedly, with a challenge of his own.

"If you are really serious about philosophical teaching in Athens, you will need established credentials when you arrive. You must have a proven teaching background, with a base of devoted followers — as well as name-recognition in philosophical circles, ready to run your own school."

"But I can...." I interject again, but am immediately over-ridden.

"You will then represent a viable competitor in your own right. The other schools, Aristotelians especially but also Platonists as well, will still do everything they can to resist you, and close you down. They will smear your name, as corrupting the youth of the city,....and debunk your teachings as perverse, against the gods,.... or worse still, as trivial pedantry."

He pauses, but this time, I remain silent, listening — having learnt my lesson.

"Nonetheless, they will be compelled perforce to respect you — only if you have a prior reputation and the numbers of students to prove it! Ultimately, they will have no choice but to begrudgingly recognize your school, though they will never accept it. You are too real, too practical, for their abstractions. The time has come for you to begin serious teaching, rather than just talking about doing it. Instead, you waste your precious time tutoring the entitled sons of

Colophon, sybarites, and drunken profligates all of them."

Tough talking! I feel like I am being tossed around on a stormy sea, down in a trough one moment, trapped at the bottom with no where to go,....then in the next moment, suddenly lifted to the top, riding the crest of a wave, where anything is possible.

I'm left blinking, speechless and immobile.

Valerius continues in his bluff, no-nonsense manner, laying out my future life as if it is a step-by-step business plan in the making — or else a military campaign in which he is the general.

"What if you were to arrive in Athens as a renowned teacher, accompanied by your followers, from the Ionian city of Lampsacus? Would that make a difference?"

"Why yes, of course," I quickly reply, "Lampsacus is a respected seat of learning, well-established. But that plainly doesn't apply in my case."

Apart from its wide recognition for scholarship, I don't know much about Lampsacus, other than its location on the Asiatic shore of the Hellespont. Then there's its rather sordid reputation for worshipping Priapus, god of procreation and fertility, who is said to have been born there. Statutes with erect penises everywhere you look, apparently.

Valerius continues, speaking with measured assurance,

"This is your one chance, a steppingstone to Athens. You talk to me about free-will,....so now is the time to demonstrate that heavy responsibility: the moment of choice is upon you,....you alone. It's all about packaging the goods: wine in delicate blown-glass, rather than cheap clay amphora. Speaking of which, Lampsacus is also famous for its fine wines."

He winks, and smiles, with a cheeky grin.

We both chuckle knowingly, a private joke, at his deft ability to generate goodwill and lightness in the conversation — precisely at the point where it gathers gravity and seriousness. He's in fine form, enjoying himself — classic Valerius, all sophisticated simplicity, in a seamless mix. In spite of all my misgivings and bruised vanity, it is difficult not to like him, and his playful love of humor.

We lift our glasses together, yet one more time, then I return to his proposal, as unexpected as it is provocative. He is calling me out on my advocacy of free-will: am I just preaching it with my lips, as empty words, or do I dare to live it with my life?

"How is it my choice, as you call it," I blurt out, haltingly, "when I don't even have the drachma to travel there,….then there's living expenses?"

I hear myself wavering, unaccountably, in the face of everything I've ever really wanted! The hidden cost of free-will is the weight of personal responsibility for my own active choices: to be a philosopher, or not!

"I will cover your travel to Lampsacus and all expenses" comes the rapid-fire response from Valerius, reverting to his demure, tuneless business voice.

"You can embark on the Hector, one of my trading galleys, with Master Panyotis at the helm,….very experienced. Pirates are becoming an increasing scourge in the bottleneck of the Hellespont, so that in return, you should bring along all your weaponry to assist the crew if needed."

I nod my agreement, silently. I tell myself: "It's what I've always wanted!"

"I can also arrange an introduction to Idomenous, a pleasant fellow, older than you, and comes with his own local following. He will help you get established in Lampsacus, and deal with official-dom now that the Macedonians are in charge. They tend to be unpre-dictable, and quick to take offense. I know Idomenous is having trouble with Platonists in his home city and is looking to form a alliance to counter their intrusion. He is offended not only by their teaching, but also by their bluster and arrogance towards anyone who disagrees with them."

I find myself becoming enthralled by Valerius' expansive vision of my future — illuminated as much by his personal charisma, as by his attention to detail.

"If you form an alliance with Idomenous, who is well known in Athens by his opposition to the established schools,....then you will have gained a recognition of sorts among the inner circles of philos-ophy. The important thing is that even as a rival, you would not suddenly appear in their midst as a complete 'Unknown'. Notoriety is fine. The more effort they expend on nasty personal attacks, the more they establish your credentials regardless — you get name-recognition either way."

"I don't wish to appear ungrateful," I query, "but what do you ask back in return for such bountiful generosity?"

Valerius falls silent in thought. A spectrum of emotions flits across his countenance — surprisingly, a profound sadness which I had never witnessed previously — nor even suspected would lie beneath his sunny presentation. He seems frozen, seemingly in a different space and time, not present. It is as if for a brief moment, I am seeing deeply into the man and his pain. Sensing my wide-eyed stare, he recovers — at once, avuncular and charming as ever. This revealing moment in time is not lost on me however.

"I had the pleasure of meeting Chaerestrata, your mother, back on Samos", he replies, "She provided great assistance to me at the time of my wife's early death in childbirth. I owe her a debt of gratitude, but then she too passed. You have my sincere condolences. I wish to honor the memory of your dear mother and repay that debt, in some small way, by assisting you."

We both lapse into quietness. Time passes — I'm not sure how long before Valerius speaks.

"May I ask what happened to your mother? I hear different rumors, and don't know what to believe?"

Under the circumstances — a good deed not forgotten but repaid in kind, one sadness begetting another — it is hard for me to feel offended. I answer after a short pause.

"She took her own life." I hear my own voice, flat and wooden. It sounds definitive, even convincing,....as if I am merely stating an everyday fact beyond dispute.

But did she? Valerius obviously thought highly of my mother, so his question is not one of idle curiosity. The day is turning out to be full of surprises, not all pleasant. At the same time, I can't say that Valerius has opened an old wound — if I take an unstinting look at myself, the wound has never healed beyond a superficial shrug.

❧❧❧❧❧❧❧❧❧❧❧❧❧❧❧❧

Valerius concludes his promotional rally and raises his electrum goblet to mine. I fumble for the right words, taken aback, rudely gulping down his wine.

I'm not sure if I'm intoxicated by the wine or the slowly dawning magnitude of Valerius' offer. Either way, it's one of those unforgettable events when as the day progresses — beginning normally but gathering momentum — I realize at a certain point in time, that an invisible line is crossed and my life has changed, irrevocably, forever. I am left with a peculiar feeling, an intuition, that there is more to Valerius' interest in me than what he is admitting.

Thankfully, Valerius replies for me, as I am lost for words — such an exceptional state that Servilia, had she been present, would shake her head in disbelief.

"Of course, you need time to think about it," he says calmly, "I understand that."

He raises his goblet.

"I salute your promising future!"

PART IV:
"Secrets"

Chapter 22

Mytilene, Lesbos
310 BC

I begin with an introduction, my voice surprisingly strong and unfaltering — hoping that no one will notice that my heart is beating out of my chest.

My first ever public address: in this case, to the good citizens of Mytilene.

Epicurus: "We live preoccupied with the dread of death, always a shadow waiting for us at any time,....which stops us from being fully alive in the present. Instead, we lead unhappy, fearful lives of pain and suffering. We hope in vain that the capricious gods will be merciful to us. We are told that we should accept the sacrifices of this life, since we will find pleasure and tranquillity in an afterlife.... of which we know nothing."

A rising babble of murmurings begins, lead by a pot-bellied, squat figure with a bald dome and droopy nose, further distinguished by the clumsy gait of a clubfoot. These few flaws — not uncommon — become minor blemishes with this unlucky fellow, when set against another most conspicuous deformity. Where the left ear should be, lies a conical mound of discolored scar tissue and at its center, a small crater — as if a volcano in miniature has been mistakenly stuck to the side of his head.

My mind wanders distractedly as I talk — he habitually cants his head to the affected side. Due to its weight? I try not to stare, out of politeness, at the misshapen picture. He wears a coarse-hair cap of sorts, pulled down with the intent of concealing his ears — only that as his agitation rises in tempo, so in turn, does the cap, exposing his protuberance.

The recognition when it comes, bursts upon me abruptly, like a clash of cymbals inside my brain. This man before now, 'One-Ear', is that same brute who grabbed me in the docklands alleyway.

I remember him watching eagerly, drooling, while 'Red' went about his weird sadomasochistic death rituals — with myself as the sacrificial goat. After my whacking blow to Red's gonads, there was no way he was going to catch me, hopping along with his clubfoot — I had wondered at the time why there was so little pursuit.

'One-Ear' raises his voice, harsh, throaty and guttural.

"How do you know there is no life after death when we have priests and temples and (he pauses, pointedly)....they even make blood sacrifices? Do they mean nothing?"

"One-Ear" (Agesilaus)

He winks at me knowingly, murderously, as if to emphasize

the veiled threat embedded in his seemingly innocent question. He wants vengeance for his failure in the docklands. As my impressions of 'One-Ear' coalesce into certainty, I struggle to regain my composure. A faceless crowd one minute and then abruptly, his glaring disfigurement in the next, bobbing up-and-down before me — as if a ghoulish apparition. I can't take my eyes off it.

The shock, when it comes, hits me with a physical shudder — I am debating mortality and the dread of death with the very same roughneck who assaulted me, only a few days ago. There was no 'philosophic' debate on that sorry occasion — only preparations for what would have been my certain murder. Now....here I am, with the same fellow, debating the afterlife!

I have no time to examine the irony of the situation, nor betray any shiver of recognition. I scan the crowd furtively for a red tunic — relieved that my worse fears are happily disappointed. I am in no immediate danger. Regardless of my discomfort, if not panic, I must continue my presentation at all costs, as if all is well.

Epicurus: "We have no material evidence of life after death, only what is passed down to us by these priests, priestesses, and oracles. We are fed these superstitions to keep us in check, to live in fear of punishment,....since our true natures apparently can't be trusted. Death is only non-existence,....but if we don't exist anymore, then how can we pine for a life that no longer exists — when we ourselves no longer exist? All we have is 'Now', this moment in time, not to be squandered in fear, but rather to be free, and seek out all the goodness and pleasure that this life has to offer...."

"You want to make satyrs and harlots out of us all!", One-Ear bellows, cutting into my lecture, "Then off to the woods we go, nymphs and satyrs of Venus, and we can all be at it! Bacchic rites for everyone!"

A ripple of bawdy laughter and guffaws spreads across the

crowd — other shoppers stop to join what looks like a lively spectacle. 'One-Ear' follows a simple tactic he has used many times: shock the speaker speechless, while titillating his listeners. I notice that the young man braces himself, pensive and frowning, against an adjacent column, apart from the rapidly swelling crowd.

Emboldened now, 'One-Ear' has gained a following of like-minded hecklers — a regular feature on the promenade, well-known for his lewd antics. An agitator for hire, not least of all by 'Red'. In keeping with his reputation, he continues his sharp remarks, playing to the blood-lust of the mob:

"You tell us that we are all unhappy people, living in dread, and you are going to save us. All hail, our new god!"

At this, One-Ear bows before me theatrically, with his arms outstretched, as do several of his followers. While most of the mob are jeering, still in good humor, there remains a separated group, remote and serious — who are clearly offended, rather than entertained. No friends of mine, however.

From my earlier survey of booths, I recognize several prominent Aristotelians. They speak in subdued voices, as if plotting and scheming. There is much finger-pointing in my direction — they are deciding what to do with such an unwanted intruder on their territory. I have enemies, it seems, in all directions. One-Ear looks back at the Aristotelians from time to time, exchanging nods and hand-signals.

A Scythian Astynomoi turns up, representing authority — onlookers pull back, making way for him. I remain silent, refusing any further debate with One-Ear: no longer a cool philosophical discussion, guided by reason and respect. Rather, it has regressed to the status of a cheap sideshow — a stage for his own scurrilous antics.

Is he alone, still acting as a mercenary for 'Red', or as seems more likely, an agent in the service of the Aristotelians? My lack of response is clearly disappointing for him — if his misshapen sneers are any indication. The roiling crowd runs its course like a spent animal, reduced to a harmless babble. I stand quietly for several minutes,....then pick up the discussion again as calmly as I can muster.

Epicurus: "Know that the naked thighs and fulsome breasts of Venus are nothing but a baited Roman trap to drag you down to their own primitive level of shameless orgies — Dionysian madness, no less. If you be inclined to worship, then we noble Greeks — who carry the blood of ancient Trojan heroes — are born of the Eternal Feminine: virtuous Athena, goddess of war certainly, but she is also tempered by purity and wisdom. Yes, we should seek out the good things in our lives that give us pleasure, without doing harm to others, in balance with our better natures. We should do nothing to excess,....whether it be wine, gluttony, greed, lust, or any other appetite. Our own natures, our better selves, will surely regulate us, moderating our appetites,....since excess inevitably leads to unhappiness and rancour."

'One-Ear' tones down his sarcasm now, at least to a tolerable level....

"So we all should just do whatever we want, whenever we feel like it? Elysium Fields already, and we don't even have to die first to get our reward?"

I pause briefly — a wave of raucous laughter crests, then falters. 'One-Ear' seems to be losing his cutting edge.

Epicurus: "As for the gods, they surely exist,....but reside within our own minds, operating through us,....which is yet another reason that we should trust our own better selves. This is why we don't see them visually,....other than in the images we make of them, statues and carvings, which spring naturally from within us."

Abruptly, an apple smashes on the column behind me, only a little splatter reaching my linen tunic. I suspect 'One-Ear', frustrated that his audience has grown tired of his same old snipes. Neither 'One-Ear' nor the Aristotelians are anywhere to be seen now, arousing my earlier suspicions of collusion between them.

I am struck by the twisted irony: to be deeply relieved that it was the Aristotelians — rather than 'Red' — who commissioned One-Ear to disrupt my first effort at teaching! Agora-phobia, be damned. Should I be flattered that I was important enough to warrant such a hazing from the Aristotelians?

I keep to myself the newfound knowledge that 'One-Ear' is a local mercenary, a possible misstep by 'Red' — since the Mytilenian authorities can apprehend 'One-Ear' anytime. This could enable them in turn, to set a trap for 'Red'. Knowledge is power, and I may need this leverage at some time.

Meanwhile, I need to be vigilant.

Chapter 23

"One-Ear' may have slipped away, but the mob remains — roiling, loud and incoherent. The overall effect is that of a single entity, like the Gorgon-headed Medusa, projecting a collective sense of venom. They move forward towards me, cautious but threatening, the rear members pushing those in front, compacting together, many-legged, reinforcing my first impression of a malevolent creature closing in on its prey.

I stand my ground, anxious but resolute, since to back away would be inviting further harassment, even pursuit. At the last moment, the Astynomoi — a burly, rugged figure with the distinct deep facial scars of a slashing sword — pushes to the front of the mob, which opens up before him, snapping out commands as he goes.

The many-legged 'creature' disassembles, breaking up into small groups and singles, amid much grumbling and cursing. My first teaching has ended in chaos — yet I feel oddly triumphant, as if I had held the line in a great battle. It must be the Athenian hoplite in me, old training that comes in useful.

The Scythian then turns to me, stern-faced but surprisingly diplomatic, recommending that the crowd 'is not ready for my doctrines'. I am welcome to visit the agora anytime 'of course', but 'it would be in the interest of everyone' that I should refrain from further teaching 'at this time'. While his concerns are framed as advisory only, there is no mistaking their categorical nature,....or from whence such commands have come.

Having no choice in the matter, I readily agree, thanking him for his timely action, his courtesy, and of course, his 'recommendations'. Then, a peculiar thing: he nods to me, and leaves — but not before pausing briefly to hand-wave a greeting at the mysterious young man, still standing by the adjacent column.

The young man now introduces himself as Hermarchus, son of Agemortus of Lampsacus. He is visiting relatives and friends in Mytilene as his father's family has ancient ties with Lesbos. Some of his friends include the agora Scythians — who in turn dislike the arrogance and aggressive polemics of the 'booth' philosophers. He singles out the Aristotelians in particular, who consider themselves to be the elite, often fomenting trouble in the marketplace.

Since he was educated and trained as a rhetorician, he expresses a keen interest in my presentation, cut short as it was by the unruly mob. He invites me to a communal dinner — a meeting of like-minded young people.

"Take care," warns Hermarchus, "To many Mytilenians, your unconventional views on life and death seem dangerously sacrilegious. Even a great teacher like Socrates was put to death unjustly for displaying a similar lack of piety. No hemlock for you, please."

Fending our way anonymously through the crowd, I'm glad to depart the promenade and agora after today's upheaval. We then tread in the general direction of the famous theatre, towards the hill on the western side of the city, absorbed in animated conversation.

Hermarchus: "I like it that you emphasize personal responsibility. You ask us all to reflect on the outcomes of our behavior and choices. But that's not for everyone. Saying that men should be guided by their own moral compass, rather than fear of the gods, will condemn you as lascivious — perverting the morals of young people, with which Socrates was also accused."

Epicurus: "I protest. That's not my intention."

Hermarchus: "I'm sure it isn't, but you had a taste of mob violence today,....even though it was contrived. It would not help those to come who may follow your wise teachings, if you were to be convicted as a heretic,....or found guilty of sedition against society."

Epicurus: "What do you mean by contrived?"

Hermarchus: "You have not heard the last from the Aristotelians, who use One-Ear's thuggery to drive away newcomers. One-Ear threw the apple at you, then retreated to avoid the Scythian."

Epicurus: "Why can't the Scythians stop it?"

Hermarchus: "They can only do so much, since the Aristotelians have political pull with their Macedonian masters. Remember that Aristotle himself lived here for a while, and was teacher to the great Alexander. The Aristotelians believe that gives them a special tenure."

Hermarchus continues, with a short explanation of agora politics.

"The other philosophers who have been able to establish themselves pay the Aristotelians for 'the right to be heard'. One-Ear collects the levy, otherwise they suffer your fate. It's all a big, sordid business. Only the Cynics are exempted,....since they eschew money, and never draw large crowds anyhow, only scoffers."

At this point, my anger takes over.

"That's extortion! These are philosophers whose proper 'business' is the study of morals and ethics, for the betterment of humankind. Instead, you tell me they are hypocrites....and worse still, criminals!"

Hermarchus laughs heartily at my burst of self-righteousness, tears in his eyes.

I join him, amused at my own naivety once again. My easygoing acceptance of people and situations, already battered and bruised, takes another shock.

So ends my inglorious debut as a philosopher-teacher!

Chapter 24

The Hector, a veteran of Valerius' trading fleet, continued its passage to Lampsacus without me. Three days out of Mytilene, already nearing the Hellespont lighthouse, the good ship is under full sail, riding a following sea and clear skies.

With luck, the Hector will secure a berth at Lampsacus in record time. Luck is supposedly in the safe hands of Poseidon and the water Gods, with an assurance of calm seas by the sacrifice of a wild boar. Be that as it may, the destinies of ships and men remain subject to the Goddesses of Fate....

Preparing to enter the Hellespont narrows, with little room to manoeuvre amid treacherous shoals, Master Panyotis is at the helm, skilfully navigating his stout vessel. The dangers of the Hellespont are the stuff of legend — mythical Sirens whose ethereal beauty and entrancing song lure mariners to their watery graves. Ulysses had himself lashed to the mast, asserts Homer in 'The Iliad', while his crew of Argonauts plugged their ears with wax. The Hector and its crew are not so fortunate — no siren-song, but just as fearsome: a fast pirate galley appears astern, gaining rapidly on

"....the Hellespont lighthouse"

the unwieldy old veteran.

The crew can hardly believe that the Hector is so unlucky, as to be twice intercepted on a single voyage. In this case, luck has nothing to do with it. The Hector is not a random target of opportunity, but the sole object of a carefully conceived plan.

'Red' had been among the congratulatory crowd at the Mytilene dockyard, as I had conjectured, spying on our good ship for its departure schedule and cargo. He had purloined the Artemis, a replacement vessel for the damaged Sea Wolf. Once again, he is after a rich prize, but moreover, seeks revenge for his wounded pride. There will be no mistakes this time around.

'Red' probably expected that I was also aboard, which would be an added bonus for him. He has a personal score to settle with me, beginning with the 'Sea Wolf' — the several crew lost to my slinger-shots, as well as the nasty facial scar he carries as a permanent reminder of that humiliating sea battle. Then there's the embarrassment of my recent escape in the Mytilene docklands, no less than the indignity of my deft kick-to-the-groin, crunching his manhood — it is not only his pride that calls out for revenge!

Master Panyotis considers the option of running his ship ashore, beaching it, in the hope that his crew may at least have a fighting chance. He calculates quickly, his practiced eye weighing up relative distances and speeds, concluding that the situation is hopeless. They would be overtaken before they could beach.

Escape is impossible. The crew knew what destiny has in store for them: fight, and there was the likelihood of a quick, violent death; surrender, and face a lifetime of slavery, far away, probably in the slave markets of Assyria, or Phoenicia.

My own Hoplite training forbade any form of surrender, but as the fates would have it, for better or for worse, I wasn't aboard.

Master Panyotis calls the crew to order, stating that he would not make a decision for them. Since they are seamen and not trained hoplites, every man's life is his own to choose: whether to fight or surrender, the matter should be put to a vote. The outcome is unanimous — surrender, with one exception, notable but not unexpected. Master Panyotis, of course.

In accordance with the crew's decision, the master orders the lowering of all sails, and unfurling of the sea-anchor. As the pirate vessel trims its sails to come alongside, Master Panyotis slips below decks, wielding the ship's double-bladed axe. He orders the crew to remain clearly visible on deck, huddled in a rowdy group, surrendering but disorderly, cursing their fate — all the while obscuring the master's absence. Heavy axe blows ring out from the bilge, deep below decks, sending vibrations from stem to stern. Experienced seamen, they know only too well the intention of their stalwart master,....as well as the likely consequences.

The crew of the Artemis throw grappling irons, tethering alongside their prize, ready for boarding. All are flushed with the heady triumph of finally winning such a rich prize after so much disappointment. Leaping aboard the Hector in the rush to secure such a bounty, the pirate horde — so gleeful only a minute before — lets out a wretched cry of alarm....and anguish. The Hector has begun to settle deeply, unnaturally, wallowing between the troughs. As if there was any remaining doubt, waves are breaking over the stern.

In a salutary action, becoming of a brave Athenian mariner, good Master Panyotis has scuttled his ship. In workmanlike fashion, the master had punched through the hull in several well-chosen places along the entire length of the keel. He would deny the pirates their prize of the vessel and more so, its valuable cargo.

At once distraught and enraged, 'Red' leaps aboard the Hector in a single bound. Scimitar in hand, he races below decks, cursing and slashing senselessly at the cargo as he goes. Soon after, realizing that the ship is doomed, he drags a bloodied Master Panyotis back to the upper deck of the Hector, now awash.

The crew are promptly herded together as witnesses. Howling and crazed with unbridled anger, 'Red' braces his muscles, launching a swift and tremendous sweep of his two-handed scimitar,.... Master Panyotis is beheaded at once, showering 'Red' with pulses of spurting blood. Scuttling his own ship has cost the master his life, as he knew it would.

The Hector's crew, cowered into submission by their master's grisly fate, are then transferred to the Artemis. A beating follows, painful but superficial, more as a warning, yet not so much as to affect their auction price at the slave market — the pirates only remaining gain in this otherwise futile attack. Grappling irons retracted, the veteran old Hector is cast off on its final voyage.

The hungry sea washes greedily over the gunnels of the stricken ship. Swirling in the white froth of its breaking waves, is the sightless head of Master Panyotis.

'Red' had retained the Hector's pinnace and sail however — pulling one of the bedraggled crew aside. Expecting to be next in line for a beheading, the intended victim begins shaking and crying pitifully, collapsing prostrate on the pitching deck, begging for his life. At Red's command, the hapless seaman feels himself lifted and with his struggles to no avail, callously thrown overboard.

Instead of a watery grave, he lands heavily, painfully on one of the cross-beams of the Hector's pinnace. With a few provisions and makeshift sail, he is promptly cast adrift, quickly carried away by the wild, foaming sea.

Rather than an act of clemency, the horrified seaman will continue to serve the pirates' cause in a different role — as an erstwhile messenger of terror. Since Master Panyotis is widely respected in the maritime community, his frightful fate will serve as a dire warning to others: the scuttling of captured ships will be summarily punished.

Buffeted by breaking waves, the heavily-laden Hector rears up by its bow, where air pockets became trapped below decks. Stern first, with much hissing, gurgling, and bubbling, proud Hector that had sailed the length of the Mediterranean for eighty years, weathering tempests and shoals, slides beneath the surface of the covetous sea that had finally claimed back its own. Forever gone from the world of man, the world of sun and light, the Hector plummets downwards in its death throes, into the cold, dark depths.

Where once there had been a noble vessel, no marker remains other than a pitiful flotsam of ropes, a few barrels, the remnants of a linen sail,....and the master's severed head, sightless, still bobbing eerily in the noonday sun, amid the swirling, sparkling after-wash.

Chapter 25

Many long months have passed, and Mytilene is now my home — avoiding the agora and its den of vipers, masquerading as philosophers. The bloodening, though painful at the time — a necessary rite of passage — has left me with a newfound fighting spirit. I once tried to reconcile my life experiences as a philosopher and warrior by thinking that the warrior needs the philosopher to provide a moral basis for his conquests. My trouncing at the agora revealed only too plainly which is the more treacherous of the two.

Strangely enough, it wasn't long before my gruelling experience gained a certain gossip-driven publicity, even notoriety. A small cohort of 'thinking individuals' became curious to meet such a person, foolhardy or downright crazy, who would stand his ground against the Aristotelians. I suppose I should thank 'One-Ear' as my closet publicist.

Maybe not!

I use the local palaestra and gymnasium now, free from the mob agitators of the marketplace. Thinking individuals of all stripes are welcome to join our vigorous discussion — including Metrodorus, from Lampsacus, already a shrewd and inquisitive young philosopher. I crave the intellectual traffic in ideas, to and fro, between us. Trying to 'push' people into accepting my ideas, convincing them by the sophistry methods of the agora, doesn't work for me!

This is where my sensibility has undergone a dramatic shift. As Valerius had predicted, I was overly earnest to spread my message

— but in so doing, I was insensitive to the backlash which so often arises from new ways of thinking and living. However self-evident to me, my ideas had represented a radical shift away from the traditional conservatism peddled at the agora. Rather than 'pushed' into a tenuous belief by clever sophistry, I want companions who are 'pulled' to my ideas by virtue of their plainspoken truth.

These good friends are still a select few, but their number grows daily. Lecturing at a distance invites an attitude of passive reactance — instead, we sit around together and discuss topics naturally and equally in a pleasant garden setting. This is Socrates' real legacy: the groundbreaking idea of a lived 'Demos' and 'Kratos' among equals.

A self-learning, self-teaching community of Democracy.

Only now, when I am beginning to feel secure, even confident,.... am I overtaken by calamitous news. An event which is long past the newsworthy date, has finally caught up with me — a kick to the belly, taking my breath away. I am shaking in shock and tears, to the very core of my being.

It's the merchant galley 'Hector', my host ship of friends, the old tub that brought me safely to Mytilene, at the dawn of my public life. A sentimental association for me — on that rolling and pitching deck I first took my destiny into my own hands. After the offloading of cargo, I bid farewell and wished them a speedy passage through the risky Hellespont narrows.

I recall parting with mixed feelings, wondering if I had made a rash decision which I would later regret. Suspended on a precipice, at that precise moment in time when I needed to enact a life-changing choice, I found myself unaccountably dithering. My once solid resolve began to crumble. I was turning my back on Valerius' carefully laid-out plans and his generous patronage, burning my bridges.

Do I stay onboard, wistful of a future that might have been, ashamed of my cowardice — or depart forthwith, impetuously casting myself into an unknown future laden with risk?

In the end, good-natured master Panyotis and his vagabond crew, frustrated with my reluctance, took matters into their own hands. Hardy souls themselves, they were driven by the swashbuckling spirit of adventure.

"Now be off with you, my lad," the master had growled, in his aloof, good-natured way, his final words of parting still ringing in my ears, "trot out your stuff, as well as you can, and be done with it!"

"Master Panyotis....trot out your stuff as well as you can"

Hermarchus was busily purchasing fresh fish at the south harbor — months previously — when he had overheard the ghastly story. Another lost vessel and crew, victims of piracy in the Hellespont. Hermarchus had expressed requisite sadness, made a shrug to indicate the fatalism of existence, and gone on his way. He had no reason to connect these events with myself.

The name of the vessel and other finer details, including its original berthing at Mytilene, were lost in the gruesome telling of the main events.

It so happened that one of the missing freemen aboard the Hector was a friend of Tolmaeus, a distant cousin of Hermarchus. Only today, a few hours ago, Tolmaeus and Hermarchus had met coincidentally at the agora.

Catching up on family news and latest happenings, Tolmaeus had casually mentioned the tragic loss of a friend aboard ship in the Hellespont, several months previously. Tolmaeus recalled his nostalgic last meeting with his friend — only made possible because the vessel had berthed unexpectedly at Mytilene on its outward passage to Lampsacus.

"A little cargo to offload in the morn, but mostly, there's this landlubber from Colophon," said Tolmaeus' seaman friend, "We's don't take no visitors as a normal thing, not set up for it,....but sure are mighty glad that we did so with this one. Some landlubber was he, that whipped out a sling to fight off pirates, cracking heads aplenty. Never saw such a thing — he can come with us anytime he so likes."

With gnawing disquiet, Hermarchus suspected that this unfortunate galley might be the very same one on which I had arrived, and made further enquiries. Tolmaeus remembered that the galley was named for one of Homer's epic characters.

"No, not Ajax, Achilles....neither,....nor Odysseus,....it was the Trojan hero-prince of Homer's 'Iliad',....Yes, Hector — that was it."

The galley had already fought off one pirate attack with great success, which was widely celebrated at the time. That was the clincher!

Always a caring friend, Hermarchus immediately rushed to follow up his fearful speculations with me. I had always been reticent with him on the sensitive subject of my arrival in Mytilene — the telling of it didn't cast me in a particularly good light. I had abandoned carefully prepared plans and wise advice, launching myself impulsively into an untried and dubious future. In glossing over the trivial details, I had failed to mention the name of the galley to Hermarchus!

Among friends, I am perched on a stone bench in a shady glade of gnarled old olive trees, ancient when Sappho was a girl. The public Palaestra, the rectangular area used for wrestling instruction and other athletic activities, lies nearby, partly enclosed by colonnades.

Unlike the Agora, the Palaestra and adjacent Gymnasium are strictly policed by a Gymnasiarch and his deputies who report directly to the Macedonian governor. The authority of the Gymnasiarch ensures a superficial tolerance among the various philosophy teachers who frequent the complex and its adjacent olive gardens.

I am talking with friends, followers, and interested listeners when Hermarchus approaches at a fast pace, his usual placid demeanour replaced by one of grave concern. Not a good sign. He is sweating profusely and breathing deeply from his exertion. He asks to speak with me privately on an urgent matter. Now, I am definitely alarmed. Between panting breaths, he shoots me a question in such pressured-speech, that I fail to understand.

Finally, I get it.

"Yes, it was the Hector that transported me to Lesbos. Why do you ask? What's happened?"

This is the torturous, convoluted means by which I finally receive — only by a string of coincidences — the sad news of the loss of the Hector, master Panyotis and his crew, many months after the event. I was indeed, an Outsider with no inkling of any happenings in that distant everyday world that lay beyond the safe retreat of my shady olive grove. What I am told is all that Hermarchus knows: an abbreviated, much-repeated, thus exaggerated, version of the events as they unfolded. Painful in its colorful detail, the pertinent facts are undoubtedly correct, too horrid not to be true.

Moreover, it seems that the pirate vessel was the Artemis, commandeered by my half-forgotten nemesis, none other than 'The Red Devil' himself. Once again, Red intrudes into my life.

Contrary to the truism, misfortune has indeed travelled by a slow wagon to eventually run me over. So much time has passed since the tragedy, adding further to my overwhelming sense of guilt. I have been going about my life unperturbed, lounging about under the shade of the olive-trees, free and independent, satiated with fresh fruit and nuts, building a foundation for my future — while my friends have suffered, having either no future, or a bleak one at best.

As the lone 'survivor' of the ill-fated Hector, emotional loss and despair overcomes me — my mind is flooded with all the fond memories of the crew and Master Panyotis, all lost!

Damn the risk. I'm going to the Scythians, despite the unproven rumors that have our Macedonian overlords in secret collaboration with 'Red'. Should 'One-Ear' be apprehended and questioned, mercilessly I hope, then the trail may lead them to 'Red'. It's the least I can do, to gain justice for my crew-mates.

If only I had done this at the time of my alleyway assault, seemingly a lifetime ago, then the Hector and her crew may have been saved! I must make every effort now to put an end to Red's regime of terror. To do otherwise, will leave me skulking around, dewy-eyed and downcast — running away from my own shadow for the rest of my pitiful life!

Sometimes, philosophy is that simple.

Chapter 26

I take heart from the courage of Master Panyotis — who at a vital moment, challenged my self-doubt, that I must firstly, trust my own intuition — since "there be no mistakes, my lad, only chances at learning". If Red is pure evil, then the Master shows me all that is best in humankind.

Would I have sacrificed myself, following his example? My passage was fully booked to Lampsacus, in which case I would have certainly confronted the pirates at the Hellespont. The Master's fate still takes me back there — asking the same question over and over, in moments of private reflection.

"Why was I spared ? To what end?"

I find myself thinking about the master's last moments before his callous execution. What were his thoughts and feelings, knowing the horror that surely awaited him? How does one even breathe, when in the next second, he will breathe no more? The future ceases to exist — compressed into the immediacy of that last, precious second of life.

By what guiding light did I decide, in a twilight state of semi-consciousness, lazing on that sun-drenched deck, to depart the Hector at Mytilene? Timing is everything! Did my battle against the pirates bring out the half-forgotten warrior in me, to strike out on my own?

Hermarchus shrugs, offhandedly. "It's divine intervention," he adds, "the gods must have something else in store for you. It wasn't meant to be."

I am surprised, somewhat ruffled, at his superstitious explanation. I can't believe in an inevitable destiny that somehow is mapped out for me by Providence — a love of fate which we must not only accept as pre-determined, but also embrace — as the only measure of control left to us. I choose to believe in the destiny I carve out for myself — by the act of my own free will, moment by moment.

While not discounting the gods entirely, I don't believe in their agency to direct human affairs. They might perchance do it covertly….under cover of my own free will. If so, then this is a slippery argument — a cheap way to avoid taking a position.

Yet,….I'm compelled to take a position, as it defines who I am. If I don't have agency over my own actions, then I cease to be a free-acting individual, responsible for my own behavior — I remain merely a pawn of providence. This is where I part ways with superstition,….to follow instead, the self-determination of Master Panyotis, scuttling his own ship. He may have lost his head, only to be honored by all, ever afterwards.

I come back again as I must, to my relentless questions, 'Why me? For what?'.

I was lost in a mire of superstition, shameful guilt, betrayal, and onerous self-doubt. I beat myself up with these self-righteous questions — until now, right now, I have reached a certain precipitous point. I turn around in my mind and examine these questions clearly and squarely, as if I am seeing them for the first time in the light of day.

Up to this time, I have never doubted the basis of these questions, their right to haunt me. My epiphany breaks through in a startling flash! The Hector has sunk,….regrettably; it's in the past, so asking retroactively how things could have been different is a futile exercise. Worse still, it's a waste of energy in present time, which is needed for living now. Master Panyotis is right: my "chance at learning" had come.

These very same questions, repeated again and again in different forms, were surely tedious for poor Hermarchus, who had to listen patiently to my endless ramblings. Yet they were also necessary for me to get to this place in my mind. The questions generate a mindset in search of an answer; yet they themselves — in their act of asking — lie at the heart of the problem. Master Panyotis had little time to overthink matters as I am presently doing. As an honorable ship's master, he simply took the necessary actions which he intuitively needed to do.

With the help of Master Panyotis, I had disembarked from the Hector at Mytilene....because I intuitively needed to be the free agent of my own active choices. However well-intentioned he may be, Valerious must realize that it is my life to live, not his. Whether my choice was right or wrong, predetermined or spontaneous, plays no part. Reaching my present position — the emotional acceptance that these past actions were indeed honorable and authentic — has been a heart-wrenching process for me.

Clouded with grief, I felt compelled to second-guess my own past actions. What if I had remained onboard? What if I had immediately told the authorities about 'One-Ear' and his connection to 'Red', instead of cowering away in fear? What if….and so on, and so on, alpha to omega. I created a set of wordy questions, a smoke-screen, to deceive myself — nay, punishing myself to atone for my self-inflicted guilt. I denied the simple but painful fact that I couldn't trust my own intuition and be done with it,....instead of adding a baggage of guilt. Master Panyotis would surely scold me for such useless self-deception.

I had woven an unsolvable Gordian knot for myself, round and round in circular reasoning, when the only answer — following the Great Alexander — was to cut straight through it! This is where Alexander parted ways with Aristotle, his old tutor — appointed by his father, of course, King Philip II of Macedon.

This shift in perspective, from searching for answers to scrutiny of the questions themselves, is illuminating — my 'Swerve analysis' in action. Floundering about with vague concepts like 'Destiny' and 'Providence' create mental blocks that get me nowhere. I direct my thoughts instead, at my own subjectivity: I begin to question the presumptions hidden away in my own questions — all those embedded ideas that I have taken for granted.

Yes, I agree wholeheartedly with the 'examined life' recommended by Socrates. There comes a point however, at which life needs to be fully lived, spontaneously and intuitively — rather than made subject to constant auditing. If everyday life is reduced to a mere object of enquiry, to be cut up and examined retroactively — then it can't at the same time, be lived fully as a flowing, lived experience. Neither is right or wrong: Life is a matter of balance between the two activities,....and I have lost my balance.

All my soul-searching over the loss of the Hector has paralysed my ability to live fully in present time — I am using my thinking to run away into my head, to create a meaningless puzzle out of an unfortunate grief. On the positive side, this inner conflict is a significant step forward in my awareness as a philosopher. I suspect that it's an occupational hazard in my line of work!

I only hope that Ulysses, the eccentric Pelican mascot of the Hector, made good on his escape!

Chapter 27

My guilt over Master Panyotis has been put back firmly on the shelf where it belongs — which leaves me with a hoard of down-to-earth questions in the wake of the Hector's loss.

With the assistance of Hermarchus, and his knowledge of local personalities, I am able to gradually tease out further details. The redoubtable 'Red', cunning as ever, released one of the crew in a pinnace to spread the tale of Master Panyotis' gruesome execution. The pirate chief hoped that such fear-mongering would act as a deterrent against any further scuttling of captured galleys. 'Red' may be sadistic, but he is also cunning!

From what I can gather, it seems that the lucky sailor met up with another merchant galley in the Hellespont: the Antigonus, also owned by Valerius, en route to Notium, port to the city-state of Colophon. The Antigonis was the same galley that berthed at Mytilene, several months ago — when the first shocking reports of master Panyotis' heroic death were circulated. The Antigonus then continued to Notium, passing on the tragic news as it went.

The only freed survivor of the Hector refused to remain on board the Antigonus, fearful that the galley would attract more pirates,…. and his own re-capture. With a replenishment of supplies, he hoisted sail in the opposite direction, hugging the Ionian coast for safety in his small pinnace.

Passing the ruins of ancient Troy, thence further into the Hellespont strait, he was last sighted entering the inland sea of the Propontis.

The master of the Antigonus reported that the survivor's only goal was to return to his native village and family somewhere near Colchis in the adjoining Euxine Sea. The sailor swore that he would then remain in his village to the end of his days — such was the terror of his last voyage onboard the Hector. He was done with the sea.

I must believe that the master of the Antigonus, upon his arrival in Notium, was ushered into the presence of Valerius — who would have questioned him closely about my wretched 'fate'. The good master could only answer what was passed on to him by the loan survivor: that Master Panyotis was executed, the Hector scuttled, and 'everyone else' sold into slavery.

I thought it very improbable that my last-minute departure from the Hector at Mytilene had been reported by the lone survivor. It was an irrelevant detail and not pertinent to the tale, overshadowed as it was, by the horrifying nature of the calamity. My fate was therefore unknown to the Antigonus' master — who by default, could only advise Valerius that regrettably, I had been enslaved with the rest of the crew.

I had avoided telling Valerius that I had jumped ship at Mytilene, rather than continuing to Lampsacus as originally planned. Acknowledging that I had taken matters into my own rebellious hands would probably have incurred his wrath — even retribution of some kind.

Instead, I decided to withhold any news of my whereabouts and activities until I had achieved success and status in Mytilene. I could then make a triumphant return to Colophon — my achievements would then be mine alone. My 'obvious success' would vindicate my decision to remain in Mytilene, leaving Valerius silent, with little to say. Like a naughty child, hoping not to be caught out, I believed that everything would fall into place, just as I wished it to be. I think it; therefore, it is! That matters may be otherwise, never entered my head! At least, that was my self-absorbed, rather smug fantasy.

Servilia was sure to be impressed!

Now, everything has changed!

Then comes the aftershock: I realize that the latency of the news — the delay in time it took for the loss of the Hector to finally reach me — has many repercussions for me personally. By this late stage, it is reasonable to assume that Valerius, no less than poor Servilia, could only conclude that I was a prize specimen in an Assyrian slave market. Otherwise, I had been cruelly sold as a human mule, at the mercy of the fearsome 'slave-breakers', fit for laboring until I dropped.

Many months have passed since the loss of the Hector, yet those people who love and care for me, such as Servilia, my father, even Valerius, are likely to be grieving over what they still believe to be my woebegone fate.

I could imagine the pitiful scenes — that I was languishing away in shackles in a fetid prison-cell. Worse still, a skeletal shadow trudging under a bloody whip in a foreign salt-mine? A dozen other morbid scenarios may be preying on their minds. I think of the unnecessary distress that I had unwittingly inflicted....then remember that at least, I am alive and free.

I compose an open letter immediately, to Valerius, Servilia, my father, and others — offering my fond greetings and profuse apologies. I am quick to advise them of my good health and public teaching in Mytilene, ending with the assurance, " that I will be returning to Colophon very soon, as my busy teaching permits, and look forward to that happy event."

Prophetic words indeed, as events close in upon me — while in my blindness, or ignorance, I innocently ponder the hair-splitting abstractions of philosophy!

Chapter 28

Our band of friends grows larger with each passing day: we hold our symposia in the convenient shade of the olive grove — men and women alike, with full freedom of discussion. The many interesting topics keep me fully absorbed, causing me to drop my guard, unmindful of what is happening about me. The rabid Aristotelians however, had not forgotten such a dangerous heretic — now that the 'scoundrel' has rudely taken up full-time residence right under their very noses, in their midst of their sovereign territory.

There are emerging signs that matters at the Palaestra and Gymnasium may be going awry — even I could hardly fail to notice two new arrivals, each standing in comical contrast with the other. While one is gaunt, congenitally balding, with a whiff of the cold-blooded ascetic about him, the other is corpulent and unkempt, shaggy locks down to his shoulders, almost bovine — most unforgettably, he carries a fetid odor wherever he goes!

'Not local' says Hermarchus, ever wary of outsiders, probably with good cause, considering Mytilene's history of invasions, and roughneck culture.

Both men cluster together, showing little willingness to mix. If they talk at all, it is only to whisper between themselves, though they listen intently to our rambling, sometimes heated conversations. If asked to contribute to the discussion, they protest — they are only beginners, whose ideas are too unformed for any useful exchange.

Their reluctance to mingle freely is at first, put down to shyness.

Without meaning to be disrespectful, it isn't long before their hairy contrast becomes too much for the friends. The pair henceforth are known to us, in reference to their hirsute status, deficient or surplus, as 'Baldie' and 'Shaggy'.

"Corpulent with unkempt, shaggy locks, almost bovine"

If covert Aristotelians, they are woefully obvious as spies, skulking from one group to the next — sent to report on our 'subversive' activities. Despite these misgivings, our ethical code always remains one of inclusion and welcome.

Meantime, our discussions have drifted to cosmology and the nature of Nature, especially the physical composition of all matter. The speculations of Leucippus and his famous student, Democritus, are introduced. I recall the lively symposium, sometimes fierce, always convivial, spanning several days.

The established truth means little to us — a place where fact and fiction blur, only to serve the cause of conformity — hindering the story of human progress. Starting with Democritus, we begin with the fresh idea that all matter consists of infinitely small, solid particles that are indivisible: therefore in Greek, 'a - tomic', or atoms — moving on preset paths within a void.

"Indestructible and invisible, these atoms comprise the 'building blocks' of all creation. Atoms can also spontaneously 'swerve' away from their set paths, becoming intertwined and clumping together. By this process they build up into visible objects of different kinds, such as rocks, seas, mountains, plants, animals,....and ourselves."

"That different objects vary in their appearance, with a wide range of tastes, smells, textures, and colors, depend upon how the atoms come together, so that each of us sitting here is different from the other. In fact, these smallest particles fill the whole universe with other worlds beyond number."

There are of course, the normal flurry of excited questions, pert answers, and wholesome haranguing, befitting a group of strong-minded individuals.

Abruptly, the babble of conversation ceases.

A long silence follows, of such eerie quietness as one may find upon entering a prehistoric cave. One of the 'observers', as we now refer to them, actually stands up to speak. It is 'Baldie', who for the first time, poses a question:

"You say these atoms of yours congregate to form other worlds floating in a void of black nothingness. Yet how can this be so when Aristotle comes to an opposite conclusion: that a void is physically impossible? The universe must consist of matter, even if we can't see it — just as we can't see your imaginary little atoms!"

A most unusual question from a self-proclaimed beginner, as my fears of Aristotelian mischief come true. Awkward laughter ripples nervously across the group: Baldie's response is treated as an innocent quip — a light-hearted attempt at humor. They politely give him the benefit of the doubt.

I have not failed to notice however, that Baldie walks back and forth as he talks. This is not exceptional in itself of course, though it remains a distinctive characteristic of the justly named 'Peripatetic' school, that of Aristotle. The great man walked while he taught, believing that it facilitated thinking, and his followers adopted the same practice, maintained after his death, as a signature ritual.

I keep my growing fears to myself, and Baldie resumes, regardless of the tittering.

"Such matter displaces and supports the moon and the sun as well as our own planets. This is merely a common sense logical deduction, as Aristotle makes absolutely clear. You have no evidence that your invisible atoms exist, much less, the multitude of unknown worlds that you describe. We can be certain however, about the visible planets that circle around us, and that's all there is to know. The rest is nothing but overripe imagination."

This is definitely a tear in the delicate fabric of politeness — no longer humorous! One of the friends, I couldn't see who it was, then fires back testily,

"If so, then what is it that makes up Aristotle's celestial matter which as you declare, supports the sun and moon? Of what ethereal stuff is it comprised? If this presumption is taken to be true, without any evidence, then following your logic, surely the idea of atoms and void must then be equally true,....or else, equally false? Unless of course, the Aristotelian 'matter' has already been drained away by nymphs, leaving only the Epicurean Void, then all our questions, yours and mine, are fully satisfied!"

The group erupts in hilarious laughter, not disparagingly, but as one would do with a well-told joke. Humor is part of our community spirit and helps to dampen hurt feelings.

'Baldie' gives no response other than returning to his seat, tight-lipped and sour-faced.

Alarm bells are ringing in my head.

Chapter 29

I notice that Hermarchus also, remains stern-faced — unlike his colleagues, he is not amused by the sarcasm directed at 'Baldie'.

Over the passing months, I have come to recognize a kindred spirit in Hermarchus, loyal but also practical in ways that I am not. I see him rolling his eyes, while at the same time, I fear for his long-standing distrust of people — on the other hand, I trust people too quickly. Maybe that's why we get along so well: we cancel out each other's faults.

I look to him in difficult situations, much like the oracle of Apollo at Delphi, for help in my decision-making. Judging by his worried appearance at present, we are headed into troubled waters.

Regardless of the growing tension, our group discussion has its own momentum and moves forward — as our ideas evolve over time, it is important to catch and record the general agreement on important matters. Such record-taking, sporadic at first, has happily evolved into a regular activity at these symposia: we have our own self-appointed scribe, ready with her scrolls, reed pen, and lamp-black ink. Since we all contribute in different ways, it is our rule that no particular individual be mentioned in the summary:

"All these many worlds are associated with stars, which are other suns just like our own sun, with planets circling around them. Contrary to the naked eye, and the doctrinaire teachings of Aristotle, this includes the startling but inescapable conclusion that our own world also, circles around the sun. The sun doesn't rise in the east,

to give us a morning, but rather, the morning dawns because our own world is 'rising' as it rotates on itself."

At this point, in keeping with his thuggish bearing, 'Shaggy' raises objections, inserting himself loudly in the discussion — almost a bellow, shaking his copious mop of odiferous hair from side-to-side as he speaks. The effect is immediate and priceless! The companions scatter away from him in all directions, holding their noses. Enjoying the effect, 'Shaggy' takes his standing position as speaker with mock drama and ceremony,

"Your outpourings are nothing but heresy. Aristotle tells us that our earth is the primal hub around which the universe revolves just as it was created by the Prime Mover, the gods themselves collectively, which you are choosing to defile."

It becomes immediately apparent that, unlike his reserved accomplice, Shaggy's style is one of hard-nosed in-your-face aggression.

"You need no more proof than your own common sense to look up and see that the earth is the still center of the turning wheel, the original spark of creation...."

Meanwhile, Shaggy's pompous mannerisms have enlivened the crowd. Taken with the comical side of it, they are bent on having a jolly time after all the serious discussions. The howls and cracklings reach such a pitch that Shaggy's solemn arguments only add to the rising crescendo. Undaunted, he bravely carries on for several more minutes, finally petering out before throwing up his hands in disdain.

It is unclear whether 'Shaggy', if not interrupted, would have introduced additional reasoning to create a more compelling case. I was genuinely interested to hear what followed. He had commenced his response with what was obvious to the naked eye — the concrete 'facts' that are readily apparent in Nature. In this case, the 'apparent' movement of the sun, moon, and stars around the earth.

I expected that, following the sophists, he intended to build upon this 'factual' base, ending up with a monumental — and apparently reasonable argument — constructed layer upon layer, to overwhelm an unwary audience.

His fundamental assumption, based upon an appeal to 'common sense' — the information provided by our own senses — would then remain unchallenged, hopelessly lost in the elegance of a grand exercise. If this was to be the plan, his long-winded statements, loaded with prejudice and spite, only served to undermine his well-reasoned sophistry — as well as providing much-needed entertainment for our lagging group!

On the other hand, I remain perplexed about Shaggy's 'apparent' self-defeating behavior. Why would anyone who is obviously skilled in the art of sophistry (unlike 'Baldie'), allow his emotions to undo that very same training, thereby negating his powers of persuasion? I don't understand this, which only feeds my increasing sense of unrest. It's almost as if he was acting out something that was rehearsed beforehand, designed to raise the hackles of his audience.

Unfortunately, the raucous laughter and jeering from my throng of friends, inconsistent with our philosophy of tolerance, brings an early end to the morning's presentation. While this uproar is unseemly, it is no more so than the inflammatory accusations levied by the Aristotelian.

Rumor has it, whispers Hermarchus, that Shaggy cultivates his wild, knotted hair and lack of personal hygiene for defensive purposes — matching his aggressive personality and misshapen body. Distracted and repulsed, newcomers reel backwards beyond the reach of his invisible, but no less potent, emissions. Without ever having to ask for personal space, it is freely conceded to him, only too readily. I feel saddened by Shaggy's plight, that — despite the warring circumstances — we have mistreated him when we had an opportunity to do otherwise. Not the behavior expected of enlightened philosophers.

In a showy act of defiance, our two unrepentant 'observers' excuse themselves abruptly — yet with exquisite politeness — an obvious parody of the treatment they had received….or provoked. As they leave, I note that their manner doesn't appear to be one of failure or even dissatisfaction with their effort; strangely enough, I would describe it as smug, even gleeful!

For the first time, the prospect of a different explanation crosses my mind. Had they planned for a reactive disturbance from their audience and carefully engineered it, as an entrapment? If so, their strenuous accusations of heresy are a mere subterfuge — intended to create noisy agitation and dispute, that would not pass unnoticed. Such a noisy rupture would attract attention and disciplinary action from the Gymnasiarch and his deputies! Only too well, do I recall Hermarchus' warnings. Too late: I fear the trap is sprung!

Hermarchus, usually tight-lipped, addresses the group in such grave terms that instantly command everyone's attention:

"I fear that the early departure of our two observers is an ominous sign, foreboding of things to come. If such is proven to be the case, may the gods forbid it, then let all of us attend my private residence in small groups, so that our community may carry on the fine work we have commenced, under the tutelage of good friend, Epicurus."

The friends are dismayed, somewhat distressed, so that I feel compelled to remind them of the ethical and moral philosophy that we share and espouse to others.

I stand up before them and speak from my heart:

"I beg you all to follow the advice of friend Hermarchus, which I wholeheartedly endorse. We should disband for today, but we will meet again and continue our discussion at a time to be determined."

"Before we do so, I wish to bring our discussion of the last several days to a close with a few summary remarks. Just like dust motes caught in a bright shaft of light, swirling and intersecting, atoms may swerve way from their pre-determined path at an invisible level."

"At the visible level, individuals can also swerve away from the pre-determined paths of their instinctual thinking or habitual reactions, by choosing one life direction, idea, or partner, over another. The outcome of this unexpected change in direction, we refer to as 'free will'."

"May you continue to follow your own Swerve in all those choices which guide your life."

"Until our next meeting."

The benign shelter of our olive grove, a 'palisade' of goodwill, is breached. The omens of an ill wind have found our gentle and peaceful retreat, the consequences of which can only be a matter of time.

I didn't have long to wait.

Chapter 30

Be straightforward," says reliable Hermarchus, "come to the point — don't trifle with him."

I have always taken the goodwill and neutrality of the Gymnasiarch for granted. I had been warned however, that apart from his prestigious position, he is a personage whose authoritative bearing commands immediate respect.

I feel like an errant schoolboy, sulking and despondent — caught out in the act of wrongdoing — now reporting to the master's office for punishment. Walking along the Gymnasium colonnade, I admire its famous hunting frieze spanning the length of the inner architrave, and at the far end — the patina-bronze door of the tablinum of the Gymnasiarch of Mytilene.

This is the moment I have been anticipating since the hostile departure of the 'observers' — so much that I have dreaded waking up for the last several mornings. I knew it was coming. Hermarchus had expected it and tried to warn me against allowing them into our group. I had insisted that our community of friends was open to everyone; once we start making exceptions, we not only lose our diversity, but also introduce a policy that easily lends itself to misuse.

That was the past, and now the moment of reckoning has arrived.

Strangely enough, pacing along the colonnade, chatting with friend Metrodorus, I experience an unexpected kind of release

— that matters will just unfold as they may. My reprimand will soon to be over, certainly embarrassing, but perhaps also an education of sorts. I had been naïve to think that philosophy was above politics. I assumed without questioning, that an implicit code of respect and tolerance existed between philosophers — only to find regrettably, that all the foibles of base humanity have no exceptions.

In a sense, I remain oddly flattered that the Aristotelians continue to see me as a dangerous competitor capable of attracting followers away from them.

If they believe in the eternal truths which they expound so earnestly, then I wonder why they feel so vulnerable? Truths should speak for themselves, shorn of personalities, be they an Aristotle.... or even a poor Epicurus!

I lift and release the heavy ring attached to the door plate, the dull metallic resonance announcing my arrival. Metrodorus shakes me amiably by the shoulders, an act of togetherness, and departs silently as the bronze door creaks open with a shudder.

I am ushered along the mural-lined walls and picturesque mosaic floors, into the presence of the Great One, in obedience to his summoning.

The Gymniasarch is preoccupied in his reading, sitting to one side of a magnificent obsidian table, covered in rolled scrolls. An oil-lamp burns to one side; otherwise the

"The bronze door creaks open"

191

spaciousness of the great room is lost in semi-darkness. I continue standing in the shadows — a disciplinary action I presume, though it gives me time to take his measure.

He remains self-absorbed, inscrutable, seated on his carved klismos chair, dramatic with its curved back rest and outstretched, gilded legs, almost a throne. Patience has never been one of my virtues, as the Gymniasarch fusses with his scrolls. I dare not make a sound: to do so, would be a show of puny weakness, unbecoming of an Athenian hoplite. I will deny him that satisfaction.

Still standing, no shuffling, unflinching — with legs growing more leaden every minute! I distract myself by the deceptively simple exercise of converting my sensory observations into silently worded sentences, arrayed visually in my mind. There is for example, a distinctly musty smell emanating from the scrolls, some of them tattered and weathered, appearing to be quite ancient.

The Gymnasiarch however, is a ruggedly handsome man, with a intelligent, sculpted face, whose every gesture signals strength and firm resolve. No dithering here. He wears the sartorial garb of a Tyrian purple tunic, with a sash of Pompeian red, over a muscular, tanned body. It's the 'unexpected' though, which captures my attention: a meticulously-trimmed pearly-white full beard — a contradiction in appearances that befuddles any estimation of his age.

My overall impression is that of a refined, dignified bearing, even imperious, befitting a man of his lofty status. A sheathed dagger with garnet-encrusted hilt is fastened loosely under his belt. The symbolism is striking, probably intentionally so: an intriguing combination of cultured governance along with an ominously sharp warning!

Finally, his eminence turns towards me and nods a bland,

wordless acknowledgment. It looks like I may exist after all, though no doubt, contemptible to his aristocratic eyes!

He even speaks, a great concession to a poor lowly scholar from Colophon.

"It seems you have offended many people, not least the gods, with your impious speeches, such people who have come to me, willing to bear witness against you, and for you to provide me with good reason without further wasting my time, why you should not be imprisoned immediately, awaiting lawful trial, as it is incumbent upon me to do so."

The Gymnasiarch continues at length, legalese rolling off his tongue in grave monotone, outlining the weighty charges levied against me. It seems that the two Aristotelians have done their work well with much added embroidery, over-stitching, and color-ful patchwork — weaving an imposing artifice of impiety, heresy, inciting a public disturbance, sedition, as well as 'the corruption of young minds'. I must have been a very busy fellow!

This fanciful construction was capped with the insinuation — so outrageous as to leave me gasping, breathless — that I was in league with the pirates! The Aristotelian overlords had gone all the way, creating this 'cartoon' of a sly and devious mind. I am also an informant, it seems, disembarking at Mytilene to use my teaching as a ruse — avoiding any semblance of a connection with the capture of the Hector.

In addition to the other outstanding offenses, I am therefore charged with complicity in the murder of good Master Panyotis! This accusation is the clanger, designed to unseat me — the rest was just preamble, small movements to build up the pressure of appre-hension, propelling me to this fearful endpoint. Unbelievable! The law of unintended consequences was never more plainly written.

I experience an odd mixture of laughter and anger simultaneously, as if there is an inner conflict with each one struggling to gain outward expression. Circumstances demand that I suppress both, the effort of which produces a choked sigh.

I sniff at the faint odour of Oxycrat, a refreshing blend of honey, water, and grape vinegar, while the Gymniasarch sips from his ornamental eye-cup. This does nothing for my parched throat. He looks up, bemused at my discomfort — and continues with his litany of my evil wrong-doings.

Furthermore, if 'more' was needed, it seems that my meditative strolls along the harbor each evening, unbeknown to myself, have been transformed into heinous acts of spying — a convenient cover, used to evaluate vessels arriving and departing, as future pirate prizes. Viewed through this prism of legal paranoia, my every action has become tainted. Job, well done, 'Baldie' and 'Shaggy'!

The Gymnasiarch concludes his weighty recital of charges.

"The list of witnesses against you is a long one, and the body of evidence, while circumstantial in regard to some lesser matters, is nevertheless substantive when aggregated, and demonstrates a reasonable likelihood of criminal behavior. This is an initial indictment, and you have the right of response, which shall be duly noted. Since there is a high risk of absconding, and these are very serious charges, you will be imprisoned awaiting a public hearing."

His voice is noble and cultured, a deep baritone, as he pauses expressionless, the bureaucratic face of high officialdom, awaiting my reply. Though I hear his solemn words, their effect on me is a different thing altogether — wispy and feathery, far away. It all feels unreal, as if this is happening to someone else — as if I am watching it, impartially, from outside my own body.

Is it really I, Epicurus of Colophon, son of Neocles, hoplite of Athens, who has been thrust into this bizarre predicament? I was expecting to be verbally chastised — targeted by an Aristotelian conspiracy with powerful political connections. Instead of a stern warning however, I am summarily charged with an exhaustive list of grievous crimes — not the least of which is that of an accomplice to murder, carrying a penalty of death.

Who would have believed that my 'fellow philosophers' would condemn one of their own, whose only crime was that of public speaking? The indictments are so overwhelming, it feels as if a great weight is pressing down upon me. I even begin to doubt my own self. Crazy thoughts cross my mind. Would it be easier just to give up, and plead for mercy? Confused and distraught I may be, but I must....must....must regain my composure and commence my rebuttal, or....suffer the unthinkable consequences. I never imagined today that I would be fighting for my life.

"As a philosopher, I will speak only to the charge of impiety which is the principal reason that I have been brought before you. As such, I invoke the freedom of thought and speech, without which, philosophy is reduced to nothing but mindless dogma."

"As for the other charges, I will say little in my defence. To do so lends them a credibility which they are sorely lacking. Apart from the so-called 'witnesses', all Aristotelians or their proxies, such charges are baseless and fabricated to the point of being ludicrous."

My voice has been quavering so far, with a mix of feelings, fear and anger mostly, and seems to be echoing in my ears, as if I am a silent spectator to my own responses.

Yet my dander is surely rising as my true voice begins to emerge, and along with it, a growing defiance come what may, in the face of such outrageous injustice.

"I will now state the platform of my philosophy and leave it to you to judge its impiety or not, as the dice fall, for I am truly a philosopher in the spirit of the great Socrates, and must call out the truth as I see it."

"Let me say first that I believe in paradoxes, as against the false dualities implicit in the works of Aristotle. Such dualistic reasoning makes his subjects, whether societies or the physical world, appear to be more 'black and white' than their true natures, which are 'shaded in grey' and loaded with contradictions."

The GYMNASIARCH of Mytilene

The Gymnasiarch gives me a patronizing scowl,....then offers an indulgence for which I am totally unprepared, though it is most surely welcomed — he waves for me to be seated in the one remaining klismos chair. Most irregular, to be seated in his esteemed presence. After all that I have been through, I'm perplexed. Anything is possible. Is this some trickery to let down my guard, as a prelude to flogging? Fiend, or Friend?

He nods for me to continue.

"In regard to the gods, then think of them as arising from Eros, the primordial god, who came before all the others, and abides within us, through us, making love possible, and by the union of the sexes, the ongoing procreator of life. I see no conflict between my teachings and the gods, through the medium of Eros."

Chapter 31

The Gymnasiarch sits facing me, listening closely to my words, pondering over each statement. A pin-drop silence follows — he seems to be struggling with what he would say next. He leans in, scowling under his beetled brows, speaking now in hushed tones, choosing his words carefully — even kindly:

"Valerius sends his regards, and asks that you return to Colophon immediately. He is an old friend, from my early merchant trading days."

Epicurus: "But I'm facing several charges, including murder."

Gymnasiarch: "The Aristotelians are in the service of our Macedonian overlords, which makes them a problem for me also. Their spies are everywhere, watching you at every moment, even as you entered my chambers today. In my position, the separation between justice and politics becomes a very grey area."

"I know that the charges against you are unfounded — apart from a few minor breaches — but when political forces come into Aristotelians would stoop, as well as the wide-ranging reach of their power. The Gymnasiarch assures me, much to my relief, that their power is confined to Mytilene, having to do with personalities and politics, which is not the case in Athens.

My newfound guardian describes the details of my 'escape': I am to remain safe within the gymnasium chambers until late evening. My watchers will assume that I am manacled in a prison cell, and will likely relax their vigilance and depart. The Gymnasiarch will generously supply them with ample wine to speed the process along. After changing into slave clothing, I will slip out a rear door under cover of darkness along with two other servants in similar dress, and head for the north harbor. There, I am to board Valerius' galley Antigonus and remain below decks, waiting upon the early morning flood tide — thence set sail for Notium....and Servilia!

"If you are detected," says my host, sharply, "I will say that you escaped. Then there is nothing further that I can do for you."

Following my escape from Mytilene, the Gymnasiarch will provide a short explanation that I had reacted badly to the duress of a 'long searching interview'. Dying unexpectedly from latent medical issues of the heart, I am to be cremated without ceremony befitting such an impious criminal. The Gymnasiarch is adamant that I must have no contact with any of my Mytilene followers whatsoever — even trustworthy Hermarchus. I may advise him confidentially only after I have arrived safely in Colophon.

Though he received my last message — that I was alive and well in Mytilene — Valerius remained concerned for my safety. Knowing that the city is a 'frontier' trading cross-roads with a tumultuous history, he wisely suspected that matters may be fomenting against an upstart intruder such as myself. The Gymniasarch confirmed Valerius' fears and offered his cooperation for my return, fabricating the showpiece of my trial as a convenient cover for himself.

At the same time, he used the trial to show that my accusers would go to any lengths to silence me. Judicial murder means nothing to them! I had no idea, contentedly teaching away in my little cocoon, blissfully ignorant among the olive groves, expecting no more than a mere rap on the knuckles.

"I won't always have a worldly Valerius," I think to myself ruefully, still grappling with the shock that I was the target of such infamy, "nor a cultivated Gymnasiarch to snatch me out of trouble.

I need another plan."

I thank my erstwhile host, and signal my agreement. While it is not my style to sneak out the back-door, I'm willing, even anxious, to make an exception on this occasion. I feel for poor Hermarchus, a collateral victim of the deceit, who will mourn 'my passing'. I hope that he will forgive me when we are reunited.

But the Gymnasiarch is not through with me yet.

"There still remains another pressing matter, and this time you can assist me."

"Yes, of course", I quickly reply, mystified that the honorable Gymnasiarch of Mytilene would ever request the assistance of a fresh-faced, wandering philosopher.

"It's a straightforward matter that can help the grateful Mytilene community which in turn, will make my premature release of you all the more palatable in some quarters, if needed."

Taking my silence as agreement, the Gymnasiarch continues in his commanding manner.

"At some risk to yourself, you performed a great civil service and came forward to the authorities, implicating a certain resident, Agesilaus, a common nuisance at the agora — who you may know by the distinction that he has only one intact ear. Acting upon your information, he was apprehended but not without putting up a struggle. Unwilling to divulge any information at first, it took only a whiff of torture before he was snivelling for his life."

"We needed to ascertain the movements of an infamous pirate, known locally as 'The Red Devil' — who I believe, is familiar to you. He kept a nondescript hovel in one of the squalid dockside regions, which he used from time to time as a city base. This enabled him to spy on shipping arrivals and departures — scouting and selecting only the richest prizes for his piracy." I notice interestingly, that the Gymnasiarch refers to 'Red' in the past tense.

Eyes trained on me, he continues.

"The alleged piratical individual was eventually confronted as he left the said residence whereupon he immediately took to the sword, though he was surrounded. A savage fight then ensued, in which several of our brave men went down, though not without wounding said individual."

"Though I instructed that he should be taken alive, such was the ferocity of his defence, with no quarter given, that there was little option but to run him through, rather than risk further lives."

The Gymnasiarch speaks in elongated, weighty sentences bursting with legalese phrasing which passes for cultivated speech in such provincial centres. If it wasn't for the inherent nobility of the man, I would find him pretentious.

"The unfortunate event of his death created a further problem: no citizen of this community has encountered 'The Red Devil' and lived to tell about it. We can't be sure that we have our man beyond a reasonable doubt: it could for example, be one of his murderous underlings. His immediate resort to the sword, and the skill in its deadly use, argues for a positive match. On the other hand, he was not wearing the signature red tunic that you described in your original statement to the city officials. Of course, we know him to be exceedingly cunning so that he may have relinquished the tunic after it enabled your ready identification of him."

"But 'One-Ear',....I mean Agesilaus, could surely identify him for you?"

"That brawler for hire resides in a dungeon under our feet, and will do so for a very long while. He has no credibility however, and will say anything to have his shackles removed. He did identify the body, but I need to have that confirmed, if only for my own peace of mind. You might be able to provide me with some identifying bodily features, apart from his obvious reddish hair. We can then confirm your identification by examining the body — presently soaking in a vat of vinegar for preserving purposes."

"Yes,....I may just be able to do that for you," I say, remembering back to my vivid confrontation with Red, eyes-locked, imprinted in my memory, when the Hector was inbound to Mytilene.

"He has a tattooed face, with pitch-black eyes, but most significantly, my sling-shot grazed his right cheek, leaving a noticeable scar: I saw the scar again when he ambushed me here in Mytilene. I had my chance with the slinger and I came so close to getting him, which would have saved so many lives, including Master Panyotis. It's a great pity."

The Gymnasiarch becomes suddenly animated, jumping from his chair impulsively, so much out of character for him. I recoil, alarmed that once again, I have said something that offends him.

"Then we have the scoundrel, at last!"

The Gymnasiarch shouts in jubilation, thrillingly, forgetting himself. Recovering his officialdom, he turns to me, beaming with a fond, avuncular smile.

"You have put the matter to rest, m'boy, much to the relief of all shipping plying the Ionian trade routes. You have performed...." He pauses, stumbling for words, surprised at his own difficulty, normally so facile. "Yes,....Yes, indeed,....it's a meritorious service! We still have to smuggle you out at this stage,....but now we have some insurance should the stuck-up Aristotelians kick up a stink. Good work, slinger!" His words tumble out at a fast pace, flowing, even garrulous — at least for the moment, until he regains his stiff, official composure.

And so it is over — Master Panyotis is avenged if that is any solace, and the scourge of piracy is lifted for a time. I feel gratified, yet deflated by the whole hellish experience. I remain sad for all the lives that have been lost unnecessarily, dead or enslaved, but changed in some way forever, including in no small way, my own.

While the Gymnasiarch has once again returned to his reserved self, he has decided nonetheless, that such an occasion deserves libations as a celebration. It's not everyday that a rogue pirate chief is dispatched to Hades.

A slave arrives, bearing a tray of cheeses, exotic fruits, and sumptuous wine. I have time to spare before my closeted departure — a friendly exchange ensures , so different from my first guarded experience with him. I take the opportunity to ask him about my torrid time at the agora, still troubling for me.

"Let me give you some sage advice," the Gymnasiarch says, which if I'm not mistaken, comes with a tinge of affection, "Your teachings are certainly not orthodox, and will always be threatening for some people."

"The other schools, your 'competitors', will take advantage of that to shut you down. You may even forfeit your life, which is why you should pay attention to what you say, and where you say it."

"You surely realize by this stage that you can't teach in public places, like the Agora or Palaestra, either here or anywhere else. You need to learn from this experience — it's not so much what you do, but where you do it, and who is listening. You need to grow a hard, worldly carapace, if you are to survive!"

Epicurus: "You mean that I should give up teaching?" The Gymniasarch arches his eyebrows sharply in annoyance:

"The slightest movement causes an agony"

"No, that's not what I said: put simply, you take a great risk if you teach in public forums. You are likely to be summoned before officials like myself who will not be so forgiving. That's another reason why I gave you a foretaste of what could happen. It may have been a nasty shock, but that's what waits for you should you continue on your present course. You will be punished as a heretic and blasphemer....certain death."

"You could be hanged, roasted alive, impaled with a stake, beheaded, but here on Lesbos we have devised something very special — an execution so terrible that begins at the spot where the backbone ends. The slightest movement causes an agony that widens the wound, eventually cleaving the organs apart, so that death comes slowly by degrees, sometimes taking days."

As he intended, the Gymniasarch has my full attention — I shudder at the thought of such a cruel fate. He's made his point.

"You have nothing to fear however," he says, patting my shoulder reassuringly, "you may teach whatever you wish so long as you do so on private property. It might be your own house and garden, or that of a friend or patron like Valerius."

"That's the politics of philosophy!"

Chapter 32

After my long absence, I wake with the dawn, sluggish, once again in my childhood bed, safe within my father's farmhouse. Other than weariness, I feel no sentiment of 'homecoming' — the old dread lingers however, nightmarish memories that drove me to escape. I take a barefoot stroll — all is hushed and sparkling fresh — feeling the pebbles and briars under my toes. Alive! A new day calls me forth, possibilities abound, thoughts of Servilia going about her day, lifting my spirits.

Orchards of figs, apples, and pomegranates radiate out from the house, punctuated by scattered olive groves. Then comes my father's 'pride and joy': patiently tilled garden beds, with vegetables and herbs of all varieties, protected by a stout wicker stockade. Long-haired goats graze outside the enclosure, casting covetous eyes occasionally, at the grand feast laid out before them — yet forever beyond their reach. I feel for them.

My father's farmhouse (Colophon)

My father seems glad to see me, though reserved, in his usual flat, taciturn way, unreachable beyond his defences, stronger than wicker.

His emotional vocabulary does not extend beyond a superficial enquiry: "What about the weather during your voyage from Mytilene" — he recounts, yet once again, tediously, his own stormy passage from Samos to Colophon, fleeing from the Macedonian invasion. I nod my understanding. Mute. I have learnt not to expect anything more. A long time passed as a child before I realized that this was his own problem — not something wrong with me. This startling revelation came upon me suddenly one day, while I was distracted — tilling his fields for planting barley — though it was also disturbing nevertheless: a wistful loss for what could have been. I accept him now, without asking anything more.

His chronic dark moods have abated, at least for the present, which is a welcome relief.

During my absence, Marius has assumed a caretaker role, becoming more a friend to my father, rather than a household servant. I'm relieved that my father has a companion now — his isolated, curmudgeonly temperament is always a household concern. Marius possesses that mysterious art of navigating my father's erratic mood swings without becoming a target.

Beside the house stands the 'Black Hill', unchanged and monumental, as if I had never left. My thoughts fly to Servilia — so many lively discussions atop that mound, sacred for both of us, high above the dreariness of our daily lives, our hillock of dreams. Laughing at my most self-serious philosophies, she poked and prodded for flaws and openings, a cherished melding of like-minds and young bodies — or else, huddled close together, cross-legged amid the blooming wildflowers, we shared our future plans between intimate whispers and furtive kisses.

I am surprised now, even hurt a little, that there was no message from Servilia or Valerius upon my arrival — surely they must know of my return! Is Valerius up to his old tricks: leaving me waiting in suspense? I let it go, without brooding on it: a wiser, happier man for doing that!

The narrow, winding goat path up the hill, eroded by countless hoofs over the ages, has become a natural watercourse for winter storms, further loosening the scree underfoot. My thoughts wander — as I sidestep between the masses of stones — to those blessed times when Servilia and I gathered poppy-flowers for the table. Nearby, lies a copse of gnarled old olive-trees, bent over, almost kneeling, as if in supplication to the prevailing north wind.

The dappled shade of the olive-grove hides a cairn of basalt rocks, assembled into the rough shape of a pyramid, a forlorn grave — the solitary burial site of my teenage companion. Here lies Melanchaetes, the black-coated dog who was my sole comfort during those lonely, dark years following my mother's disappearance on Samos. I was 16 years of age at the time.

I sit down on the bench, painstakingly built upon my first return to Colophon, after my military training. This same ancient olive grove with its ample shadow was also my private retreat, a getaway from the world — once again the weathered bench comes into service, now encrusted with lichen. I look back over my past life, taking stock, combining the old with the recent, gathering together the scattered shards, half-forgotten experiences and colorful characters, before I visit Valerius tomorrow. At the caldera!

At 18 years, I was called upon to complete my military service of two years in the Athenian ephebate. I deeply resented leaving my childhood home on Samos, though looking back, it was probably the toughening and strict discipline that I needed.

Brutal and soulless perhaps, but it pulled me out of the morass of grief in which I was firmly stuck. I had no time to think of my mother's fate. During my absence in Athens, my father (and Melanchaetes!), along with other Athenian settlers on Samos, were forcibly relocated to Colophon by Perdiccas, the Macedonian.

Melanchaetes, crippled and failing by this time, his scampering days long past, had patiently waited for my return. Reunited once again and assured that I was safe, he allowed himself to gradually drift away. I took him outside in my arms, rolled up snug in a blanket, clasping him close to me so that I could feel his laboured heartbeat. Lifting his head from the blanket, with his eyes still vibrant and alive, he took a last lingering look at the trees, sky, the hill of bright, red poppies,....then ever so gently, lowered his big, black head, finally lapsing into a peaceful sleep — his breathing becoming increasingly feint.

I stood frozen, timeless, our two hearts beating together, until there was only one. I was just 20 years of age — tears welling up and rolling down my young face.

Lovingly, tenderly, I carried him alone, up the hillside, stopping for breaks, whether for tears or fatigue. The loyal friend of my youth had gone, a marker in so many ways, of the shortness of life, yes, but even more, of the invisible bonds of love that all of us crave in our hearts, be it dogs or people.

With shovel, blanket, trinkets, and a ceremony of gratitude, I laid my faithful companion to rest on the summit, with a familiar view for eternity: swathes of tilled land in the foreground, turned umber-colored by recent ploughing.

Beyond the rustic village, fields of golden wheat-stalks, dried and ready to be scythed, stretch away to the horizon. Melanchaetes knew the pattern of the seasons, and often capered with the village dogs among the rustling stalks.

"I put my faithful companion to rest on the summit"

I gathered together a cairn of heavy rocks — the labor helped. No animals would disturb his last resting place.

A ritual, sorrowful parting. Trundling back down the loose shingle at sunset, tired and aching, I went straight to bed. In the space of four years, I had lost my beloved mother, my homeland of Samos, and my very best friend. Canine or not, Melanchaetes and I were a tight little family of two. My only real family for many years. As for my father, he retreated even further into his private prison of sadness, regret, and anger,....often beyond reach.

I try not to dwell on such thoughts now, while Servilia is never far from my mind. We often played together as children do, only to grow apart for reasons that are still unclear to me. There were fleeting glimpses of each other from time to time — occasionally we would encounter each other, awkwardly, swopping snatches of teenage gossip to fill the silence. Returning from Athens as a grown man, a hoplite warrior, I came upon her during my tutorial duties — a friend of my student.

Awkward no more, I was smitten by the grown woman she had become, as if Aphrodite herself had entered the room: graceful, quick-witted, exuding a mature self-confidence and poise I had never seen before or since. I could think of nothing else for days. Servilia became a frequent presence in my life, and surely in my heart — I couldn't get enough of her! And so it remains to this day.

In the meantime, we have both taken deep draughts from life's experiences, albeit in different ways. In my case, nothing clarifies one's priorities like the imminent prospect of death — I still get flashes of that dank Mytilene alleyway. Bathed in a sinister half-light, with that sadistic pirate proceeding in his workmanlike manner, gleefully considering the varieties of painful deaths he could inflict on me, the sun glittering on his blade, seconds from slitting my throat. Such terrifying episodes — I think of the Gymnasiarch's accusations of murder — with death hanging in the balance, have sharpened my sense of the fragility of life.

I need to grasp love with both hands while I can — gone are the days I took life for granted. With my newly whetted appetite for life, I know what I want. Following my escape from Mytilene, Servilia has become everything to me, grown ever more feisty and irresistible in my fervent recollection.

Tomorrow can't come soon enough!

Chapter 33

Hardened by my adversities — when once I called them 'adventures' — I have returned to the Villa of the 'Domos Solis Domina'. Somehow, it seems smaller.

Home of Valerius and Servilia, the villa is otherwise known locally as 'The Caldera', Nature's volcanic cauldron. It is also prophetic, in that I had escaped, just barely, from another varietal of cauldron, fraught with emotion and politics. I have come to think of it now in positive terms, as my professional 'rite of passage' that was always fated to happen — my 'coming of age' as a philosophy teacher.

Once again, I am ushered into the tablinum of the master, overflowing with all the blandishments of wealth and power. Valerius sees me — rushing forward and hugging me, breathless — expressing an uninhibited, contagious joy. My previous ambivalence towards him evaporates at once, replaced by my own jaunty response, surprising even myself. Servilia must be waiting for a private audience, biding herself for our own 'very special' reunion.

Valerius and I settle into our couches, half-reclining, both of us chattering away with good fellowship. Much has changed between us, mostly unspoken. We both realize that my very presence is due gratuitously, to a tenuous thread of good fortune. He asks many questions, about poor Master Panyotis, Hermarchus, the Gymniasarch, and so on, until my throat runs dry.

"Do you have any more of that fermented grape juice that you offload on unwary guests, to get rid of them?"

He apologizes, and upon his signal, electrum goblets appear, matched by his best imported Samian wine. Finally, oil-lamps are lit, with their flickering shadows dancing lifelike on the kaleidoscopic wall frescoes. As for Servilia, she and I both value our privacy in matters of personal intimacy.

I wait for Valerius to mention Servilia in the normal course of our conversation. I thought perhaps that she would make a grand entrance once the menfolk had progressed with their libations.

Much to my dismay, neither event has happened.

I'm growing increasingly uneasy. Since twilight is now upon us, expediency finally compels me to ask after Servilia. Valerius' mood at once becomes somber — his face drooping into a sad, languid pallor. For the first time today, the changes in his appearance catch my full atten-tion, though not even a year has passed since our last meeting.

I am appalled at his sagging jowls, watery eyes, and splenic complexion. His posture is noticeably stooped. He also has a pronounced limp, which causes him to grimace as he walks, with the aid of a cane.

"Valerius....his posture is noticeably stooped"

I realize with alarm, that he has been avoiding the matter of

213

Servilia's absence. He had probably been waiting for me to ask, while I was waiting for him to tell me. I lean forward, beads of sweat instantly forming on my brow, my heart seeming to beat out of my chest.

"I don't know how long I have to live, but nevertheless, I must tell you now about matters that have long being witheld from you," says Valerius, "since you are now a grown man of the world, and must take full account of them. I see you that you are concerned about Servilia's absence, so let me start there. First, she is alive and well,....so put your mind at rest. It's also a great relief to me that she is so loved by you." We are both close to tears, which also feeds the mutual bond between us. I don't know what to expect. Valerius begins his story, lowering his voice and adopting his matter-of-fact businesslike manner.

"Now that I have reassured you, I must start at the beginning. As you know, the Antigonus is one of my trading galleys. There was a single crewman of the Hector who escaped from the pirates using the ship's pinnace, and promptly returned to his home village, somewhere past the Hellespont. Before doing so however, he met up with the Antigonus, and described the cruel fate of the Hector and Master Panyotis."

"The crewman was clear that all on board the Hector were enslaved, and bound for the Assyrian markets. After discharging his cargo at Mytilene, the master of the Antigonus returned to Notium and promptly reported the loss to me. Servilia and I naturally assumed that you also were lost to us forever — given over to the infamous slave-breakers of Phoenicia, from whom no one returns alive."

"Many months passed before I finally received your message from Mytilene that you had disembarked earlier from the Hector — most wonderful news....you were alive and well. I immediately enlisted the help of my old friend, the Gymnasiarch, to monitor your activities as I knew only too well that life is cheap in Mytilene. This is why I had originally planned for you to begin your teaching at Lampsacus, a much safer place."

I think back to my misguided plans, hanging my head with a heavy sigh. Waves of emotion — shame, guilt, sorrow, remorse — course through me overwhelmingly, each in their turn. I remain stiff and frozen-faced.

"Meanwhile, poor Servilia was heart-broken, stricken down beyond reach," Valerius continues, ruefully, "I watched with mounting concern, powerless to intervene, the slow degradation of my poor daughter's sanity. I've known mourning myself, but this was something else....something deeper."

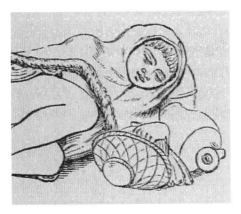

"Finally....she would collapse with exhaustion"

Weeks went by, and she refused to leave her room, hardly eating, softly weeping at first, then gradually regressing to fearful sobbing, filling the villa with her keening and heaving. I had never before witnessed such wailing — Servilia's whole frail body became caught up in one massive convulsion. Finally, exhausted beyond measure, she would collapse with exhaustion."

"Her emotional extremes were the worse: crying out for you

in desperation one moment, then in the next, venting her anger, smashing urns and cursing thunderously at everyone in sight — her devoted servant-girls grew frightened to approach their mistress, as was I. As things got worse, I feared that driven by blackest despair, she would take her own life."

"Then came that miraculous day, when she emerged, haggard and pallid, but eerily calm, as if transformed by some marvellous epiphany. Her slaves feared that she had broken down completely, descending into a mindless refuge of madness, wandering the Villa's grounds. Rising early, she found me, as it happened, during my morning devotions at my wife's mausoleum temple — she knew I would be there. We sat on the bench outside the temple, side-by-side.

"I listened attentively to her story, watching her closely all the while, only gently nodding — in deep appreciation for the mysterious gift that had been wrought, so unexpectedly. We hugged, holding the embrace, then strolled back to the villa wordlessly, arm in arm, in reverence for our loses....for you....for Hypetia. It was like one of your Greek fables in which the unsullied, young soul, carried aloft by her purity and innocence, is resurrected back from Hades and his dark Underworld — back to the world of sun, flowers, and birds."

"She told me that with you gone, she was nothing but a husk frozen in time, meaningless and empty — until the previous night, when she had a 'dream', more like an omen: unforgettably vivid, beyond anything in her worldly experience. She was incarnated as Persephone, daughter of Demeter, a symbol of death but also Spring and renewal. Returning from Hades to the Earth above, Persephone was reunited once more with Demeter, the mother she had lost."

"With tears in her eyes, Servilia told me that her own mother, my beloved Hypetia, then appeared in the form of Demeter, cloaked with a brilliant aura and scents of myrrh and fresh cedar. Kissing her softly on both cheeks, Hypetia pleaded with her daughter: akin to the mythic Persephone, she should return to Eleusis and the temple of Demeter....the only place where Servilia had felt fully alive, at peace with her mother, sanctifying the union. Spooked not in the least, but rather a revelation beyond measure, her destiny was foretold from that waking moment onwards."

"Her devotion to the Eleusinian Mysteries had saved her. Whether by blind faith or godly interference, I care not. A mythos playing out in real life....though the bargain was a hard one for me to swallow: losing you, and now she also would be leaving. As for Epicurus, she had concluded that if you weren't dead already, you should be considered to be so. There was no hope of your salvation from such a grisly fate. In the process of her grief, she had reached a state where you had to die beyond all hope, in order for her to live."

"I remained afraid for her life, but in the depths of her solitude, a plan had emerged, to which I reluctantly agreed. I would gladly have agreed to anything, if it would keep her alive."

"She has dedicated herself in your memory, to the Eleusinian Mysteries in honor of Demeter and Persephone. She resides in the sanctuary of Eleusis near Athens,....she is there now, as we speak. Only women are permitted as residents — she will be initiated into the sacred rites of a priestess of Eleusis, as she tells it, along with its 'intuitive, mystical knowledge, the fusion of opposites, organic, devoid of moth-eaten abstractions and metaphysics', and so on. While I see all this as incoherent blabbering, my opinions don't matter, only that my daughter has returned from whatever demonic pit in which she was trapped. I am permitted to see her twice every year, outside the sacred temple, in which she will be taking vows of celibacy and solitude...."

Suddenly flushed, I interrupt.

"We must leave immediately for Eleusis," I demand, in a pressured, strident voice, that I would otherwise never dare to use with Valerius, "we must save her before she takes her vows."

He startles, wagging his finger, but is not offended, remaining calm and compassionate. I can appreciate that it is his loss also, as much as it is mine. He shakes his head in such a profound, heart-wrenching gesture of hopelessness that it touches my heart.

"The Eleusinian sanctuary, with its secretive Mysteries, would certainly never be my first choice for my only daughter," says Valerius, "Servilia has risen from a very deep grief, when I had despaired for her recovery. Now, she has found her own peace that works for her. We both need to respect her choice. Though this may not be what she had planned for her life, she has matured in ways I previously couldn't imagine. I hardly recognize her."

"She seems so tranquil and serene, transforming her grief into helping others with their own losses, as her special duty of care. I suspect your past talks with her may have had something to do with that choice — she mentioned something called 'the Swerve'. If you truly love her,....then I beg you not to undo that very adjustment by which she has finally come to terms with your dreadful fate. It's a strange life that so mixes sacrifice with gratitude."

Valerius sighs deeply, dejected and downcast. The lengthy explanation is clearly a struggle for him, emotionally and medically. He pauses, takes several breaths, and continues unabated. The irrepressible businessman, pragmatic as ever, rises to the occasion.

"I think her level of grief was of such intensity that she 'died' to herself, the person who she once was, which was the only way she could survive your 'death'. She had to let go of everything from the past, you and I included — to become someone else, reborn at the sanctuary. She couldn't survive if she was to go through that again, waiting on the sidelines, for you to 'die' a second time."

He pauses, pursing his lips, hesitating to say any more.

"Besides, it's too late....she has already taken her first vows."

The final blow. I fall silent, crushed, thinking over all that Valerius has said. I run through his words, over and over, in my mind. If only I had known about the Hector sooner, I could have written from Mytilene, so that this disastrous web of events would not have occurred. Putting excuses aside, the folly is mine alone. I feel that I must be cursed. Wild thoughts surge across my febrile mind: that I should have offered my throat to 'Red' when I had the chance! I know that I'm angry, and try not to take it out on poor Valerius.

Without Servilia in my life is akin to losing a part of my own self, my better half. It feels as if all those worldly experiences — which she shared with me together — that have me who I am, have been erased. I feel 'lesser' for her absence.

Reeling under the shock of Valerius' news, I suddenly recall the odd manner in which he had begun his tale of woe — mysterious words, 'matters long withheld', that caught my attention at that time. Secrets? My concern for Servilia had then distracted me, and the moment had passed.

Roused from my misery, agitated still, I peppered poor Valerius with rapid-fire questions.

"Let us both visit Servilia, and then she will be overjoyed to see me, and drop all her plans! Will you join me? What about if I just speak with her, without asking her to leave Eleusis? And also.... what is all this about your health?"

Finally, I spit out the question that has been sitting on the tip of my tongue throughout our long discussion — but crucially, one that Valerius has avoided, purposefully it would seem. It can wait no longer.

"You were also referring to something else, apart from Servilia. What did you mean when you started speaking of matters that had long been withheld from me?"

The time has come for me to lay aside that primal fear which springs from a dim sense of something monstrous, half-seen, forbidden — lurking on the fringes of awareness.

Chapter 34

Given the late hour, Valerius kindly requests that we call a halt to further conversation. I readily agree, disturbed by his obvious fatigue. My pressing question is left hanging, begging for an answer. He takes it for granted that I will stay overnight at the villa: it's becoming a second home for me.

While the circumstances would dictate such a cordial invitation, I also detect a deeper motive. He needs me as a living connection with his faraway daughter, reluctant to let go, a loving bond which I understand and moreover, share with him. We have struck up a mutual trust, beyond friendship, and 'Servilia' is her name. Nor can I forget the undeniable fact that he saved my life.

Unspoken, we now cling to each other in joy, love, and loss. It is true that nothing in life is wasted, not ever pain and suffering — the means by which Valerius and I have come together, a closeness which I would have thought unimaginable only a short time ago.

At my request, he allows me to sleep in Servilia's bedroom, infused with her longing and despair, that had served for months as her solitary retreat from the world. It may be a melodramatic contrivance, but I need to feel close to her by any possible means. Yet healing sleep is denied to me, and lying in the dark, savoring her lingering perfume with each breath, my restless mind wanders over the day's events.

I have come to accept as I must, that Servilia is lost to me, at least for the near future. She is alive, as am I,....so that hope still remains. Furthermore, Valerius promises to tell her of my miraculous 'resurrection' at their next meeting, in several months. I begrudgingly agree with him that a personal meeting with Servilia at present would likely be too much: her new life needs adequate time to take hold.

I don't want to be culpable for regressing her backwards to that catatonic, fragile condition I have previously witnessed. Nor do I wish to place her in a conflicted situation in which she is 'torn' between her past love and her present vocation. The shock of responding to me, all at once, could mean undoing the newfound stability and sense of identity she has achieved at the sanctuary. This would be selfish of me — not an act of love!

I must reluctantly, place her safety above my own feelings. She will need time to digest the fact that I am alive, at which time a later meeting may become possible. Meantime, I need to get on with my life, albeit a desolate one without my beloved Servilia. I carry her in my heart.

Come the morning, Valerius and I breakfast together, somewhat awkwardly, as we struggle to keep our conversation light and positive. I sense that we both recognize the dark abyss into which our feelings could readily plunge. I provide further editions of my 'adventures'; he describes the many vexing issues involving the management of his estate, outnumbered as he is, by an an army of servant-slaves; we both lament the greed and tyranny of our Macedonian overlords, and so on.

All good-natured chatter of course, on every topic other than the array of questions I had put to him yesterday regarding himself, Servilia, and most intriguing of all, whatever mysterious matters that had been hidden from me 'for so long'. Avoidance however, creates its own demise: the more we suppress the obvious, the greater the tension set up by this suppression — until the dam bursts its banks, and the obvious breaks through with a deluge. So it is with Valerius, and he is the first to break the taboo.

"Let me start with the first of your questions, the 'hidden' matter," announces Valerius, always the businessman, coming straight to the point, "since the answer to that question, a long, uncomfortable, regrettable answer, will color all your other questions."

"I'll try to keep this brief. As you know, my beloved Hypetia died in childbirth, though baby Servilia survived, the remaining joy in my otherwise empty life. What you don't know is that I have another child, a boy, or I should say, a man now. Following Hypetia's death, I fell into a deep melancholia, not unlike Servilia's recent bout."

"I couldn't make even simple everyday decisions, whether to put on one tunic or another. I just stood there, paralyzed, until a servant dressed me. I slept in snatches all day, then spent my nights wide awake in worry, regret, and grief. Nothing made me happy, my appetite became outrageous, and a large amphora of wine would be gone in a week. I isolated myself from people, even servants, and thought about following my wife to Elysium, or wherever we go after death, probably the underworld of Hades in my case."

"Hades wouldn't have you," I say, as consolingly as I could manage, "but worse still for a Roman, would be your rebirth as an Athenian."

He appreciates my weak attempt at humor, laughs heartily, and fires back a salvo.

"Oh, no please! Better in Hades, amidst the Gorgons and Harpies, than to be an Athenian! We Romans always ponder the warning told by your own Sophocles concerning the treacherous Athenian victory over your Trojan cousins."

"Instead of honest and manly battle, you employed the insidious trick of using a gift horse to gain entry into that fair city. So no gifts of solace please, lest I end up like your cousins."

I should know better than to spar with Valerius, well-read, with his impressive library of scrolls. He appreciates the lightness of my diversion, though he tells his tale by halting bursts, clearly painful for him. He continues, nevertheless.

"....the insidious trick of using a gift horse"

"My servants became so concerned about me that at last, they sought the advice of an itinerant healer, skilled in medicinal herbs, who visited me with her clutch of potions and extracts."

"While I resisted the interference at first, I nevertheless started to improve, gradually in the beginning, then more quickly, as life started flowing back into my soul. I asked her to come more frequently as I got to know her, then I asked her to stay overnight. She declined politely, saying that she was married, but I remained very fond of her. We continued to talk about everything and she became a close friend. She also helped me with managing Servilia, who had only just started to walk."

He pauses to catch his breath, not without clutching his heart. I wonder why he is so forthright with me on such private matters, but he certainly has my undivided attention.

"Years came and went, and I became aware that our increasing familiarity was slipping into affection. We were still living at Samos: this was long before the Macedonian exile of Athenians."

"I continued to pay her for her visits, and I appreciated all that she had done for me. Remarkably skilled with herbs, she was also an excellent listener. Talking with her over the years helped me to adjust to my loss, probably more than the herbs. We carefully dodged around our personal feelings for each other."

"Then one day, many years later, she arrived unexpectedly when it wasn't one of her regular visits. I was alone, and she was distraught, crying inconsolably. She wouldn't stop, so I put my arms around her, which helped. Her husband was having an affair. She had followed him, and caught him with another woman, who worse still, was also one of her close friends."

"So it was a double betrayal for her," I say, "She had trusted her husband, and trusted her friend. So you took her to bed to comfort her?"

Startled by my direct statement of the 'facts', Valerius takes a deep breath, swallows, and nods ever so slightly, almost invisibly — I'm pushing him into places he doesn't want to go, as if he is opening Pandora's box, as the myth would have it, letting into the world that which is forbidden, shameful. At the same time, I'm losing patience, anxious to get to the point of our 'discussion'.

I had never seen Valerius, the paragon of masterful composure, so uncomfortable, so obviously agitated. He avoids looking at me, but stares straight ahead at the wall, rubbing his brow, in stony silence.

We sit there, as I listen to his heavy breathing mingled with sighs. Finally, I speak for him.

"I'm guessing that it didn't finish there," I say, softly and gently, to avoid any impression of judgement.

"Both of you began a relationship that continued."

I hesitate to say what's on my mind, struggling instead, to frame the right words: something descriptive, perhaps noble, that doesn't come loaded with a sordid morality.

"It was a special friendship for both of you."

Chapter 35

He nods at the wall, pursing his lips, over and over.

At last, he shakes his head vehemently, immersed in his own mental dialogue, as he wipes runlets of tears from his eyes. It's a heart-rending experience to watch — a mishmash of pain, regret, loss, and profound sadness. I sit fixated, in breathless silence, not without a few tears of my own.

Valerius begins speaking once again, regaining his composure — a calm, deliberated voice.

"I finally told her that I loved her, but she wouldn't answer. I implored her to leave her loveless marriage, but her own guilt compelled her to stay. Her husband admitted that he loved the other woman, but would remain as her husband, and not leave her. So she felt that if he stayed, then morally, she couldn't leave either. They were locked in a stalemate, and went their separate ways at home — though apparently, it was a very tense, unresolved arrangement."

"Did her husband find out about you?" I ask, hesitantly, with beating heart. It's the obvious question to ask, but Valerius is fragile, gravely ill, and I want to avoid any cutting remarks. I don't need to hurt the man who only recently rescued me from a ghoulish execution.

I didn't need to worry. He looks up at me tenderly, bent over with dewy eyes, and if I'm not mistaken, coyly, even lovingly. It's a poignant moment, loaded with unsaid meaning. I feel awkward, perplexed, not knowing what to do, or say.

He replies, "The husband confronted her and screamed at her, but she locked herself in her bedroom — they had separate rooms by this stage. I think he guessed she was having an affair, but didn't know who. She became very cautious in visiting me, so that I saw much less of her."

"You mentioned the Macedonians. Was she one of the early Athenian settlers on Samos?"

He nods. I knew most of the settlers, so I try to put the pieces of the puzzle together. Now it's my turn to fall silent, as things begin to drop into place ominously. Time passes, as if a heavy curtain has descended upon us.

"You used a means of preventing children, I suppose?" I asked at last, as innocently as I could.

Valerius nods again, and I feel a flood of relief — a deep sigh, at which he also sighs. A long, bothersome pause follows, after which he speaks softly.

"Despite everything, she became pregnant and once again I begged her to move in with me. She told me that there was no longer any sex with her husband, so the pregnancy had to be ours. I proposed marriage to her,....but she would not budge. Her vows, taken before the gods, were sacred for her. As she reached an advanced stage in her pregnancy, so her visits became less and less frequent. She told her husband that the child was his, that he had forgotten a tryst one night after the olive harvest, when they were both drunk. He remained deeply suspicious however, with frequent accusations, shouting that he had been honest and open, while she continued to lie. At last, the child came — a boy."

"I saw her just once after the birth. She was very sad and hopeless, announcing that this was her final visit — which understandably, sent me into a blind panic. Nothing I said mattered. She had made up her mind, and that was it."

At this stage, I fear what may be coming. I fight against it, cling-ing to the hope that events are merely an unrelated cosmic coin-cidence — that it can't really be true. Our conversation has now withered to a standstill, both of us distraught.

There is one more obvious question that I should have asked much earlier, but did not. I must have known the truth intuitively, even at that early stage, but shied away from it. I had kept up the conspiracy of denial between us, hoping that some new evidence would miraculously surface — steering my forebodings away from the precipice of despair that I saw looming ever closer, before me. My heart is beating out of my chest.

"What is this woman's name?" I ask, in a measured, raspy voice, not my own, articulating each word slowly and carefully.

The efficient businessman replies, without missing a beat — anxious I think, to share his onerous burden. Family secrets come at a cost.

"You knew her very, very well."

He uses the past tense, because....she is dead.

Valerius must be my biological father,....which makes Servilia my half-sister!

Mouth agape, I am struck dumbfounded!

A chill draught cuts through me. I manage a gasp, followed by a stream of guttural whimpers and murmurs, all incoherent — then throw my head back on the lounge, closing my eyes as if to shut out the dreadful reality. If there be gods, please make it go away. My mind is reeling in overdrive, thoughts racing in all directions at once, disoriented in time and space.

This is why he had promoted my travel plans, hoping that I would find someone else. All Valerius' suave arguments and apparent goodwill only served the purpose of concealment. Damn these family secrets — now I am dragged screaming into the family battleground. While I was lolling about on the sunlit decks of the Hector, lost in a dreamy fugue, my intuition had sounded the alarm, knocking furiously on the doors of consciousness: I shouldn't trust Valerius' motives — all was not as it appeared!!

I was right, but for the wrong reason.

As if he is reading my mind, Valerius breaks the morbid silence that fills the widening space between us.

"Yes, I admit that I had wanted to separate you both for obvious reasons," he says, putting his paternal hand on my shoulder, "but you are also my son, my own flesh and blood — and I really believe in your talent. That much is true. I can see so much of myself in you. So I made plans which I though were best for your future ambitions."

"....and strangely enough, best for you, too....especially you," I add, wryly, "....to keep a lid on the past, when you preyed on a vulnerable, married woman, my poor mother!"

After a fit of coughing, which sends servants scattering for water, Valerius continues.

"You changed those plans while they were in progress, and it is your right to do so, since it is your life. I rescued you from the ghastly accusations of those rabid Aristotelians, because I didn't want you harmed in any way. I owe you that, at least....and much more!"

A few candid words....that set me back to thinking. Adopting any attitude other than merciful, would be an act of cruelty, compounding the slew of misfortunate, misguided events — painfully, all too human.

Valerius pauses, takes his prune juice, a few olives, barley bread, and cheese — then settles back into his chair, rubbing his hands together, as if he was massaging his thoughts. Yes, it's over, and come what may, the telling has been told! I don't know if he is expecting a reply? I remain immobile, lost for words. I'm still reeling in shock, struggling to accept the unpalatable.

I wonder to myself absentmindedly, whether Valerius' 'seduction' of my mother was part of the ancient Roman attitude of having 'an heir and a spare', in which case I was 'the spare'. As a male, I continue the line of succession. Servilia would not find the same level of ready acceptance by the Roman gentry of Colophon. Is this why she never felt that she could please him, and win his approval? Is this what she meant by her oft-repeated 'father in my head'? I shake my own head, to push away such disturbing thoughts.

We both sit staring at each other, made mute and insensible, by all that has passed between us. I struggle to sort out my own thoughts: Valerius' 'seduction', or my mother's 'infidelity'? I think back to the cliff and the sandals: my father's mysterious disappearance on that dark, windswept night — his certainty that my mother had leapt off the cliff. Thoughts tumble over each other. I startle. Abruptly, Valerius speaks up, surprising me with his steady, resolute voice.

"You are indeed, sprung from the seed of my loins....looking at you, I see myself — my only son, and I acknowledge you as such. Whatever their misdeeds, know that you were....conceived in love. More than that, I actually like you, enjoy your company, and respect the accomplished man that you have become. I'm proud of you,.... though I take no credit for that."

He stops breathless for one of his frequent pauses, pauses that tug at my conscience, then picks up the thread.

"It must have been hard for you, without your mother. As for your father, as much as I know him, he is a hard man to like. Neither do I expect you to call me 'father'. I have been mostly absent in your life, though I have watched you from afar. I don't know where we go from here, or what kind of relationship we may have — or not have — in the future. That's entirely up to you."

Another pause, followed by several dry hacking coughs.

"I have loved two women with all my heart, and they have both died tragic deaths. How many times have I wished it was I, rather than either of them."

"You may ask: why tell you now, even why tell you at all. Simply, my health is failing and I don't want my legacy to be.... one of lies. I kept it a secret all this time because Chaerestrata had wanted it that way. I promised her that I would do so,....and to my everlasting regret, she sealed my silence with her unexpected death. Now, I have gout that's becoming worse, as you have seen me hobbling about with my cane."

He sips on a glass of wine, which seems to fortify his pallor.

"I use those symptoms however, to mask a greater illness: that my heart is congested with an excess of phlegm, or so I have been told, and I am not expected to live many more years. I told you now, despite your mother's wishes, because I believe the living have a greater right to the truth, than do the dead. The dead should not control the living from the grave. I hope that in time, you may forgive me — and your mother also."

I listen intently to his explanations: confessional, apologetic, testimonials of love — what a mixture! I should feel angry perhaps, but strangely, I really don't. There remains a singular question however — like an annoying bee buzzing in my mind — about poor Servilia, my sister.

"Does she know? Have you told her?" , I quizzed. I miss her

acutely — a wave of longing engulfs me — though no one would know from my flat, wooden demeanour. I give nothing away, other than a rapid intake of breath: a sigh of resignation. Valerius tells me that he hasn't done so yet, but will explain it all, as he has done with me, when she is sufficiently stabilized and secure in her new life.

"You were her lover, suddenly murdered," offers Valerius, in his straightforward manner, "then you come back larger-than-life, only now transformed into a long-lost brother she never knew existed". Mind-blowing stuff, even for me. Not forgetting that other lingering wound beyond healing: baby Servilia who killed her own mother during childbirth. It's a lot to swallow at one gulp.

Like me, can Servilia trust anything at present? Everything is fluid. All those anchors that she and I took for granted, the truths that kept us moored to reality, are gone in a flash. We are floating freely, directionless, at the mercy of forces that drive us one way, and then another.

Even now, she doesn't know what she doesn't know, out there,....

....waiting for her.

What more is there still to come?

Chapter 36

Valerius and I agreed to meet again in a few days time. I am still coming to terms with his newfound status — it's a struggle for me to shift ground, and think of him as 'father'. Then there is another issue to consider. Though he attempts to mask his symptoms in a manly display of courage, I can plainly see that Valerius is struggling.

Whether friend or stranger, illness has always evoked in me, an immediate empathic response. I see it as a legacy of my mother's care-giving influence, when I accompanied her as a child on her rounds as an herbalist and folk healer. Her soft yet charismatic presence and sage advice were perhaps, just as effective as her herbal compresses.

Meanwhile, there is ample time to reflect upon Valerius' startling revelations. Out of nowhere, I find myself with a new father and sister, who now belong to me, just as I belong to them. Facts are one thing but emotional feelings are another — they take time to grow and flourish. They can't be summoned up — with a blithe snap of the fingers — by Valerius' goodwill talk of 'family' and 'loving parents' that he is using to soften my 'illegitimacy'! Time is running out for him and he wants matters to be settled and healed. Always, the businessman!

Valerius' revelations create a confusing meld between my family-of-origin and my new 'secret' family. While Servilia's espoused father and mother are also her biologically parents, yet the same can't be said for me.

This new knowledge makes me a bastard of sorts, which I think, interestingly, is the reason why I have always felt a profound sense of unworthiness....forever an outsider peering in the window at others' happy lives, with the door latched and locked against entry. After all these years living with 'my parents' since infancy, it is strange and unsettling to think of myself as a 'bastard'....at my age!

Was I the unwanted outcome of a clandestine liaison between Servilia's father and my beloved mother, Chaerestrata? Is that how my father saw me, reducing him to a cuckold? Nor could he throw any stones, much less any accusations — that would surely rebound back on his own infidelity!

Yet here I am, living-and-breathing, a troublesome inconvenience? — the bodily outcome of that illicit connection between the two families. If only the fallout stopped there! Instead, it widens still further, in the love-making between poor Servilia and I, both of us innocent pawns in a conspiracy of silence — our shared bloodline. What was once a carefree, tender intimacy has forever become something tainted and unspeakable — better than any jealous rival could ever arrange.

What an incestuous mess!

Chapter 37

Valerius was understandably alert on any occasion when his only daughter and I were together. Spending time alone meant careful planning: scheduling her visit when Valerius was occupied with business, usually at Notium.

Servilia would sneak out of the villa aided by her girl-servants, playing cat-and-mouse with the guards, under the pretext of visiting her girlfriends — caught up in the secrecy, her loyal friends they were only too happy to cover for her. At the time, I mistakenly believed that Valerius' scrutiny was driven by his overreaching possessiveness. That there could be any other reason had never occurred to me, any more than the radical idea that he was not only concerned for Servilia, but also harbored a special interest in me.

My very appearance reminded him of his lost love — the walking, talking 'outcome' that ensued from seducing my mother — used in turn, to soothe an earlier unbearable loss, that of Hypetia. Now both women are dead!

As if the gods had singled out Valerius for special punishment, he must watch as the offspring of both losses then replicated this entanglement into the next generation. Valerius must carry a great weight on his shoulders! I wonder at his secret inner life — unreachable, impenetrable, even by Servilia.

Then there's the matter of my mother's suicide, which is not Valerius' fault, though he is surely implicated. As a folk herbalist, she would be required to visit many households, her healing activities providing a natural cover for infidelity. It's sordid for me to think of my beloved mother in such immoral terms,....though Valerius speaks well of her, even admits to loving her, if I am to take him at his word.

It's true that most people were smitten by her.

I think of Neocles, my father (now, stepfather?) who raised me, fed me, yet a man of few, if any friends. With his mood swings, he was never a good match for my mother's free-spirited, effervescent personality. He also, is implicated in her tragic death.

I can't help thinking that the 'excitement' generated by my father's clandestine affairs was a kind of vicarious treatment for his chronic melancholia. He was free to present himself as a different person, having a charming 'secret self', while he lived two parallel lives. Yet there was a tragic circularity to all this — his betrayal also fed the guilt of his chronic melancholia, which in turn, found its outlet in further betrayal.

One pathetic self would 'whip' the other!

Not long after my mother discovered his serial affairs, my father orchestrated a very public rupture with his then current girlfriend — capped with a melodramatic brawl on the street. Of course, the end of the affair also ended the excitement of his other 'secret' self. Within a few months however, he had entered into yet another 'hidden' relationship of stealth and intrigue.

My mother and I were not supposed to know about this fresh betrayal, despite his telling pattern of behavior,....and so the compulsion repeated itself yet again. 'Secretiveness' loses much of its restless appeal, if those who are betrayed, continue to remain blissfully ignorant. The enticement lies in walking the tightrope of tension between discovery and deception. Young children know this excitement when they tease their playmates, "I know a secret!" followed quickly by "And I'm not telling."

My father's struggle was not only with my mother however, as his inner conflict and confusion came to the forefront at times. Within this self-destructive compulsion, 'the two selves' would betray each other — leaving clues to undo the other, so that arguably, the single true self could then emerge, integrated and free — which of course, never actually happened. In a sense, he was addicted to his own inner conflict: the excitement of the 'secret' struggling with the flagellation of guilt which it spawned, and so on!

At least that was the explanation that my mother and I artfully constructed, as a means of coming to terms with his unpredictable glumness. We came to believe that his inner conflict was the real, deeper basis of his tempestuous mood swings. It was useful for us to think of it this way, as a chronic illness — his 'demons' as we called it.

He would become uncontrollably angry at a slight inconvenience, then later seek forgiveness to the point of embarrassment. Between these two poles, there were lengthy periods when he would isolate himself, mute and unapproachable, in a dark space of self-hatred. At other times, often lasting several weeks, he would emerge as a caring, gentle and loving individual.

My father, Neocles, as I have often said....was a hard man to love.

⁓⁓⁓⁓⁓⁓⁓⁓⁓⁓⁓⁓⁓⁓

Since my poor mother's death, Marius tells me that my grieving father, regretful perhaps for his wrongdoing, has had no liaisons with other women. Furthermore, his moods have stabilized greatly, though the dread melancholia retains its stranglehold. It would seem that the explanation adopted by my mother and I was more accurate than we could have imagined — though at such a price. My mother's death provided a partial resolution of Neocles' inner conflict — she was the necessary focus of his marital betrayal. On the other hand, her death also added a fresh baggage of guilt.

For me, he will always be my father who suffers from an unfortunate illness, like the recurring 'fevers' suffered by people who breathe the 'bad air' around swamps. I have now come to a point where I have turned the whole matter on its head and choose to think of it in positive terms. I am lucky to be blessed with two fathers, Neocles and Valerius, different in every respect. One dry and predictable though melancholic; the other, sociable but manipulative. Both flawed, beset by demons, as are all of us, not least myself. The fact that my 'two fathers' are such different personalities actually aids my adjustment. In the recesses of my mind, they don't compete with each other — both are neatly assigned, each in their separate, sealed box.

Lingering questions still remain. I continue to ask myself whether I have other unknown siblings out there? I also wonder about the telling signs that I ignored in my mother's own behavior prior to her disappearance? Did my self-appointed role as her lead defender and advocate, intently focused on my father's misadventures, blind me to her deteriorating condition?

If so, I should have listened to the emptiness that she increasingly raised in our conversations, in one who was normally so vital and expressive. Instead I dismissed her pain, because 'I' needed her to be back to normal, for me. Are we all so selfish at heart?

Chapter 38

To forgive is to forget, or so Valerius tells me, but there lies the problem. Too much has happened! The unfolding nightmare clutters my brain with sticky cobwebs that catch every passing thought, illuminating nothing, going nowhere,….stuck.

My waking hours are filled with these wild thoughts that, no matter how much I fight it, always turn back to my origins, and the many questions that follow — the treadmill of emotion starts all over again. Who I am is not who I thought I was! Try as I may, it seems that I can't just let it go and move on with my life. Something is still missing, holding me back. I mooch about aimlessly, with a hangdog face — inside, I'm bursting, ready to explode.

I find myself lost in a family battleground not of my own making, left with a legacy of dark secrets: betrayals that are hidden away and tightly guarded — unseen, unknown malignancies that cripple future generations, myself and Servilia. I'm flummoxed by it all — everything that I once cherished and took for granted — as it unravels before my eyes.

I need to talk with someone! Someone who is at once comfortable with all the bizarre circumstances, yet at the same time, can listen to me impartially — to sort out the tangle of emotions and facts. Accessible, supportive, wise, unbiased. Quite a list. But who? I'm sitting in my old bedroom, rocking myself, musing over this question — when I hear the splash of water outside the door.

Marius is washing the kitchen floor, in his characteristic unhurried manner. Even these small movements, the measured to and fro of the mop, seem to be imbued with thoughtfulness, a transcendence, as if he is savoring a grand task. There is an innate appeal to this, yet curiously, I find it disturbing to my sensibility of action and achievement.

"Marius....remains discreet and trustworthy"

Marius is my father's age, though the comparison stops there. Unlike Neocles, Marius is large-boned, sinewy, with prominent jug-ears and thick, bushy hair. Strangers find him intimidating at first, then by stages, intriguing, and finally, endearing. While he maintains his servile schedule of chores — including the top-knot that singles him out as a slave — he is otherwise treated as an 'invisible' member of the family. Witnessing everything that happens in the main house, he remains discreet and trustworthy. He lives and eats alone, humble and kind-hearted, in a small detached cottage. In being respectful to all, he gains immeasurable respect by all.

I known little of his origins. My father has alluded to the rumor that Marius was a tribal 'holy man' of some kind, a Zoroastrian who worshipped fire, from one of the nomadic, warrior tribes of the eastern steppes, in the region of Scythia. So quiet, he goes about his chores like a benign spirit, bearing no grudges, needing no correction, nor seeking any approval. In the shadowy half-light, his ebony skin takes on a sheen that profiles his muscular figure.

My father is away teaching school, doing what he loves, so this is the opportunity I wanted. I approach Marius and ask him if we could talk privately in his cottage. He agrees immediately without question, unblinking — as if it was an everyday request and I had asked him to clean my room.

We sit together in his cottage, with his chair off to one side. The door is wide open — I have an unrestricted view of the flourishing vegetable garden and adjacent orange grove. I find that it is easier for me to talk openly when I don't have to stare at someone directly in the face.

"If I am not who I thought I was, then who, or what am I? I've lost my way, Marius. Stuck at a crossroads."

I assume, correctly as it turns out, that Marius is fully informed. My father also, uses him — patient, and impartial — as a sounding board for his many woes. I needn't explain any background: all the better.

"People are not perfect," he replies dryly, then in the manner of an afterthought, adds a laconic twist, "anymore than you are!"

"Do you mean that I should just forgive them," I ask, tersely, "as if all the lies and secrets mean nothing, when the consequences are life-changing?"

"What is it that you are forgiving, or not forgiving, in this case?"

I have the impression, totally unfounded, that Marius loved my Mother. Most people did.

"I find it difficult to forgive the lie that Valerius and my mother continued to foster, year after year, upon which Servilia and I built our lives. Each of us trusted our parent, and that trust was sorely misplaced."

"They let you down," Marius remarks, barely above a whisper, "Betrayed your trust?"

"The very foundation of our lives has been torn apart, much as one casually rips a papyrus sheet in two. We're ripped open, vulnerable!"

"Why don't you speak for yourself, without including Servilia," came the pointed reply, "I'm sure Servilia can speak for herself."

I'm stunned, and more than a little offended, at Marius' wry reply. Is it just factual bluntness, perhaps with an edge, or did he really mean it to be a cutting remark? I have to remember that I asked for this meeting.

"So I'm angry,....me alone, as you say. Forget Servilia," I reply, testily, "so where do we go from here?"

"So your mother should have told you then? When? At what age?"

This loaded question, heavily loaded indeed, sets me back. Firstly, it puts the responsibility on my beloved mother. If I object, Marius will say that she was my primary parent-figure, so that she should have told me the truth. It was her responsibility. I have to admit reluctantly, that he is right on that count.

In addition, Servilia has been summarily removed from the discussion, along with Valerius. I feel like I'm being pushed, yet he only asks questions? I need to think ahead where he is going with all this. It's difficult for me to let down my defences.

I lose any sense of time as I attempt to follow the implications of Marius' volley of questions. I was expecting weighty advice, but I have received none whatsoever, which perhaps, may be a good thing. After a lengthy period, I offer a half-hearted reply to Marius' query.

"Well, she probably should have told me the truth about my real father long ago....when I reached an age where I could reason for myself, let's say twelve years old."

"And what would be your reaction at twelve years old? Would you have been relieved and thankful?"

"I'm sure I would have been very angry at first," I admit, "but I'd get over it in time."

"And what would happen around the household before you got over it, while you are acting out your anger on everyone?"

I see where he is going with this, as I suspected.

"You mean that I would refuse to believe it," I murmur, "and ask my father directly if I was his son?"

"Would you do that, even if your mother said not to do so?"

His query is deceptively simple, yet why do I feel a conflict churning within me? Time passes....as I become fully absorbed in his question — seemingly so innocent yet loaded with hidden meaning. I struggle evasively to find a way out, but decide at last, to be brutally honest.

"Yes, I would probably ask him. Even if I didn't, he would certainly have questioned me about my anger, and would probably find out anyway. Once he starts on something, he doesn't let it go. Besides,....he already had his suspicions."

"He already had his suspicions?" Marius repeats, framing my statement as a question, raising his voice ever so lightly.

I stare intently at the garden, rubbing my temples, thinking about my own statement — was I just been compliant to give an answer that Marius wanted, any answer to go along with his line of questioning, or was it really the truth? Yes,….as I think back to that distant past — Yes, it is true! My father did indeed, have his suspicions!

Probably more than that, as I delve back in time, straining to recall. I remember his offhand sarcastic probing, levelled at my mother, who mostly ignored him.

"Yes", I reply simply, quietly — I see the 'pathway' of associations and causes stretching onwards, ahead of me.

"So what about you? You tell me that your father had already suspected that you were not his son. Does that mean that you also had your own suspicions?"

The question is disturbing, even provocative, as I suspect Marius intended it to be. I stare at the garden. It looks like the asparagus is ready for harvest, though the beets still have a way to go.

Memories begin to emerge, feint traces at first, forming into broken snatches, then finally, clear and startling. Asparagus is my father's favorite vegetable. Or is it to be step-father? What is it that constitutes a 'father', if I am forced to choose: biology, or parenting?

Neocles has a nuggety build, prominent jowls, an aquiline nose and black, bushy eyebrows, matching his dark complexion. My features on the other hand, are opposite to his profile in almost every way. A slight build, though sinewy and strong, I inherited (from whom?) a thin, bony face, stub nose, almost no visible eyebrows, and blondish, wavy hair.

I had reached sixteen years — that callow age of questioning everything — including the noticeable disparity in physiques between my father and myself. I remember now. We had a brief conversation about it, if 'conversation' is the appropriate term for such an volcanic exchange.

I was intrigued — but not alarmed — by the differences in our profiles, nor in my innocence, did I make any moral inferences. For me….it was just that….merely a question. Just that, and nothing more. I recall that my father was obviously very annoyed, even more than normal. Naïve as I was,….I remember now that I followed up with another question — asking him unabashedly if he was really my father, or whether I was adopted? I wasn't particularly worried either way — just curious, as young juveniles can be, not fully understanding the consequences.

My father erupted in fury, eyes bulging — I cowered backwards, fearing that for the first time, he was about to strike me. Thinking better of it, he stormed out of the house, cursing loudly as he went. I was both shocked and surprised by his reaction, which is what I most remember now — at best, he was a sullen man, given to fits of anger — but this was something I had never seen before. Extreme ….even by his standards.

Being a powerless cuckold really didn't sit well with him!

The truth should have been obvious, made even clearer by my father's abnormal reaction — yet at the time, I blithely ignored its meaning, and quickly dismissed it.

"And what would happen then," says Marius softly, relentless in his enquiry, "if your father truly believed that you are not his son?

"I imagine that there would be a huge fight between my parents. My mother would probably leave, when he begins yelling at her. She won't tolerate his abuse."

I hear myself say the words innocently, then uncannily, without any effort on my part, the words become memories that change into jumbled scenes, all running together — the rain pelting thunderously on the tiled roof, and my mother and father yelling and screaming; as I lie on the flagstone floor where my father pushed me, Melanchaetes barking at him, as he marches me back to my bedroom; the flood of scenes coming in flashes, playing and replaying. Despite their rousing impact, I remain aware that these scenes are not happening in real time,....I have entered some kind of trance,....yet remain powerless to stop it.

My brain is racing on by itself. I am caught between two worlds, past and present, experiencing both at the same time.

Chapter 39

I blundered onto the unconscionable truth, buried within my memories, and I didn't see it coming! A flashback that sprang fully-formed into my conscious mind.

My mother's disappearance happened on the exact same day as my discussion with my father in which I had unwittingly questioned my own paternity! Until this moment, I had never connected these two events, yet in that instant of recognition, my world changed forever.

In my father's volatile mindset however, my innocent questions had served to corroborate his long-held suspicions. He may have assumed — incorrectly as it happened — that I already knew the truth; then with his paranoia in overdrive, I had deliberately concealed it from him as part of a devious conspiracy.

I begin to understand the roots of my father's anger. It remains blatantly self-righteous, of course, since it conveniently ignores his own checkered history of infidelity. According to his self-serving moral code, then any illegitimate progeny ('that's me') — rather than infidelity — becomes his yardstick of immorality! The presence of such unwanted offspring are evidence of a calculated defiance by my mother, acted out purposefully against him — designed to leave him as the pitiful simpleton of a callous betrayal, a cuckold no less.

I sit here, immobile, stunned. I stare out once again at the same asparagus, unchanged — though the same can not be said for me.

The whole, thorny issue of my paternity — and the attempt to conceal it — is inseparably linked to my mother's death. I am the incarnated 'dirty little secret' of which my father accused my mother in their final argument: the reason that drove her away, running off blindly into the stormy night. Without me, the flesh-and-blood material 'evidence', her infidelity would be no more than his own.

My head is reeling. First, my father is not really my father, then next, my beloved Servilia and sexual partner, is really my sister. Finally, I uncover yet another trauma, even more calamitous — that I am the probable 'cause' lurking behind my mother's death.

My very existence as well as my mother's infidelity, no less than her fate, are one and the same thing! The truth was there all this time, staring me in the face. I simply needed to connect the dots, which amazingly, I had avoided doing. Marius helped me uncover that which I already knew, albeit locked away, concealed in the depths of my being.

What was once the 'Unknown Known' now rears up before me, like a mired beast — the Chimera of family wretchedness, come alive! Too much to know! Madness would be a most welcome relief — to allow one's self to slip away gently into a black void of blessed nothingness.

Now I understand Servilia's plunge into darkness, retreating from an overwhelming reality.

I get up off the chair, floundering, unsteady. Tears fill my eyes, rolling down my cheeks — my face feels strangely contorted, frozen into a grimace. I stagger out of the cottage, somehow reaching my bedroom. Marius is talking to me, repeating something, over and over. Though I can hear his words, they sound muffled and distorted, distant, as if echoing down a tunnel.

I lie down, closing my eyes, eager to shut out the chaos of the world. All these separate scenes however, and incessant talking faces, still continue their inane revelry, playing out as they will, like a collage of crazed puppetry.

My mother's raw, bewildered state, and even her 'senseless' death, becomes 'sensible'....though even less acceptable, now that I am surely implicated.

❦❦❦❦❦❦❦❦❦❦

I wake alert and calm — it's morning, and my head is throbbing. I remember lying down, in a state of collapse, during the previous afternoon,....after my enlightening talk with Marius. I must have been emotionally exhausted; no, more than that, an emotional crisis, the like of which I have never experienced before or since.

The clamour and aromas of breakfast break in upon me — frying pans rattling, pots boiling over — adding to my headache. At the same time, it's a familiar, comforting commotion,....reality imposing itself: I'm insatiably hungry. My nose knows — father is serving his favorite dish of staititas pancakes, sizzling in olive oil, made according to his own inventive recipe of spelt flour, honey, and curdled milk, topped with sesame and melted cheese.

"My father is serving his favorite dish of staititas"

When my father cooks, unlike Marius, he has a well-earned, infamous reputation for using almost every available kitchen utensil. Coordination and efficiency do not figure in his temperamental strengths — though his staititas however, more than compensate for the messiness. Cooking means he's in one of his perky moods, a good sign. I smile to myself. Life goes on, like breakfast — unabated and messy.

Half-awake, I slip into a morning reverie. While I may have been happily sleeping, it seems as though my brain has been busy, working overtime. I'm inundated by a parade of fresh thoughts — I watch them pass by for inspection, dispassionately, detached from them, as if I am seated in an amphitheater, many rows back. Curious, entertained, but not overly involved.

Was my mother's death a self-inflicted punishment? The shame of a betrayal and deception that conflicted with her own high moral code of goodness towards others,....as well as her own sense of herself as a good person. She had endured this nagging conflict and shame for sixteen years, but could do so no longer!

My parents had their frequent arguments of course, though this one was exceptional. For the first time, it centred on her enduring shame, her "dirty little secret" — my paternity — that struck at the crux of her high moral code. The weapon of retribution had been slowly assembled, but this last argument pulled the trigger on her life-and-death struggle.

So be it.

I leave this circus arena of wild thoughts, fully awake now, and spring out of bed for a pleasant, domestic breakfast with my father. He's pleased to see me, jocular and engaging, even unseemly merry. Following an indulgent breakfast — more than I needed — I compliment his culinary skills. His staititas really are delicious....filling the void. He beams with satisfaction, and his simple joy gratifies me.

A gift given is a gift received.

Only,....Who is to clean the kitchen pots and pans,...but myself!

Oh, Marius, where are you? He knew my father was cooking today, and prudently, remembered that the far garden bed urgently need tilling. Duty calls!

Pulling on my tattered chitonium, a relic leftover from my younger days, set aside for kitchen chores — I catch myself in this frozen moment of time. I feel unleashed, unblocked, flowing in a way that is new for me, ready to move on with life.

I am at peace with my mother....and strange as it is to say, 'both' of my fathers, the old and the new.

Chapter 40

Valerius greets me with his trademark Roman legionnaire salute, the iconic symbol of his homeland — which interestingly, does good service as a marketing prop for his business.

Such a greeting not only sets him apart from commonplace Athenian merchants. It also indicates that he is an outsider who is not embroiled in partisan city-state politics. Servilia has told me that, within elite business circles, he is famous for his eccentric gestures — often donning the field kit of a Roman legionnaire — played

out amidst much wine and general merriment. His trading partners, surprised at first, have not only come to accept such irregular embellishments, but moreover, now eagerly expect them.

They were not to be disappointed in his showmanship, when for a change, he chose to wear a gold wreath crown while closing a recent business transaction. He also adorned himself with the metallic trim costume and double-face mask of the god Janus. Ever sensitive to others perceptions.

"Valerius in Roman legionnaire costume….his showmanship"

Valerius dug into his own Roman pantheon and chose the mantle of Janus as a distinctly Roman god. Janus has no local Greek equivalent, so it would not offend the sacerdotal sensitivities of the Athenians or their overlords, the Macedonians. Commerce and Politics, he knew, are always interwoven.

Janus was doubly appropriate, he explained to his merchant friends, since his carefully chosen regalia also conveyed a business-related message,

"I am the glitzy bright god of beginnings and transitions," he declared, godlike, arms outstretched, "looking backwards to the past, all our successes, and looking forwards to a prosperous future, all the opportunities still to come."

If quizzed about his outlandish costumes, Valerius replies innocently that he only wants to inject some much needed levity into what would otherwise be a rather joyless business transaction.

"There's no appeal in doing business," has become his stock byline, "without the lubricant of laughter and play."

He artfully cultivates this lustrous image as a shrewd business strategy. At the same time, it's also a spontaneous expression of his own gregarious personality — making others smile with goodwill is intrinsic to his nature. The fact that this same irrepressible quality also makes him a natural salesman — not to mention a wealthy gentleman of high repute — is almost a secondary spinoff. Not surprisingly, his boisterous parties and exotic costuming become memorable as a frequent topic of conversation in the rarified circles of the rich merchant elite.

Tight-lipped, dour merchants have been known to convulse with laughter, bent double, holding their sides. In doing so however, they are talking about him. Whether the perception is that of facile publicity, or crass notoriety, it matters little to Valerius — so long as people are smiling, which in turn, reinforces his dominance in the competitive marketplace of merchant shipping. To meet him, is not to forget him.

Other traders have even come to copy his shenanigans, paying the ultimate compliment, by recognizing the halo effect of his astute marketing — although there can only ever be one Valerius, for whom it comes naturally. There is something at once engaging and distinguished, almost magical, in his larger-than-life personality. Beyond the glimmer and sparkle, Valerius knows that simple trust is what really matters. He remains at heart, the consummate purveyor of genuine goodwill, in business or otherwise — and irresistibly, people love him for this!

Today however, his outstretched arm trembles noticeably as he presents the salute — we both tacitly agree to ignore it.

Privately, I am worried and, with family in short supply, I don't want to lose this other lost father just as each of us in our own clumsy ways, are fumbling to know each other. He compensates with an offhanded heartiness that is endearing in its warmth — the old laughable Valerius, true to form. He's hard to resist, infectious even, and helpless, I embrace his love of life.

"I'm concerned for your future," he remarks, suddenly turning serious, "my good friend, the Gymniasarch of Mytilene has given you sage advice….to avoid teaching in public places like an agora or gymnasium. Your teaching is provocative, and I know that is your just intention. I also agree with it, just as I attract attention in dressing up outrageously for my business meetings. But business is one thing,….peoples' core beliefs are another thing altogether. You wish to provoke peoples' minds for their own sakes, towards a greater good, which is an honorable motive — there are others however, for whom your words only provoke anger. This can lead to violence,….directly or through the manipulation of officials such as the Gymnasiarch."

Valerius takes to his couch, and indicates for me to do the same. His movements are painfully slow and deliberated. My respect for his wisdom however, has grown immensely since our first meetings. Once settled comfortably, he continues.

"Your teaching must be restricted to the private residences and gardens of powerful patrons who can endorse and protect you. I had arranged all this for you with my merchant friends in Lampsacus.... but you are wilful and stubborn, just like your dear sister, so you chose Mytilene instead, a hotbed of political dissidents. You taught openly in the public agora, inciting anger and fomenting trouble.... which can quickly escalate to mob rebellion in a marginal city like Mytilene. Spurred on by the Aristotelians, you played into their hands. Officialdom was left with no other option but to come down hard on you, which may easily have cost you your life."

I lower my head, avoiding his penetrating gaze. Valerius doesn't raise his voice, yet his measured speech is more compelling than any dramatic gestures.

"Yes, I agree. I didn't trust you, as I should have done, and must apologize. I gave you small return for your bounteous generosity."

"You avoided the sad fate of the Hector," he continues, in his rational, monotone manner, "only to put yourself in equal peril. In your innocence, you failed to realize what is common knowledge.... that the Aristotelians have a monopoly on philosophy teaching in Mytilene."

We are both sitting on lounges now, rather than lying, bent forward towards each other, quite close together, each of us intimate and attentive to the other. No longer, does any boundary separate us. While he relates the sorry tale of my misadventures, what I hear is fatherly concern rather than judgement,....nor do I feel any need to be defensive.

The conversation is draining for him, and he leans back, in a spasm of coughing. His resilience is impaired, yet he trusts me in exposing his vulnerability. While he recovers, I pick up the thread.

"In my future teaching, I must pay special attention to my safety. As a free-thinker, I'm a sitting target for other traditional schools, whose spirit of 'competition' extends to violence,.....even judicial murder. I never counted on that. But I have another matter that requires your advice and experience?"

He smiles at my request, flattered perhaps, much as a caring father would seek to guide a prodigal son. I feel as if we have broken through an invisible barrier. He doesn't want me as a snivelling 'repentant sinner' — nor does he seek to control my life, as I first thought. I put my question before him, with more than a touch of wishful thinking.

"Avoiding public forums for my teaching however, raises another question. How can I gather a community of likeminded friends for discussion and debate if I am sitting comfortably at home, lost in my own thoughts?. First and foremost, I'm a teacher!"

My 'father' nods as he listens attentively, pausing carefully to consider all options and consequences, then replying in that characteristic tone that I have come to appreciate — slow, even, and thoughtful.

"You need influential patrons, at least initially, until you become established in your own right. Such patrons, high-ranking merchant friends of mine, will endorse your teaching, and facilitate your political entry. They will introduce your ideas, thereby raising interest in their social circles, or at least idle curiosity — enough that their colleagues and friends will attend your garden symposiums — so that they can provide comment when they in turn host their own dinner parties. You become the latest gossip! The rest is up to you."

At this point, Valerius, my 'father', grabs my hand to lend significance to his words. The human touch, literally.

"You are safe so long as you remain in your patron's garden. You may think this emphasis on safety is a negative, that isolates you from possible followers. Instead, I invite to turn the whole idea on its head, since it is actual a positive — a shrewd strategy. Your residential garden symposiums set you apart. The other philosophy schools actively solicit followers in public areas — as if they are mere tinkers and hawkers, selling their wares amidst the raucous of the agora, or other public places."

He gasps, breathless, his once resonant voice becoming feathery with fatigue. A long pause follows....then he gathers his strength, and raps up with his closure.

"Your school is then immediately different from all the rest.... made appealing by its meditative garden setting, consistent with its practical, yet philosophical goals."

As the experienced trader, shrewd negotiator, and strategist, he leaves his punchline to the last.

"Let them come to you; you don't go to them!"

PART V:
"Followers"

Chapter 41

The moon shines at night due to reflected light from he sun! A most astonishing conclusion, opposed by priests and commoners alike, when first announced by Anaxagoras from his homeland in Ionia.

It was he who introduced 'Natural Philosophy' — the idea of objective reasoning about Nature based upon careful observation — to the newly minted Athenian philosophers. Such was his influence that Pericles sought a consultation before constructing the Parthenon.

Alas, Anaxagoras was also behind those fateful debates that erupted into the long, disastrous Peloponnesian War. After a series of grievous losses, the Athenians looked for scapegoats. As an influential foreigner, Anaxagoras was an obvious target for the mob. Narrowly avoiding execution, he eventually found a safe refuge in Lampsacus — a city-state with a long history of tolerance and inclusion.

Upon his death, the good citizens of Lampsacus celebrated Anaxagoras' wisdom with a grandiose marble altar including a perpetual flame and plaque, 'Mind and Truth'. A Festival in his honor continues to this day.

With its reputation as a safe haven, Valerius chose this city-state as an ideal retreat in which to begin my mission, as did Anaxagoras in past times. Lampsacenes extend goodwill towards others and welcome foreigners....expecting that such friendship will be returned in kind. A colony of Athenian Platonists had recently turned up, for example, bent on making fresh converts, and were received with traditional kindliness.

The generous Lampsacenes were stunned however, when the new arrivals abused the magnanimous welcome offered to them. Exceptionally zealous, they put aside the familiar tropes of Platonism. In their place, they favored a fiery brand of radicalism in which they somehow regarded themselves as 'the anointed ones', called upon to convert Plato's idyllic 'Republic' — the just and the good and the beautiful — into an earthly reality. They would become the elite 'Guardians' described by the great philosopher in his famous treatise.

In as much as Plato hated tyranny, he remained a privileged aristocrat and never totally trusted democracy. This gaping uncertainty in his treatise later prompted him to include the Guardians — a compromise measure at best — that opened the door to abuse, begging the question: should people be made to see what is good for them? As the Lampsacenes pointed out wryly, Plato himself had once tried — and failed miserably — to create his 'universal republic' in Syracuse, only to be sold as a slave until saved by his friends....so why did these latter-day missionaries think that they could do any better than their courageous master?

The arrogant pretension of the newcomers, not surprisingly, did not sit well with their provincial hosts. Furthermore, their 'noble cause' was not helped by an exclusive philosophy that denied freed-slaves and women entry to their symposia. It was not forgotten that the venerable Anaxagoras, revered by the local citizenry, had been exiled from Athens, barely escaping with his life.

As the saying goes, arrogance begets hubris. It wasn't long before the strangers were hauled ingloriously before the Macedonian ruler, King Lysimachus — to be expelled in disgrace at the point of a spear.

Their despotic attitude had made a mockery of the enlightened philosophy which they had inherited. This was not how Aristocles, known endearingly as Plato ("Chubby") had run his school in the Academeia district of Athens — which in time, became 'The Academy'. On the other hand, I had not forgotten the Gymniasarch's warning on the importance of political context: Valerius contacted his merchant partners with ties to the Lampsacus community, seeking sponsors and patrons for me. The ground has been tilled and furrowed — now it's my turn to sow the seed.

The expulsion of the Platonists reminded me of my own impulsive attempt to push my way into Mytilene philosophical circles. The planning of my entry into Lampsacus however, has been meticulous, and further blessed by good fortune. To my great surprise, I find a veritable absence of philosophy schools following the forced departure of the Platonists.

I can't help wondering whether Valerius' long reach had anything to do with the downfall of the Platonists? His close friendship with the Overseer to the court of King Lysimachus provides me with peace-of-mind, if nothing else. Intervention or otherwise, providence has provided me with a wonderful opportunity.

⁓⁓⁓⁓⁓⁓⁓⁓⁓

Located on the eastern side of the Hellespont at its northern peninsula, known as the Troada, in the region of Homer's Troy, Lampsacus is a prosperous city-state, renown for its worship of the phallic god, Priapus.

I arrive on the harbor dock to find Hermarchus and several Mytilene friends waiting for me, a most joyful reunion. Approaching me at a brisk clip is a wiry greybeard, attired in a pure white, elegantly draped toga, followed by a phalanx of servants. After my disastrous Mytilene experience, I hold back, cautiously, not knowing what to expect.

"Hail and welcome, Epicurus of Samos, philosopher of good standing, son of Valerius Mela? I am Idomeneus, proud citizen of Lampsacus and high steward to the court of King Lysimachus, who greatly values learned men and extends his greetings and good will."

I remain somewhat shaken — an awkward situation when one has learnt to expect the worse, defences at the ready — only to find that now, my cautiousness has become an embarrassment: all the city gates are flung wide open, and invitations abound! I lamely mumble my appreciation to Idomeneus — emboldened by the mention of Valerius' name, I go straight to the issue that is uppermost on my mind.

"With your kind assistance, may I be considered as a suppliant so as to obtain court approval for my teaching?"

Idomeneus' face opens up into a generous smile. I take stock that he is a tall man, as I look up at his soft, intelligent eyes. He seems amused by my wariness.

"My dear Epicurus, you already have court approval, otherwise I wouldn't be standing here, officially welcoming you. Lampsacus has offered itself as a sanctuary and home to philosophers of good repute since before the time of the great Anaxagoras. My servants will gather your baggage. I hope that you and your friends will consider yourselves to be honored guests of my family?"

With this guarantee of protection, I am free to teach in Lampsacus. Judging by the accent he placed upon 'philosophers of good repute', I take this to be a veiled rebuke of the recently departed Platonists. Furthermore, I find out that Idomeneus is an eminent philosopher-biographer in his own right. We have much in common and soon become fast friends.

Idomeneus' residence is another sumptuous estate, resembling that of his colleague Valerius. Apart from Idomeneus' private quarters, we are given exclusive use of the complex, with its rambling garden terraces, olive glades, and fruit orchards for the picking, complete with a wide, covered portico for more formal teachings.

Idomeneus' Villa, Lampsacus
(Entrance to the first 'School of the Garden')

In recognition of Priapus as the guardian of gardens and vineyards, bronze statues of the local phallic god feature prominently throughout the estate. All are well-endowed, for good luck and fertility, of which the otherwise conservative citizens of Lampsacus take enormous pride.

The combination of intellectual curiosity, an open-minded

attitude, and a Lampsacian culture of hospitality is irresistible. As Valerius predicted, it isn't long before word spreads and our small Mytilenian group blossoms into an amorphous company — all ages, genders, creeds, and races are here — spilling out over the estate.

Terraces of lush olive-trees fall away to the sea, each with its coterie of friends on wooden benches, or else propped against a trunk in a shady bower — laughing, eating, and debating as they go. Masses of bright yellow butterflies flitter among the silver-grey olive leaves, while sprays of wild flowers — cyclamen, crocus, and dianthus — just beginning to turn, fill the terrace hedges. It seems to me, that everyone I meet is interrelated by friendship, marriage, or business — one vast Lampsacene family. My Mytilenian friends, myself as well, have become seamlessly absorbed much to our amazement, into a single, united community. Of course, Valerius knew this would happen.

We have now become, if I listen to others, the 'School of the Garden' — a simple, practical designation I much prefer over the pompous-sounding 'Epicurean School'. I wonder what Servilia would think of all this: the foundation of a philosophy school, as we spoke of it often in our faraway plans — long ago on a Colophon hilltop of blood-red poppies.

I rub my eyes, dabbing at the tears: what was once a mere day dream has taken on shape and meaning — noise as well, with scampering children everywhere, busy at play.

Chapter 42

An exhausted courier has arrived from Colophon, after an arduous journey by horse relay — signifying a matter of great urgency.

I receive the scroll in gloomy silence. As I look down at it — this detached object, seemingly inert yet I fear, comes loaded with dire tidings — I notice my hands are trembling. I dread opening it.

"An exhausted courier....signifying an urgent matter"

I recognize the the script immediately, written in a round, clear hand, each sentence beginning with a characteristic flourish,....written by my beloved 'sister', Servilia.

"My dearest brother Epicurus, one that I love more than life itself, greetings from your humble sister, ever proud of your wonderful accomplishments.

With a heavy heart I must tell you that my father, our father,

Valerius, who I know that you also loved, is now among the Immortals. Another loss. He always seemed indestructible, a fixture, like the firmament of the heavens.

Word had reached me of his failing health. I obtained permission from the High Priestess at Eleusis to travel to his bedside, only to find him in a lamentable state, housebound, exhausted and dispirited."

I had found a father, who had been lost to me, only to lose him again for a second time. My grief is profound, as it is also sad: I had been looking forward to sharing with him the fulfilment of his well-crafted plan. He had paved the way for me with his advice, patronage, and network of connections, knowing that he would never live to see his plans come to pass.

Servilia continues, "Yet my arrival was the salve that he needed. He lit up, and came alive again, full of his playful good humor. I devoted my time to him, as a loving daughter, ensuring that his last weeks were tranquil and endearing for both of us. Our time together was 'sublime', the best ever, if I can use that word to mean something spiritual that passed between us."

"It inspires me still, every time I think of it. I know that you say, 'death is nothing', and I do agree with you generally — but Valerius' death was 'everything' compressed into a short time. Our father had lived an exceptional life, as a proper Roman gentleman, trading in political favors, yet keenly aware of decorum, as well as being a patron of the arts."

Valerius concerned himself with everyone around him, his generosity extending to the welfare of his own employees, even slaves, seeking medical treatment for urgent cases in Athens or Rome. Where he strayed, it was for love, and how can this not be forgiven? It drives all of us the same way, mostly for the good; though sometimes, our everyday selves are momentarily suspended, and pining with unrequited passion — Eros induces us to act in crazy ways.

Hearing from dear Servilia under these morbid circumstances is a bitter-sweet experience. Unbeknownst to me, she has apparently followed my recent gains in Lampsacus, where I now have many friends.

Her letter rekindles old lovelorn feelings. I struggle to relinquish my desire for Servilia as a lover, no longer to be 'in love' — yet at the same time, continue to love her as a brother. Plato's dualism discriminates between these two kinds of loving, allotting them to separate categories: platonic, or romantic. In my particular case, keeping them apart is a difficult matter, perhaps impossible — I care so much for her welfare, and we share so many memories. Whatever the pain, I can't let her go, as she will always be a part of me.

It is probably better this way, now that she is a priestess herself, cloistered away in an Eleusinian temple. Happiness can never last forever, against the relentless grind of daily life — but loving from afar has its own reward: a fetish of the soul, a private altar that is forever sacred.

Servilia continues.

"Our father has not forgotten you in designating beneficiaries. First there is a generous inheritance, easily sufficient to purchase a home and teaching garden in Athens. I know that he shared a belief in you, which I do also. Typical of him, he thoughtfully added a further endowment to amply cover your living costs for the remainder of your life, which dear brother, I trust will be a long one."

She concludes, as mischievous as ever — she couldn't help herself, leaving it to the last:

"Until we next meet, and we shall, I remain your loving sister, and partner in philosophy (remember our agreement!),

— Servilia."

It was only then I happened to notice, seemingly added hastily as an afterthought, scribbled along the margins — so unexpected, heart-wrenching....as if it were a book, a history, a lifetime, all squeezed tightly into a few brief words that instantly took shape and meaning, coming alive.

Breathlessly, tearily, crushingly, I speak her words aloud, hearing the same sounds she once spoke to me:

"Where Love Lies"

Our early love, young and free, was a time before our much-vaunted 'destinies' grew within us like a fever, taking us over — the separate paths we chose. It isn't enough however, that our ambitions drove us in different directions; 'family secrets', the ghosts in the closet, finished the job — making our innocent love impossible.... such parting, inevitable. 'Choice' is one thing, always leaving the door open; 'Blood' is something else, slamming it shut forever. A resounding Bang.

I dropped the scroll, unintentionally, dewy-eyed. It was after all, the cypress season of allergies.

Chapter 43

Lampsacus, Ionia
299 BC

I am alone, lost in meditation, secreted deep within the leafy bower of a sacred olive grove, gnarled and ancient when Homer was a boy. The olive is my private signature tree, an ageless symbol of peace and love, whose precious oil has given sustenance to countless generations before me. A rustling of dried leaves, and crunch of gravel on the pathway, rouses me from my musings.

Peering through the foliage, I catch a glimpse of two figures approaching: my good friend Metrodorus accompanied by an older woman, greyish and stooped, but still sprightly and attractive — vaguely familiar. Metrodorus is unaccountably beaming, while she walks behind cautiously, half-hidden, half-hiding behind his muscular frame.

My heart skips; my breath catches in my throat, dewy tears begin streaming down my cheeks. I feel their wetness. It cannot be.... anything, anyone....other than my mother, Chaerestrata! Not dead, but very much alive....and walking, somewhat stiffly but gamely, here, on the pathway of my Lampsacus community of friends.

So many years have passed since that fateful night on Samos; as if yesterday, I can feel the Etesian howling in my ears once more. Other images spring into my racing mind. The enigma of the sandals, neatly arranged on the cliff edge. And Melanchaetes, long gone, now resting beneath a solitary basalt cairn on a hilltop of blood-red poppies in faraway Colophon. Then comes good, generous Valerius: what I took to be his 'manipulations' were nothing other than the well-intentioned plans of a concerned parent, dutifully watching over me.

"Chaerestrata....walking, somewhat stiffly, but gamely"

Peculiar it is, how random thoughts flood the unguarded mind when caught unawares. My thoughts fly to Servilia, who as a sprite young girl, was smitten by my mother's kindnesses even before I was born. A young girl no longer, Servilia now presides over the prestigious Temple of Eleusis. All these vivid impressions inundate me, miraculously compressed into a furtive few moments.

We are standing face-to-face, my mother staring at me, patiently waiting.

Bewilderingly, I find myself reaching out towards her, as so often plays out in my dreams. At the joyous moment of reunion, the image dissolves — I wake up once again, saddened, empty-handed.

I snap too, and blink, teary-eyed, but still....she stands before me, flesh-and-blood. If it be a dream, then I think perhaps, I must be dead. I care not — only my longing matters. My legs of lead find their true cause, and yet....yet again....she is still here, standing before me. We collapse noiselessly into a long embrace. Metrodorus is choked up, drenched, watching in silent wonderment, over my mother's shoulder.

We sit down on the bench together, my mother and I, holding hands tenderly, angled towards each other, as Metrodorus pads off discretely. A yawning chasm of explanation lies before us, waiting to be filled.

She breaks the unearthly silence — a voice I never expected to hear once again, at least in this world.

"I left the sandals which I know you loved as a coded message for you. I knew you would understand. That you may follow in my footsteps, which you have done many times over,....and now I find you as a great teacher, a famous man."

"But why?" I remark somewhat lamely, begging the question of the lost years we could have shared.

"I'm sorry for leaving you, the hardest thing I have ever done. Not a day passed that I didn't think of you,....but hear me out, then judge me as you will — I deserve it! I couldn't stand it anymore.... the endless arguments with your father, so I ran off into the night. I had a plan, if you can call it that. In moments of darkest despair, my thoughts turned back to that lonely white cliff by the sea, and its beckoning promise of nothingness. Now the time had come. Exhausted and frozen on that fateful night, I took a herbal medication to keep me going. The Etesian had suddenly blown up out of nowhere — gusts of wind stinging my face, blinding me. I must have taken too much belladonna and became very confused — though I somehow made it to the clifftop,....where I left the scandals for you."

She closes her eyes now as she speaks, trembling, moving her hand back and forth in time as if pacing her story.

"I remember bending over to place the sandals, crying, with the wind howling in my face,....before I took the next few steps over the cliff. I must have blacked out as I straightened up. My next memory is nothing but dizziness — losing all sense of direction. I thought I was headed for the cliff edge,....but instead I became lost in the blinding squalls. Groping my way, I wandered past the wooded edges of the bluff into the thick bracken that fills the hollows behind the clifftop. At some point, I fell into a briar-patch, that tore at my face, legs, and bare feet, leaving me so entwined and weary that I could hardly move. I must have fallen asleep, all tangled and bleeding, despite the freezing rain."

"I woke in the morning with the sun shining brightly in my face, bathing me in light and warmth; a new day had dawned, one that I thought I would never live to see again. Strangely enough, I no longer felt like leaping off the cliff,....yet I couldn't go back to the house."

She wipes away tears.

"Why didn't you come back?"

"I just couldn't go back, because I knew then that I wanted to live — if I went back, it would end up again with me dead. The gods gave me a second chance for some reason,....and I needed to fulfill that purpose, whatever it was."

⁓⁓⁓⁓⁓⁓⁓⁓⁓⁓⁓⁓

"I had to get away from a miserable man who didn't love me,.... but I also needed to get away from another man who loved me too much. Not for myself however; only as a substitute for his long-departed wife. Much as I cared for him, I didn't want to spend the rest of my life with Valerius — living in the shadow of a saintly dead woman."

I stroke her wrinkled hand as she speaks.

"Both of these men were possessive of me for different reasons — in different ways. For one man, I was a worthless harlot, yet jealously guarded and abused,....while the other adored me as if I was made of delicate alabaster, a ghostly reincarnation. I cheated on one, hoping to please the other, but....I eventually recognized that neither love was true! I had always thought of myself as a righteous, moral person,.....yet in the end, I had betrayed my own values. I couldn't live with myself."

"I stroke her wrinkled hand"

"My spirit became very dark indeed, dead inside. I saw no way out....except the relentless pull of the precipice. It took over my thoughts totally: I came to see it as the only solution to all my problems. The gods in their mercy showed me another way to go — though it didn't come without a sacrifice. It meant losing my only true great love....You!"

A close woman friend, recently widowed, agreed to hide my mother for several months, until the gossip-mongers had run dry, moving onwards to fresh scandals. She met with Valerius one last time, knowing that he was kind-hearted and would keep her secret. He reluctantly agreed to a final parting and arranged for her escape from Samos, below decks in the cargo-hold of one of his galleys, bound for Lampsacus.

Putting events together in my mind, I realize with a shock now, why Valerius was so insistent that I should establish my first teaching school in Lampsacus. Yes, there were other sound reasons, such as establishing my practice as a prelude to Athens — but he was also trying, covertly as it turns out, to bring us together again, my mother and I. He couldn't tell me, since he was bound by an oath of secrecy. Also, there was the kindly rogue in him — he enjoyed surprises! I had really fouled things up when, stubborn as ever, I jumped ship at Mytilene.

My mother continues, in her own words, her journey of 'redemption'.

"I married again in Lampsacus — Kratolus was a widower, a good, kindly man who I learnt to trust and love,....though he died only recently after a long, harrowing illness. Valerius sent word about his original plan for you; only much later, did I find out that you had slipped away at Lesbos. I greatly feared for your safety in such a rough, frontier town."

"I knew that philosophy was considered by the Mytilenians to be a frivolous thing; not a matter to be taken seriously as a guide to living, as it is here in Lampsacus. I hope you may forgive me as a proud mother if I say that you have proven your mettle in Mytilene as well as Lampsacus. Valerius wanted you to follow your destiny in Athens."

"Why did you not seek me out earlier," I burst out, impulsively, "when I first arrived in Lampsacus? Why now?"

"So much has been kept from you in the past — I feel the weight of my guilt,....and I'll understand if you are angry with me." I shake my head several times, bewildered, looking for the right words.

Chaerestrata looks into my eyes, imploringly.

"Truth to tell,....I was also concerned that you would be very angry with me; that I would lose you for a second time,....though I should have known better. Only when Kratolus was dying did he tell me that the time had come to confide everything to you. With Valerius gone, and now Kratolus as well, I needed to place myself in your hands and face the truth, whatever may come, before the gods come for me."

I lay her fears to rest.

"Thank you for confiding in me,....but I must insist that you reside with me here in our community, where you will be safe. I don't want to lose you again."

Chaerestrata has come home to me, a miracle I never expected.

PART VI:
"Epilogue"

Chapter 44

Athens, Attica

272 BC

My nomadic days — Colophon, Mytilene, and Lampsacus, as well as those rollicking adventures with the Gymnasiarch, good Master Panyotis, and my mother as well — are now long passed. Not forgetting 'The Red Devil', and his blood-curdling reign of terror — finally marinated in a vat of apple-cider vinegar! I allow myself a quiet chuckle: justice served!

Elder Epicurus (Athens)

I rest easy in my chair, savouring the moment, as the cool, salty breezes of the late afternoon waft up from Piraeus harbour, the newly founded port city for Athens. A lone olive tree, loaded with spiny leaves dancing and shimmering daintily with the sea-change, braces the open door. Out on the portico, dozing between musings,

I catch the murmur of household banter seeping in from the kitchen, through half-shuttered windows.

The pleasant courtyard with its little colonnade of bright painted columns, trellised grapevines and white oleander provides the space I need — as if time itself is paused — to lay down these idle words of my life. From time to time, I sip from an infusion of chamomile herb perched on a rickety side table. Beneficial for digestion, so I'm told. It seems I've been 'digesting' a great deal lately.

The alluring aromas of dinner tease my hungry anticipation,…. as well as kindling fresh recollections. As I write, the sing-song voices of the kitchen become confused with voices from the past, replaying in my layered memories — half-forgotten experiences come alive once again, retold here in my wild-eyed scribblings, loaded with years and tall tales.

At such times, my poor caretakers become unduly concerned that their wizened master is speaking into the ether, rather than addressing any living persons. In fact, such persons are at least audibly present, resounding in my head, sometimes with greater immediacy than those around me — who carefully protect me from all intrusions of earthly urgency.

Some intrusions make themselves felt however, ordained by my own inevitable mortality. I have developed a sinister kidney pain of late — it matters little, amidst the solace offered by my string of memories. I think perhaps, it may be a prelude to death — a last summertime of the soul — with all these many mirages of my past life parading before me. If so, it is a gentle rain, warm as a relaxing bath, a letting-go into the bright light of oblivion.

So much greater is the surprise when my armchair nap is disturbed by a commotion of sorts. I hear the front door opening and closing with a bang — greetings are duly exchanged. My most faithful disciple and bosom friend, strides manfully into the portico. Hermarchus does nothing quietly, or not at all. A man of action, his prominence in life has arisen from his audacity, even if at times, he puts his foot in it.

A capable administrator, I have appointed him as my successor: he deftly manages 'The School of the Garden', including the daily forums among the friends. His loyalty to me has been unwavering. While he already garners respect, deservedly, as a great philosopher, he is foremost for me, an old friend, my very first follower.

"….sitting comfortably, out on the portico"

With a perfunctory nod and grunt of familiarity, Hermarchus' large frame fills the chair beside me. His once straight brown hair is now thinning, becoming speckled in grey, jowls sagging with the passage of years. Then….silence, characteristic of him, a man not given to idle chatter. His monolithic presence fills the space between us, a wordless communion, broken eventually by my reminiscence — a tale he needs to hear as the lead teacher of our Garden School.

"All through these many years, the ways of the human heart have pressed themselves upon me, dear Hermarchus….gradually

moulding and shaping my human clay towards a most simple awareness — the willingness to admit I am wrong. The everyday person
blunders into 'the truth' from time to time, partaking a little and
moving on. There are those however, who blindly cling to that which
is 'right' as if coming from the gods on Mount Olympus — to be
shouted aloud from the rooftops. Because they happen to think it,
whatever that thought may be, then it certainly must be so! I, on the
other hand, skirt around such forceful assertions of what is right.
With my love of paradox, it's the next thing to an impossibility that
I should ever be fully in the right. No gamesmanship, nothing to
win or lose: taking no sides, I side with everyone — free just to be
who I am."

Hermarchus: "Surely, if you admit that you are wrong,....or
mostly wrong, then you have given away everything — with nothing gained in return?"

"Is it always right to be so right, I wonder. In fact, hardly ever, I
think to myself. Am I wrong to think that way, when it is clearly so
right for others? Being wrong, I have nothing to defend within my
walls — which is to say, I have no need for walls. What is this truth,
I ask innocently, that needs such a mighty walls for protection —
never to be doubted or questioned? I would much rather be wrong,
if that be freedom.

To be wrong all the time, without exception, demands little of
me. After all, I have a right to be wrong, if I so choose. Unruffled
and lighthearted, I become small and forgotten in the face of the
other's redoubtable truth. If I am ever to be set apart, then it is for
this — that I am wrong above all others!"

Hermarchus: "If people are convinced that they are absolutely
right, beyond any doubt, it seems to me that such rigid beliefs are
not likely to change?"

"When people see that I have no walls, no defenses whatsoever, other than admitting my wrongness, they brush me aside with irritation, hungry for fresh meat. The gods demand a blood sacrifice: struggling victims full of fight,….not willing martyrs.

After a while, knowing that I am useless for an argument, they call me 'Unassuming'. Not a compliment, I think! On the other hand, I have grown rather fond of my new name, and taken it on board as my own. Yes — I am all that now, 'Unassuming' it will be.

Then a funny thing happens. Single individuals, burdened with defending their rigid walls, speak to me slyly when we are alone. No, 'certainly not a fully fledged doubt', they insist stoney-faced,…. yet with a heavy sigh, hinting that something is off-kilter.

Happiness, promised as the just reward for true believers, eludes them nonetheless. To be always right means having to take on the weight of the world, a heavy burden — a point rarely grasped — always the struggle to stretch one's pristine rightness to fit a messy reality, covered over with bluster and gloating.

"Hermarchus flings his hands in the air"

Strangely enough, though small and forgotten, lacking any walls, they call me their 'dear friend'. They even bring me gifts of figs, pomegranates, and honeycomb, as if making an apology. I invite them to sit with me in my courtyard refuge, under the olives. I nod and grunt as onwards they talk, and talk — I listen silently, knowingly, 'Unassuming' that I am.

At some point, they stop and slowly at first, begin to ask me questions: Why do I smile so much? Don't I have cares and worries? Am I not, being a decrepit old man, afraid of Chronos and his sickle of death, knocking at my door? Every question trails into a discussion: that which was black-and-white, chiseled in stone, crumbles away into shades of grey, befuddling any attempt at order. No longer rigid and tight, confined behind walls, thoughts flow freely, loose and vibrantly alive. There is freedom in the uncertainty that lies beyond Right and Wrong — beyond Plato and his Absolutes. This is how I grow new friends for our Garden of Olives, dear Hermarchus — undoing that sense of a single 'rightness' to be defended at all costs.

Those heavy walls come tumbling down, filling the space with openness and lightness,....where once there were stern mountain gods."

"You were the best thing to come out of Mytilene," I conclude, after my lengthy tale, while Hermarchus stretches in his chair, half-asleep, "the only thing that made it worthwhile."

A long pause follows, as Hermarchus ponders over my statement, unhurried, as if savoring it. Predictably, I knew that he would take his time. Like most old friends, we have incorporated each other's peculiarities.

"Not at all. I think that Mytilene was the makings of you. It brought out your courage" Hermarchus replies, wholeheartedly, flinging his hands in the air to make his point, "You were pilloried, but it made you tough and resilient, ready for the difficult path you had chosen as a young philosopher. Never again, did you take the Aristotelians for granted, or anyone else. Your deeds went before you."

The conversation is getting a tad heavy for late afternoon; moreover, his singular loyalty to me is so touching, I feel some tears are welling. I know myself, that I have become more emotional as age has stealthily crept upon me, with its levy of ailments,....reminders of my approaching mortality.

I attempt to change the subject away from me, as well as taunt Hermarchus a little more, now that he is in such fine form, brimming over with righteous provocation and spark. I am enjoying a side of Hermarchus I had never seen before.

Hermarchus maintains his offended tone, returning once again to my enemies — this time with a fresh 'revelation'.

"Though many years have passed, it still hasn't stopped them from spreading licentious rumors about your sex life!"

"In that case, I can assure you that there is nothing to worry about. Nothing at all," I reply, flatly.

As I listen to my own words, I almost sound apologetic,....even disappointed.

Chapter 45

Friend Hermarchus seems somewhat embarrassed — even blushes — in raising the 'delicate' subject of my sexual life. I reassure him that his enquiry is quite reasonable, even expected. I'm not in the least annoyed.

"I had no sexual life whatsoever during all my time in the 'The Garden', nor have I done so for the last forty years or more! I'm afraid that there is nothing for them to uncover,....so to speak." I smile indulgently at my own unintended pun — the last refuge of second-rate orators.

Hermarchus seems confused, wanting to believe me, but troubled nonetheless.

"Many times I saw you with the bonded slaves, Phaedrium, or Erotion, or even beautiful Leontion, our most distinguished courtesan," Hermarchus surmises, doggedly pursuing the facts, as is his nature, "and you were stroking or lavishing kisses with great affection. Others were watching with relish all the while, cadging every detail to spread the gossip."

"Be that as it may, I was kissing them sweetly because I'm fond of each of them, each in her own way. Slave or courtesan: it makes no difference to me! We are all friends together, and share the philosophy of the Garden. People draw their conclusions, as they are free to do — though in my case, they are sorely mistaken."

"Surely such closeness between a man and a woman must lead to sexual intimacy as a natural consequence," says Hermarchus, following the prescribed course of deductive reasoning, "since to do so would only be following the call of Nature, as with any other natural bodily act or impulse?"

"Love is one thing, and sex is another"

"That's not the case, my dear friend. Love is so often wrongly conflated with sex. Love is one thing, and sex is another — whether one leads to the other, depends upon the nature of each. You mention our cherished women of the Garden: they all know that they have a pure friendship with me, without any expectations, unadulterated by sex. I would like to think that it's a special experience for them, as it is for me as well."

"What! How is that possible?" exclaims Hermarchus with such a concerned frown, flinging his arms skyward in a gesture of frustration.

He shakes his head in disbelief, then recovers some composure.

"My apologies, friend Epicurus. If you tell me so, then of course, I believe you."

"Your question is one that arises naturally from our long and trusted friendship," I reply, with added reassurance, "so I take no offence. Besides, my so-called 'sex life' will always remain a subject of muckraking gossip, discussed behind my back. They really think I fall prey to the magic of love-at-first-sight, when such a thing is nothing other than a 'save-me projection'....a projection of the scandal-mongers themselves!"

"Besides," I add with a self-satisfied smirk, "old men past their prime, are considered to be harmless, not to be taken seriously.... so we get away with outrageous things, stealing kisses and fond embraces, the only compensation for ageing."

Hermarchus shrugs, and laughs heartily — as if to prove my point!

We both settle back comfortably into our chairs, and a natural silence ensues, not uncommon for us. Each of us is reflecting on the recent exchange. While we are good friends of long standing, this intimate exchange — family feuds and sexuality — is new ground for us.

"The last woman was so special, so enchanting, so engaging, at a level that transcends any idea of normal sex," I continue, breaking the easy quietude that had settled on us, "that I have wished for nothing more since that time. All my sexual energy is channeled into my teaching."

Hermarchus startles with surprise. He is visibly shaken.

It's been quite an afternoon for him! I get the impression that he attributes my devotion for the 'special woman' as a juvenile infatuation of some kind, that's now become fixated and embroidered in my old age.

"Please take no offence, friend Epicurus, for what I am about to say. Could it be that you are deluded by your own idealized projection? It happens to all of us, sooner or later. We see only what we want to see, and all else fades into the background."

"At my sclerotic age, Hermarchus? I'm tickled by your question. Chuffed. And no, I'm not offended. Unfortunately, life has cured me of youthful projections, leaving bleak reality, a poor and miserable thing indeed. In her case however, matters are reversed. What was once her youthful infatuation with the goddesses has now become a blissful reality, in which she serves others as a miraculous healer."

I can see that Hermarchus hesitates, as if he is wondering what other revelations are yet to emerge....but decides to continue, perhaps more cautiously. He needs to supply a reason to support his enquiries.

"I only ask because the way you describe her makes her sound more like a goddess, than any mere mortal woman!"

"Yes, that's true," I reply, blandly, "I understand your skepticism. You're right though, more than you could realize. I have indeed been blessed by the gods, or in this case, by the goddesses of Demeter and Persephone."

I pause, before adding anything more to his shocked afternoon.

"She of whom we speak, is the High Priestess and Hierophant of the sacred Eleusinian Mysteries."

An awkward silence. Yet another shock for Hermarchus to digest! I can't help deriving a secret enjoyment from his discomfort.

More silence....He recovers, and moves on doggedly.

"What's her name?...."

"....I mean, are you allowed to tell me,....or is it one of those cases where her name is sacerdotal and can't be spoken outside of the temple grounds?", he asks, now impetuously, almost boyishly — pressing me for more information.

"She of whom we speak is the High Priestess"

Hermarchus is intrigued, curiosity overcoming his natural caution, especially for one widely known for his unflappable nature.

"Servilia." I reply, wistfully, admiring the musical sibilance once again.

"Just Servilia."

Chapter 46

It's a brisk evening with a wondrous twilight unfolding over the massif of the Acropolis — a spectrum of shifting hues, scarlet fading to yellow, thence to purple, highlighting the spectacle of the Parthenon of Pericles — with the setting sun gleaming off the golden statue of our urban Athena, a reminder of Servilia.

I marvel at Nature's grandeur, and think back over the discussions of the day and in particular, uncomfortable Hermachus delving into my non-existent sex life. Like a doddery father, I struggle to let go of my offspring, the Work and the Community which was once mine. As all stubborn fathers must, I need to face the truth: it is no longer mine to possess. It has already gone its own way on the world stage, and carries me along with it.

What began life as my own personal philosophy, has taken on a life of its own, and after my death, it will become the plaything of posterity. Certainly not mine, anymore, in any sense but name only.

I have now become the venerable object, treated with reverence, where once I was the personal subject. As an investigator, I stood outside the Work, examining an object of enquiry — while now I have become incorporated into it.

Metrodorus and Idomeneus have each named their sons after me. While I am honored, it seems that even for my close friends, I have become the walking, talking embodiment of the Work. These sons, the next generation of the community, will commemorate me in marble as a sterile figurehead.

I, Epicurus, poor son of a schoolmaster, have become inseparable from that monumental object of enquiry, Epicureanism, whatever that may be — all that I am, flesh and blood, passes over to the myth-making of others who know me not.

"The knucklebones will fall as they may"

My own philosophies have overtaken me, so that I feel as if this 'Epicurus' is a stranger to me, a constructed identity — a composite figure made up of ideas, teachings, aphorisms, and anecdotes.

I recall with affection, the dice game of Knucklebones that Servilia and I played when we were children, excited or else disappointed, by the random luck of the throw. So too, the knucklebones of destiny will fall as they may.

My guess is no better now, than it was long ago — once again to be a carefree child on Samos.

Chapter 47

Athens, Attica

270 BC

I detect a symmetry of sorts in the course of my life, something I never suspected in my active years, which leaves me feeling unexpectedly contented. Despite all the surface chaos, life is less vicarious than I had once feared, having a seamless continuity for which all the ruptures and crises of self-doubt are mere interludes along the way. Even my present misbehaving kidneys have their small place in the scheme of things.

Perception is everything for a septuagenarian, and my need for reality is fading, along with my bodily functions. Together with my walking stick, I form the perfect isosceles triangle! Such distractions perform good service in lessening my painful kidney episodes.

My loving friends of the Garden, now led by Hermarchus, have become increasingly watchful of me, intrigued perhaps, by my irrepressible 'Epicurean' smiles amid the episodes. I dare not offer any explanation, lest they think I have succumbed to senility to match my scruffy white beard!

As the ancients believed, no man may be called wise until he dies — at which time a final reckoning can be made of his wisdom. The way he handles approaching death is said to reveal the person's true character. It surprises me how otherwise sensible philosophers still cling to such ancient relics, as if all one's good works, bold ideas, and noble writings can be conveniently discarded — so that an entire life is compressed into the endgame of a few hours. In need of an example, they point to Socrates' lucid discourse while he was dying — I'm sure the master would be aghast to find that his final hours are used to bolster such an trifling belief. Pshaw on the ancients is what I say!

Only with one Other, am I simply Epicurus, late of Samos and Lampsacus, now a denizen of Athens, once a young playmate who has now become became a dear brother. Someone with whom she had once shared hilltop dreams, picking blood-red poppies, so long ago, or sat huddled together in my father's culina, with goblets of Samian wine, basking in the luminous rays of the afternoon sun. Undoubtably, all our dreams have come true, yet as the Fates decree, in improbable ways of which we had no inkling.

We continue to be deeply affectionate towards each other, just as we had hoped, but not in the manner our young bodies imagined. There is a residual dint of sadness about our destinies. Call them gods or not, the vagaries of life rule over us, immutable and unpredictable. Though matters have seemingly worked out in the end, fulfilling all our worldly hopes, they remain a hollow likeness — never exactly as we would wish them to be, mocking us with their subtle irony.

I take solace that we grasped that pleasure offered by our passions when we could, greedily without regret, young and carefree, blissfully unaware of the Fates. Such is my lived experience of life: absurd, anarchic, messy, but nonetheless, precious and for all of that, most joyful.

I look forward to my forthcoming outing in the countryside, accompanied by the son of Metrodorus, my namesake and kinsman. As if one Epicurus was not enough!

I think perhaps, it will be my last pilgrimage to Eleusis, three hours by rumbling donkey-cart, clip-clopping along rutted roads, past primitive drystone shrines, now crumbling and forgotten, overgrown with wild grape vines. Meadows of wildflowers in uproarious bloom crowd upon us on both sides — springtime, full of the abundance of Life, eternally renewing itself. We clatter our way across the gently rolling hills of Attica, dotted with tombs, stelae, and orchards bursting with fruit.

Finally, cloud-shrouded Mount Parnes looms above us, marking the Sacred Way as it winds down into the Thriasian Plain and the temple of Demeter. No trumpets announce my arrival, but rather, the hoarse braying of a jackass....for me, they are the sounds of a love-song!

Son of Chaerestrata and Valerius, this is my other family — that of my beloved sister, Servilia.

Where love lies.

Chapter 48

Boston, Massachusetts

2018 AD

Professor Fiona Roberts always thought of herself as an avowed spinster. Apart from a few guileless flings that she sorely regretted — 'collateral damage' from too many stodgy conferences — she remained solidly married to her research. Reliable and secure, it was always there, patiently waiting for her. In the harsh reality of 'Either/Or', she had resigned herself long ago to a single life as the unspoken cost of becoming an esteemed woman professor — in keeping with the Classical Greek tradition of tragedy!

How surreal it then felt, in her unguarded moments, following David's heartfelt proposal of marriage — 'totally unexpected' she pertly told herself. Then there was the problem of her flushed and gushing acceptance: heart aflutter with the prospect of being a 'married lady' complete with a husband.

"What am I doing?", she pondered, baffled at her own girlish eagerness.

"This is not the life I had planned for myself!".

Midnight, with no prospect of sleeping, she slipped on a robe, and stood by her bedroom window. Immersed in thought, she looked back absentmindedly at the lavish Kandinsky print and its riotous explosion of colors and angles, her eyes tracking the shapes downwards to the vacant bed that lay below — her single bed, with its monotone stuffed duvet, like an embalmed mummy.

"Anyways, I have no time for friends," she answered herself, "much less lovers….so no problem!"

As it happened, she found herself to be unaccountably happy — at the same time, shaken by an otherworldly quality, as if some cavalier stranger was now living within the husk of her former sedate self. She tried to make sense of it all, marshalling her researcher's mind to frame her runaway feelings into some semblance of order; to cobble together the scientific objectivity that she desperately needs.

Yes, she concluded, the Epicuriana had to be at the center of it all, since apart from David, there was little else remaining in her life. It was all very simple really, when you put things in perspective: two stories of romantic love had become entwined, separated by millennia — yet nonetheless driven by a quirky sequence of events.

Requiring a 'Herculean' effort, it was she and David who had brought to light the long-buried love story of Servilia and Epicurus. Their close collaboration in that discovery — with all its trappings of intimacy and unrequited longing, etched into a charred scroll, deciphered letter by letter, word by word — had brought them together in a kind of 'false consciousness'. They had become totally immersed in the unfolding romance of it all, even to the point of appropriating such passionate feelings as their own. Fiona had heard of this so-called 'transference' but didn't believe it, much less that it could possibly happen to her.

"It's an occupational hazard, a delusion that comes from overwork," she reasoned, "no matter how real it may feel". How to explain it to David without hurting him? She must return his ring before matters went too far!

"It may already be too late," she worried.

"Is my existence nothing but a string of 'accidents' playing out across generations," she thought, caught up in the despair of overthinking, "like the random hits on a pin-ball machine, defying science and superstition alike?" Fiona had looked askance at 'The Butterfly Effect' of Popular Science, when it first made headlines in the cinemas and tabloids. A young woman pauses for a few minutes, sitting on a bench in Central Park, lost in wonderment, admiring a newly-hatched butterfly flapping its wings — she will be late for her conference — saving the budding physician from a terror-ist bombing, with its mass casualties — only much later, does the same woman, now a research virologist, develop a planet-saving vaccine.

Not long after hearing the story, Fiona stumbled upon 'Synchronicity' in some airport magazine between flights, the offbeat 'acausal connecting principle' of C. G. Jung in which Unconscious motives are said to direct behavior from within. That she would waste her time reading such things — so unlike her!

At the time, she promptly relegated these wayward thoughts to the dustbin of 'magical thinking' — but not sufficiently, that some wistful fantasy remains lodged in her memory, now to be called up into active service. Faced with telling David, she hesitates, perplexed. She has never before felt so strongly, so passionately about anyone — which ironically, makes her doubt her emotions all the more. Across the many centuries, she felt a deep affinity with Servilia's plight, much like her own: could she trust that such headlong feelings were authentic, or just 'make-believe'? Her once smug sense of surety had deserted her, in the recent upheaval of her life — lost amidst the chaos of wedding-planning.

Fiona's writhing mind returned at last to the source of her frustrations. She harbored a question about 'The Epicuriana', one event in particular, that had haunted her ever since she had first formulated its meaning. She had revisited the scroll many times, over and over with the same result, convinced that she had missed something — a subtle shade of meaning 'lost in translation'. Much to her dismay, the question lingers, opaque and obstinate as ever! She was annoyed that inexplicably, such a small matter should continue to annoy her; moreover, that it has assumed the proportions of a private obsession.

Whence came that furtive 'first spark', she wondered — the protean impulse that had gradually coalesced, gathering momentum — ending in Epicurus' life-changing decision to disembark at Mytilene instead of Lampsacus? He had sidestepped certain death by his detour to Mytilene, rather than remaining aboard the doomed 'Hector'. If Epicurus had continued on his original, carefully-charted course, there would be no Epicuriana to read now, Epicureanism would not exist: David and I would have unknowingly gone our separate ways.

"What was it, in the first place," she asked herself, "for Epicurus to change his train of thinking. He gives us his reasons, but they sound hollow — like so many justifications after the fact. The kernel of the decision was there, right from the beginning! It came from nowhere, a fully-formed moment in time."

"So too, loving David, have I detoured from my own set course, just as Epicurus had done, so long ago. Whence indeed, comes that 'first spark' that I still hesitate to follow? Have I been waiting all along, burying myself in my work; now using that same work as a 'transference' alibi to avoid the opportunity of love? Why else have I struggled so mightily with the translation of Servilia's haunting poem, 'Where Love Lies', the struggle of her love for Epicurus — yet another fateful coincidence?"

Fiona's soul-searching turns back again to Servilia — to the timeless riddle of the Eleusinian Mysteries and the mythos of the eternal return. Suddenly, coming out of nowhere, as with David's unexpected proposal, the revelation strikes Fiona like a thunderclap — not only the lifespan, death-and-rebirth, but also the inner experience of a lived life. Every moment of life ends in a death, only to be reborn in the next moment — a fresh thought, a new direction, a life reborn to itself.

"There are no coincidences!", flashes across her mind in the moment — Fiona gulps with astonishment at the shocking absolutism of her own thought, popping up without warning.

"Could it really be true," she asked herself, bewildered, "that every step we make, every breath we take, every small act of generosity, is not without meaning?" They had both, she and David, become witnesses to the lifelong romance of Servilia and Epicurus, which in turn had wrought a lasting change within themselves — an openness to new experiences which is profound, yet disconcerting for each of them.

"Not transference," thought Fiona, ever the scientist, "but a catalyst!"

The celebratory vows include a lookalike Epicurus as the 'best man', complete with toga and golden wreath. Everyone admires the creative touch, Fiona's idea: an ectoplasmic match-maker, reincarnated in spirit, to watch over them. Lookalike or proxy — Fiona is not so sure anymore.

Vectors are set in motion, perpetually: a ceaseless synchronicity of chance encounters, moments that may take minutes or millennia to play out.

It wasn't long — within a year — before a girlchild was born, cooing with delight, eager for life.

Her name however, was a foregone conclusion....and a new beginning.

Servilia had arrived.

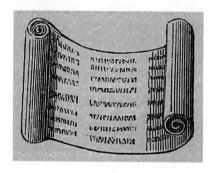

Finis

ACKNOWLEDGEMENTS

Belinda E. Pease, MFA, my ever resourceful researcher and graphics designer, tolerant of my many last-minute requests, receives my heartfelt appreciation. For different reasons, I remain indebted to University Vice-Chancellor, professor emeritus Peter W. Sheehan, who provided that vital early encouragement in my professional career when it was most needed.

Any failures of fact-checking, florid embellishments, crunching anachronisms, overwrought sentimentalities, or other unwarranted idiosyncrasies are entirely my own. The spelling of Greek words is anglicized, such as Hercules (Herakles).

The last line belongs to my lifelong companion, Pamela S. Pease, Ph.D, a partner in all matters, contemporary and archaic, affectionate and supportive, without whom this work would not be possible.

APPENDIX

I remain indebted to the following sources, which not only assisted my preparatory research for the present work but also inspired my seminal interest in Epicurean ideas, long ago, as a personal 'living philosophy' of life. The listing is given in random order.

DeWitt, Norman Wentworth:
   "Epicurus and his Philosophy", University of Minnesota Press, Minneapolis, 1954.

Slattery, Luke:
   "Reclaiming Epicurus", Penguin Specials, 2012.

Klein, Daniel:
   "Travels with Epicurus: Meditations from a Greek Island on the Pleasures of Old Age", OneWorld Publications, 2014.

Wilson, Catherine:
   "Epicureanism: A Very Short Introduction", Oxford University Press, 2015.

Jones, Howard:
   "The Epicurean Tradition", Routledge, 1989.

Greenblatt, Stephen:
   "The Swerve: How the World became Modern", Norton & Company, 2012.

Wright, Frances:
   "A Few Days in Athens" (Commentary by Hiram Crespo), London, 1822.

Epicurus:

>"The Art of Happiness" (Commentary by George K. Strodach; Foreward by Daniel Klein), Penguin Books, 2013.

Inwood, Brad; L. P. Gerson; D. S. Hutchinson:

>"The Epicurus Reader", Hackett Publishing, 1994.

Pater, Walter Horacio:

>"Marius The Epicurean, Vols I & II", London, 1910.

Crespo, Hiram:

>"Tending the Epicurean Garden", Humanist Press, Washington, DC, 2014.

Renault, Mary:

>"The Last of the Wine", Longmans, Green & Co., London, 1956.

Hamilton, Edith:

>"The Greek Way", Goggle Books, originally published, 1930.

Wasson, R.G., Hofmann, A., Ruck, C.A.,

>"The Road to Eleusis", North Atlantic Books, originally published, 1978.

Sontag, S.,

>"The Volcano Lover: A Romance", Farrah Straus Giroux, 1992.

ILLUSTRATION & PHOTO CREDITS

Cover

Jones, Sir Edward (artist,1870). *Phyllis and Demophoon.*
Birmingham Museums Trust. Unsplash.jpg, ID tV02AFxvRjg.

Author Photo

Pease, Pamela (photographer). *'Dr. Donovan in France'.*
2016.

Servilia's Poem, 'Where Love Lies'

Felis (photographer and ©Felis). *Pieces of ancient marble
Greek columns in Ephesus in Turkey.* Dreamstime.com,
ID 55638025.

Andreykuzmin. *Vintage paper scrolls set isolated on white.*
Dreamstime.com, ID 142186247

Preface

Collage:

Fletcher-Brown, Mark (photograph and © Mark Fletcher-
Brown), *Greek Statute.* mark-fletcher-brown-X_Yyb5M-
h2g-unsplash.com.

Nowak, Juergen (photographer and © Juergen Nowak),
*Landscape Greek island Samos eastern Mykali Strait Aegean
Sea.* Dreamstime.com, ID 170207650.

PART I: "Prologue"

Collage:

Steidl, James (photographer and © James Steidl). *Blank
Scrolls Open.* Dreamtime.com, ID 19920951.

Jasmin. *Olive leaves. oana-cracium.* Unsplash.com.jpg, ID xOQ_mEZh6V8.

PART II: "Beginnings"

Thravalos, Manolis (Photographer, April 27 2014). *Encore - sunset rainbow over Samos Island, Greece.* In, University Space Research Association's(USRA.edu), Earth Science Picture of the Day (EPOD.usra.edu), March 14, 2020.

PART III: "Failures"

Migfoto (illustrator). *An ancient Greek warrior with a spear and his woman are sitting and hugging. Vector illustration on dark background.* Vector wdrfree.com, ID 263662168.

PART IV: "Secrets"

Marek, Tomas (photographer © Tomas Marek. Famous *Parthenon temple on the Acropolis in Athens Greece.* 123rf.com, ID 41224717.

PART V: "Followers"

Stevanzz (photographer and © Stevanzz). *Maremma countryside panoramic view of olive trees in rolling hills and green fields on sunset.* Sea on the horizon. Casale, Marittimo, Pisa, Tuscany, Itay Europe. Dreamstime.com, ID 136206543.

PART VI: "Epilogue"

Collage:

Creative Common (CC BY 3.0) created 2010 (December 21). *Epicurus Statute.* Wikipedia.org, wiki, ID Epikur_Statute.jpg.

Nicklas-h. *Epicurus letter font, homage to the ancient Greek philosopher Epicurus (341–270 BC).* Nicklas-h.com, Epicuros_FreeFont.pdf.

Dr Fiona Roberts

Racorn (photographer and © racorn). *Casual young businesswoman or student in denim jeans and glasses standing clutching a large office binder to her chest as she stares thoughtfully at the camera.* 123rf.com (stock-photo), ID 96254931.

'Hector' Merchant Galley

Pivden (illustrator and © Pivden). *Vector - Trireme floating on the sea waves. Hand drawn design element sailing ship. Vintage color vector engraving illustration for poster, label, postmark.* 123rf.com, ID 115009970.

Map

Quennel C.H.B, Marjorie. *Everyday things in ancient Greece.* London 1929. 21.(In, Ancient Greece map from M. Quennel C.H.B book at the Archaeological Survey of India Central Archaeological Library, New Delhi, Public Resource of the Internet Archives, Book Number: 2181, Uploaded November 5, 2017)

Line drawings

Rich, Anthony. *The illustrated companion to the Latin dictionary and Greek lexicon; forming a glossary of all the words representing visible objects connected with the arts, manufactures, and every-day life of the Greeks and Romans, with representations of nearly two thousand objects from the antique.* London: Longmans, 1849.
Pages: 13, 28, 32, 41, 48, 64, 73, 78, 87,115, 150, 153,156, 159, 166, 178, 182, 193, 196, 198, 205, 206, 212, 250, 263, 265, 266, 307, 321, 328, 336, 346, 347, 351, 379, 391, 399, 405, 491, 499, 503, 532, 547, 552, 580, 584, 603, 616, 621, 642, 661, 667, 678, 683, 731.

(*In,* The Library of Congress, Uploaded to the Internet Archive, February 14, 2014. Full Catalogue Reference: MARCXML. The Library of Congress is unaware of any copyright restrictions for this item.)